Praise for the novels of

# ANNE STUART

"[Stuart is] arguably romantic suspense's most popular
novelist."
—*Publishers Weekly*

"A master at creating chilling atmosphere with a
modern touch."
—*Library Journal*

"Brilliant characterizations and a suitably moody
ambience drive this dark tale of unlikely love."
—*Publishers Weekly* on *Black Ice* [starred review]

"Stuart knows how to take chances, and this edgy
thriller shows how well they can pay off."
—*Publishers Weekly* on *Cold As Ice*

"[A] sexy, edgy, exceptionally well-plotted tale."
—*Library Journal* on *Into the Fire*

"A consummate mistress of her craft."
—*Romantic Times BOOKreviews*

"Before I read...[a] Stuart book I make sure
my day is free....Once I start, she has me hooked."
—*New York Times* bestselling author
Debbie Macomber

*Also by*

# ANNE STUART

# FIRE AND ICE

# ANNE STUART

ISBN-13: 978-0-7783-2536-9
ISBN-10:      0-7783-2536-9

FIRE AND ICE

www.MIRABooks.com

**Printed in U.S.A.**

To my fabulous agents, Jane Dystel and
Miriam Goderich, for unflagging support,
wise advice and, most of all, patience.

## ACKNOWLEDGMENTS

First off, I couldn't have written this without falling in love with J-rock and Japan, so thanks to my daughter for dragging me to Otakon. I have an addiction to Japanese doramas (twelve-hour television miniseries, which I watch slavishly, in Japanese with Chinese subtitles and I don't speak or read either language but I love them anyway).

My Yakuza is not terribly realistic, so don't blame David E. Kaplan and Alec Dubro or their fabulous book *Yakuza: The Explosive Account of Japan's Criminal Underworld*. I believe in poetic license.

And if you want a soundtrack for this, listen to the new age music from Pacific Moon, rock from Hyde and L'Arc-en-Ciel and, oh, just maybe the soundtrack to "Final Fantasy: Advent Children." A touch of Dir en grey wouldn't hurt either.

# 1

Reno bounded up the stairs, two at a time, and pushed open the door to the deserted apartment, only to stare directly into the barrel of a Glock.

Peter Madsen slowly put his gun away. "What the hell are you doing here? I could have shot you."

Reno grinned. He knew Peter thought he was the most annoying, most flamboyant operative ever to work for the Committee, that covert organization of ruthless do-gooders, and he did his best to live up to that image. He brushed an invisible speck of lint off his leather jacket and kept his sunglasses firmly in place in the darkened room.

"I trust your instincts," he said, closing the door behind him and strolling into the apartment. His pointy-toed leather cowboy boots echoed on the parquet flooring.

"How do you ever sneak up on anyone when you're so damned noisy?" Peter said.

Reno gave him his most annoying smile. There was nothing he liked better than to irritate the Ice Man. "I manage," he said. "I thought you might need a little help."

"When I need help, I'll ask for it."

Reno shrugged. "Just trying to do my duty, boss. Isobel's really gone, hasn't she? Our fearless leader has disappeared, leaving you in charge."

"Yes." Peter glowered at him. "And don't call me boss. It's not my idea you're here."

"Not mine, either. You think she went with Killian?"

"I expect so."

"Aah, true love," Reno said. "For good?"

"I hope so," Peter said.

"Why? So you can take over running the Committee?" Reno wandered over to the window to look out into the wet winter afternoon.

"Hardly. I'm passing this off to the first person qualified."

"Then why?"

Peter shrugged. "Because this kind of life demands too high a price. Isobel and Killian stayed too long—they earned the right to get out of it."

Reno snorted. "You don't seem the sentimental kind to me."

"And you're such a great judge of character?"

Reno merely smiled his catlike smile. "So explain this to me," he said in his deliberate English. "Why are we still in hiding? Why have my cousin and his wife disappeared somewhere in Japan? Thomason is dead—any contracts he put out should be canceled, and the Russian mercenaries should have lost interest. Mercenaries don't work without money, and their source of income has dried up. We should be ready to move on to new things, not wasting time cleaning up old messes."

"Maybe the Russians haven't heard. Maybe they've moved on to other things, but our intel is spotty. Either way, I'm not about to take a chance. We've lost too many operatives to risk it. Besides, I'm rather fond of your cousin."

"So am I. I also think he could hold his own against half-a-dozen retired Russian operatives," Reno said.

"Probably. But we're not going to find out. They stay hidden until we know it's safe. You got that?"

Reno didn't respond, changing the subject instead. "How is Mahmoud doing?"

"Fine," Peter said gloomily. "I'm supposed to bring home a PlayStation Three. The kid's a ruthless, soulless assassin, so Genevieve's plan is to get him blowing up virtual heads instead of real ones. No thanks to you."

Reno laughed, heartlessly. "I'll give you a list of games."

"Christ," Peter grumbled.

Reno looked around him. "So why don't we move the offices in here? There's plenty of room. Or even better, why don't I move in?"

"For the same reason we're out of Kensington. It's been compromised, and so has this place. The house in Golders Green will be fine for the time being."

Reno made a rude noise.

"You don't like it, you can come out to Wiltshire and stay with us," Peter said.

Reno could imagine just how much Peter would like that, and he was almost tempted to accept the invitation, just to annoy him. But then he'd have to put up with Genevieve's mothering, and at twenty-seven he had no more need of a mother than he'd had at seven. He did very well on his own.

There was a muffled sound of an electronic beep, and Peter yanked out his PDA, staring at the incoming text message. "Shit," he said. He looked at Reno, who was doing a piss-poor job of hiding his curiosity. "We've got trouble."

If it wasn't the first time Peter had come up with the word *we,* it was close to it. "What's up?"

"We've got word from one of our informants in America. It's about your cousin."

Reno froze, dead serious now. "You said they were safe."

"They are. Even I don't know where they've gone. That's the problem. Taka's sister-in-law, Jilly, decided to make a surprise visit. So while Taka and Summer are somewhere safe, hiding out, the girl could be walking straight into danger. And I don't have anyone to send in...."

"I'm going." Reno's voice was flat, implacable.

"You can't. You were kicked out of Japan for the time being—"

"My grandfather kicked me out, not the government. I can go back anytime. The Toussaints are back on their mountain, half your operatives are dead or missing. I'm your only real choice."

"Are you asking my permission?" Peter said.

"Fuck, no. I'm going. You can send someone else but they'll just get in my way."

"I don't have anyone else to send and you know it. I still haven't heard what happened to MacGowan."

Reno nodded. "So it's up to me. How long ago did Summer's sister leave?"

"They're not quite sure." He took a long look

at Reno. "I think Taka wanted to be very sure you didn't get anywhere near his wife's sister."

"Taka wants a lot of things. He thinks he knows best. Right now he's gone, and there's no one else. You try to stop me and I'll kill you."

"I doubt it," Peter said. "And I don't think you want to waste time trying. I'll see to transport for you. Not that I approve, but trying to stop you will take too much time. I'll send backup as soon as I figure out who's left alive."

"I don't need backup."

"I'll send backup," Peter said.

But Reno was already gone. Out into the late winter night, into the ice-cold city. London was at its darkest in the last few weeks before spring came, and during the months he'd lived there it had never once felt like home. He was heading to the nearest airport, back to the land of his ancestors, whether his grandfather approved of his return or not. He wasn't going to let anything happen to his cousin's sister-in-law. He wasn't going to let anything happen to the tall, shy-looking teenager he'd seen only once and should have forgotten all about, the one who popped up into his dreams at the most inconvenient times.

He was going to find Jilly and send her back where she belonged before she got hurt.

And then he could forget all about her once more.

The jet lag shouldn't have come as a surprise to Jilly—she'd seen *Lost in Translation* too many times. She'd staggered off the airplane in a sleepless daze, and it was sheer luck she'd made her circuitous way from Narita airport into Tokyo and into one of the cute green cabs. She handed the address to the driver, then sat back, closing her eyes.

Where the hell were Summer and Taka? She'd left half a dozen messages on her sister's cell phone and heard zip in return. If she'd had any sense, she never would have gotten on the plane to Tokyo until she heard back from them, but right now she wasn't in the mood to be sensible. She was running, running to her big sister, who'd hug her and tell her everything would be fine.

And in the meantime she'd finally managed to get her butt to Japan. She had all the practical reasons—she hadn't seen her sister in three months, there was an extraordinary exhibit of Heian-era pottery at the state museum, and if she was thinking of switching her doctoral studies in archaeology from Mesopotamia to early Japan, then an almost pitch-perfect (according to the reports) exhibit of Heian life was a necessary part of her studies. It didn't matter that the exhibit would be there for years—she hadn't discussed the change with her advisers and the sooner she made the decision the better.

So Japan, now, was a necessity. If it happened to coincide with the occurrence of the worst one-night stand in the history of the universe, with Duke the moron, then that was merely coincidental. She was going to put that abortive, messy, horrible night out of her mind. It wasn't the first time she'd done something stupid—well, in fact, when it came to men, it was, but she wasn't going to think about that now. Like Scarlett O'Hara, she'd think about that tomorrow. For the time being all she wanted was her sister, and she wanted her now. There were a dozen other reasons to be in Japan, like Taka, like his cousin, but she had no intention of thinking about any of those right now.

It was growing dark, the bright neon flowers lighting up the city, but she was too impatient to admire anything. She just had to get someplace and stay put for a while. She needed her sister's calm wisdom, and a decent bed and time to figure out what she was going to do. About everything.

It took the cab forever, and by the time the

driver pulled to a stop in the residential area in the southern part of the city, she'd almost fallen asleep.

*"Arigato gozaimasu,"* she said, shoving half of her yen into his white-gloved hand. She scrambled out of the taxi, dragging her backpack with her, and looked at the one-story building.

The taxi hadn't moved. A moment later the driver emerged, a troubled expression on his face. "No one appears to be home, miss. Perhaps I should take you to one of the big hotels in the city?" Except he spoke in Japanese, and clearly had no hope of her understanding.

But she'd been working toward this from the moment she met her Japanese brother-in-law. And his mysterious cousin. "I'll be fine. My sister knows I'm coming, and I have a key." Which was a lie on both counts, but she had no doubt she'd find a way in.

The taxi driver politely hid his surprise, either at her command of the language or her god-awful accent, and returned to his cab, relieved to have done his duty to the hapless *gaijin*. He took off into the darkened street, leaving Jilly alone to make her way into her sister's walled fortress.

She checked the iron gate, just in case they'd left it unlocked, but it held firm. She sighed. *Climbing, it is.* She headed around the side of the building, hoping for a tree or a trellis or something to give her a leg up. Not on Taka's watch—there'd be little chance to break in when your brother-in-law was some kind of uber-spy cum gangster.

The residential street was dark and deserted. If she'd thought of it in time, she could have gotten the taxi driver to give her a boost over the wall. He probably would have—he'd tried so hard to be helpful.

There were trees inside the compound, just out of reach. "Okay," she said under her breath. "I can handle this." She pulled her belt free from her jeans, refastened it into a loop and tossed it toward the branch.

On the third try the belt caught, and she was able to drag it down far enough to hold on to. Tossing her knapsack over the wall, she followed, using the tree branch to scale the boundary, dropping over onto the other side, feeling ridiculously proud of herself. Ninja Warrior, *here I come.*

She half expected sirens and bright lights, but the tiny house was dark. Summer and Taka picked a rotten time to go on vacation, she thought, grabbing her bag and shoving her belt inside it as she walked through the tiny, winter-dead garden. The house was so small it would fit inside her mother's bedroom suite, but Lianne was nothing if not pampered, and given Tokyo real estate this was probably considered palatial.

The last thing she wanted to do was break a window, but the inner door was unlocked. Probably because no one would dare mess with the grandson of a Yakuza leader. She kicked off her shoes and went in. Alice through the looking glass, she thought.

Where the hell was Summer?

It wasn't like Reno was trying to sneak into Japan. If anyone, in particular, his very annoyed grandfather, bothered to check, they'd know the moment he landed at Narita airport. He was hoping Ojiisan wasn't going to notice. If he had to choose between duty to his grandfather and saving Taka's sister-in-law from blundering her way into trouble, his choice was clear. Even his grandfather, if asked, would agree. He wasn't about to ask.

His name was powerful enough to get **him** through Customs quickly, and he rented a motorcycle and rode fast and hard toward the city, but he should have known it wouldn't be that easy. By the time he reached Chiba City it was getting dark, and he knew he wasn't alone—he'd been a fool to underestimate his grandfather's influence. He should probably let the two men following him herd him straight to his grandfather's compound. If Ojiisan knew when he landed, he could also know where Taka's sister-in-law was. His grandfather might have even taken care of the problem, which would make life a lot easier. Reno had made a promise, and he wasn't in the habit of breaking promises to family members, even if they were only his cousin's wife.

He didn't need to be the one to rescue Jilly— he'd only seen her once in his life. He probably wouldn't even recognize her.

That was bullshit—he'd know her if he was blindfolded. He'd taken one look at her and felt his world begin to crumble away.

And he liked his world. He liked the variety of women, he liked making his own rules, he liked answering to no one if he could help it, his grandfather and his cousin if he must.

The men following him, his grandfather's men, were some of the best. Grandfather would tolerate nothing less. It was going to be too bad that they lost him, and if he were a better person, he'd let them catch up with him. Mistakes weren't tolerated.

But he hadn't spent enough time in England to

become sentimental. He took the last turn heading into the heart of the city, slowing down just enough to lull his followers, and then took a sharp left, disappearing down an alleyway too narrow for his grandfather's cars. The air was crisp and cold, and he threw back his head and laughed from the sheer exhilaration of the day. He was back home, he'd managed to lose his grandfather's men and he was riding a Harley-Davidson. What more could he ask?

He took another left down the next alleyway, leaning into it, and then came to an abrupt halt. There was no mistaking the white stretch limousine that blocked his way. No mistaking the two black cars that pulled up on either side of it, effectively cutting off any escape. The headlights glared from both sides, filling the trap with an unearthly light.

He climbed off the motorcycle, pulled off the helmet he'd worn more for disguise than safety, shook out his hair and waited.

He recognized the driver of the limo as he lumbered his way out of the front seat. Kobayashi was a former sumo wrestler and his grandfather's personal bodyguard. He was huge, powerful, but not very fast, and Reno figured he stood a good chance of taking him in a fight. He wasn't about to disgrace his grandfather, however, and he simply stood still, waiting for Kobayashi to open the limo door and his grandfather to emerge.

Reno bowed low, and his long tail of hair swung forward, hitting the street. Unfortunate— Grandfather disapproved of the dyed hair and the tattoos almost as much as he disapproved of Reno's new name.

"Hiromasa-chan," he said sternly, merely dipping his head in return. He had always been a small man, but he looked even more frail in the cold winter light. He was getting old. "What are you doing here? Have your new employers dispensed with your services?"

Belatedly, Reno whipped off the sunglasses his grandfather despised, knowing the tattooed, blood-red tears on his cheekbones would be almost as offensive to the old man's sense of what was proper as the heir. "I've come back for a reason."

"I had no doubt you would have thought of some excuse. I wonder why you didn't think it was necessary to inform your grandfather that you'd decided to disobey his orders and return home."

"It concerns the sister of Taka-chan's wife."

"And you didn't think your grandfather was capable of seeing to the family honor?" His grandfather's voice was soft, deadly.

Reno bowed again. He'd almost gotten out of the habit in the short time he'd been in England, but his grandfather was enough to scare the shit out of anyone. "We didn't wish to disturb you, Ojiisan. We thought it was a matter for the Committee—"

"We?" his grandfather interrupted. "It is only by my kindness that I allow you and your cousin to work for this…Committee. But when it comes to matters of family I am the one who decides what needs to be done."

*Shit, shit, shit. Peter Madsen liked to think he was scary—he was nothing compared to the Old Man.* Another goddamned bow. "Apparently she's come to Japan to visit her sister."

"And Taka-chan and his wife have gone to the mountains until the Russians can be dealt with," his grandfather said smoothly.

Reno wasn't surprised he knew so much—it would have been more astonishing if he didn't. "We don't know for sure that they're Russians," he said.

"Yes, we do. But the arrival of Su-chan's sister is something new. Surely Taka would have told her not to come once he learned of the danger."

"Apparently it was an impulse. She didn't tell them."

The old man's expression signified his opinion

of the younger generation, *gaijin* and impulses. "When is she arriving?"

"I don't know, Ojiisan. She may be here already."

"And where would she be staying?"

If it weren't so cold, Reno'd be sweating. The wind was whistling down the alleyway, but compared to his grandfather it was tropical. "I don't know."

"Did you check the hotels?"

This was the tricky part. "I don't know her full name. It's Jilly…something. She's Su-chan's half sister and her family name is different."

The sigh his grandfather emitted was so soft that the wind could have whipped it away. But Reno heard it. "Her name is Jillian Lovitz." He snapped his fingers, and one of the men who'd emerged from the black cars hurried to his side. This was someone new since Reno's banishment. His grandfather said something under his breath, and with a low bow the man returned to the car.

"Hitomi-san will find out what he can. In the meantime, you will come back to the compound and I will see what I can do—"

"No."

The silence was absolute. His grandfather froze.

"No," Reno said again, this time in a steadier voice. "Finding and protecting her is my duty, my responsibility. I don't work for you right now, Ojiisan. I work for the Committee, as does Taka-san. I owe it to my employers and to my cousin to protect his sister-in-law."

Kobayashi could come over and crush his bones, Reno thought, if his grandfather gave the signal, and the old man looked tempted. But he'd be damned if he'd run. "It's my duty," he said again, hoping to sway his grandfather.

A tiny motion of one hand, and Kobayashi relaxed. "And it is merely a coincidence that this young lady is a pretty young woman?" his grandfather said.

"I don't even remember what she looks like."

"Do not lie to me. You forget that I raised you. Surely there were enough *gaijin* in England to keep you busy?"

He could be just as calm as his grandfather. He said nothing—he'd already said enough.

But Reno was up against a master. His grandfather was silent, looking at him out of wrinkled eyes, and the only sound was the traffic beyond the alleyway and the noise of the wind. A moment later Hitomi-san emerged from the black car, an electronic tablet in his hand, and whispered something in his grandfather's ear.

Reno would have given ten years off his life to

know what the man said, but he'd be damned if he'd ask. He and Ojiisan were at a standstill— they would both freeze to the ground before either of them blinked.

And then, to his shock, his grandfather lifted his hand and beckoned him closer.

For a moment Reno didn't move. Kobayashi would never catch him if he ran—maybe Ojiisan was bringing him closer to give his sumo bodyguard a clear shot. But pride demanded he approach, and if his grandfather had decided to dispense with him, in the end there wasn't much he could do about it.

He stopped just in front of the frail old man. "The girl arrived earlier today. She hasn't checked into any of the hotels—either she's gone to Taka's house or she found herself a *ryokan*. And I don't think a *gaijin* would appreciate the beauty of a traditional Japanese inn."

He wasn't about to protest. He had no idea what Jilly Lovitz would appreciate or not. And why the hell did her name have so many fucking *L*'s in it? She'd probably done it on purpose, just to annoy him.

"Three Russian nationals with ties to the old KGB also landed in Japan, at Kansai airport a few days ago. We haven't tracked them yet, but unless they had information as to where Taka and Su-chan went, they'd head to Tokyo. Putting your little *gaijin* in danger."

"Not so little," Reno said. "She's as tall as I am. And not mine."

"You've claimed responsibility for her. She's yours now, at least until you get her home safely. After that you will concentrate on your new work with the Committee until I call for you."

Reno blinked. His grandfather was giving in—he'd expected more of a battle from the stubborn old man. He'd even been prepared to escape if Kobayashi hustled him into the limo and back to the compound against his will.

But the old man had accepted his choice. "Are you sick?" Reno demanded, suddenly worried. "Dying?"

His grandfather made a face. "You've only been gone six weeks, Hiromasa-chan. And if I were dying, you'd be the first to know, and you'd be back here, taking your proper place in the family, not playing spy like your cousin Taka-chan. You say Jillian is your responsibility and you refuse my help—so be it. I would suggest that you don't fail. If you think I'm difficult, then you have forgotten how ruthless your cousin can be. He wouldn't like the sister of his wife to be in any danger, and he wouldn't hesitate to express his displeasure if you let anything happen to her."

"I'm not going to let anything happen to her. That's why I'm back here, against your instructions. I'll find her and send her back home, and then I'll return to England and continue my new work."

If his grandfather didn't find that a pleasing prospect, he didn't say so. "Don't take too long, Hiromasa-chan."

"I expect I'll find her at Taka-chan's house and we'll be out of the country by tomorrow."

"I wasn't talking about the girl. I have no doubt you'll find her quickly. I'm talking about something else entirely. I'm not going to live forever."

He looked down at the little old man who had always scared the hell out of him. "Yes, you will, Ojiisan," he said softly. "You're too old and mean to die."

"Disrespectful," his grandfather sniffed, looking pleased. "Go find the girl and keep her safe. And whatever you do, do not fall in love with her. We've already had too many *gaijin* in the family. You need a nice Japanese girl to marry. I'll make the arrangements myself."

"I don't want to marry anyone. At least not right now. And I don't believe in falling in love."

"Just remember that," his grandfather said. He

reached up and put a hand on Reno's shoulder, and his grip was still powerful. "And cut your hair," he added, peevish.

To hug his grandfather would have been very bad form, particularly with his men watching. Reno had to make do with a deep bow, moving back as the old man climbed into the limo.

He waited until his grandfather's army left before he went back to his Harley. It started with the guttural roar that was one of his favorite sounds in the world, and he took off into the growing darkness. Looking for someone he wasn't sure he wanted to find.

# 2

Jilly awoke suddenly, the developing darkness like a blanket over her head. She couldn't see, couldn't breathe, couldn't remember where the hell she was.

It only took a second for the memories to come flooding back. She was in Japan at her sister's house, and it was sometime in the middle of the night.

She forced her breathing to slow. She could still feel her heart slamming against her chest—the momentary panic had been unexpected and powerful. She closed her eyes again in the inky darkness. And then she heard it.

A noise beyond her closed door—someone was moving around in the front bedroom, quietly, so as not to disturb anyone.

Taka and Summer must have returned. She scrambled to her feet, relief flooding her. She hadn't allowed herself to worry about them; Taka was the kind of man you could count on to face down an army. Summer would always be safe with him.

She reached for the door, then hesitated. She was wearing flannel boxers and a tank top to sleep in—a little informal for company. It would have to do. Taka would politely avert his enigmatic gaze, and Summer would find her something to wear, make tea and comfort her.

It wasn't until she opened the door that she considered the extremely unpleasant notion that it might be someone other than her sister and her husband. She could see the refracted beam of a flashlight dance around the room at the end of the corridor. Why would Taka use a flashlight? He knew where the lights were.

And why weren't they talking? If Taka had come alone, why was he trying to be so quiet?

She froze, all her latent instincts swamping her. She knew this feeling, remembered it far too well. She'd been trapped once before, held captive by a very dangerous group of people just two short years ago. Isobel had rescued her, but Isobel was far away, and the Committee would have no reason to worry about her. No one even knew she'd come to Japan, unless her sister had decided to check for messages. This time it was going to be up to her to get out of whatever mess she got herself into.

There was no way out the way she'd come—the windows in the back room were high and narrow. There was no place to hide back there, either. If someone was searching the place, they'd find her.

And maybe there was a perfectly reasonable explanation for it all. Now she could hear low murmuring voices, and she strained to hear enough to translate.

But they weren't speaking Japanese, they were speaking Russian, and she was in deep shit.

She took a step backward, her bare feet silent on the *tatami* mats, when something came at her from the darkened cavern of the bedroom, swooping down on her like a giant bird of prey, clamping a hand over her mouth before she screamed, holding her back against his body in an iron grip.

And it was a "him." Taller than she was, and much, much stronger. Any attempt she made to struggle was swiftly countered. She kicked her long legs back, and one leather-clad leg caught hers as he pulled her back into the bedroom with rough hands, closing the door, trapping them in there.

"Hold still!" a voice hissed in her ear. She didn't know the voice—she'd barely heard him speak in the past, and then it had been in Japanese. But she knew who it was, with an instinct just as powerful as the ones that told her she was in danger.

She immediately stopped struggling. He had one arm wrapped around her waist, like an iron bar, pressing against her ribs. He loosened the pressure slightly as he felt her stillness.

"If you make a sound, you'll die. Do you understand?" he whispered in her ear, so quietly it was almost soundless. For a moment Jilly wondered who was the threat—the men beyond the closed door or the one holding her clamped against him?

She nodded, as much as his smothering hand would let her, and he slowly began to release her.

She wondered what would happen if she screamed. Would he snap her neck and leave her for his cousin to find?

He stepped back, soundlessly, and she turned to look at him. Her eyes had started to grow accustomed to the inky blackness. It was Reno, all right, closer than she'd ever been to him. In the darkness she could see the glitter in his eyes and not much more.

"Stay here," he whispered.

She didn't have a choice. He pushed her out of the way, stepping out into the hallway and closing the door behind him.

For half a minute she was tempted to try to escape. There was noise now—thuds and bumps and a sound, almost like a cry, cut off before it even began. And then silence.

He was dead, and there was nothing she could do but wait there until they found her. The only thing she had to defend herself was her backpack, heavy with books, and she picked it up, ready to fling it at the head of the first man who came through her door.

The footfalls were loud as they approached the bedroom, and she knew she was screwed. Reno had been silent as a ghost, and no Japanese would enter a house with his shoes on.

The door opened, and she slammed the backpack toward his head with all her strength.

"Holy motherfucker," Reno said in a disgruntled voice. "What are you doing?"

He switched on the light, and for a moment she was blinded. He closed the door, shutting them in, shutting whatever it was out.

She blinked. How could she have forgotten? The flame-red hair, the tattooed cheekbones, the faint sneer on his admittedly beautiful mouth.

"You probably don't remember me," she said, nervous. He was taller than she remembered, older than she remembered, wilder than she remembered. As dangerous, as exotic, as mesmerizing as her embarrassingly adolescent fantasies, and she faced the truth. She hadn't come here for her sister's comfort or for a look at the Heian-era pottery. She'd come back for him. And it had been a mistake.

"I know who you are," he said, his voice cool and emotionless, his English perfect. "Why do you think I'm here?"

"Visiting Taka and Summer?" she said.

"Taka and Su-chan are in hiding where no one can get to them."

"Why? Are they in danger?"

He looked even more irritated. "Everyone who works for the Committee is in danger. Do you usually show up uninvited? Because I know Taka would never have forgotten to warn you."

Now that her initial fear had faded, she was starting to get pissed off. Whatever had been threatening her was gone, fairy tales were over, and she wasn't about to let this almost-stranger bully her. "I am always welcome at my sister's house," she said in a frosty voice. "She's been wanting me to come."

"I don't think so. She wanted you as far from Japan as she could get you."

"Why?"

Reno blinked, his face giving nothing away.

"Ask her when you see her. In the meantime we have to get you out of here before the Russians send someone else."

"Russians? What are you talking about? What Russians?" she demanded.

"Paid mercenaries," he said briefly. "It doesn't concern you—you just got in the line of fire. I'll put you in a taxi to the airport and you won't have to worry about it—"

"Oh, hell, no. I'm not getting back on a plane."

"I'll tie you up and put you on it myself."

Had she ever thought he was fascinating? Beautiful? He was an obnoxious bully, and it was a good thing she found out now before she let her adolescent fantasies get out of control. Or more out of control, since they'd already given her a good run.

"I don't think so," she said with deceptive calm.

He cocked his head to one side, looking at her for a long, silent moment. "You'd better get some clothes on," he said. "Unless you want to go out on the streets of Tokyo in your underwear."

She'd forgotten her skimpy attire, and she could feel her fair skin flushing. Which was ridiculous—he was making it patently clear that he had no interest in her.

So much for daydreams.

She scooped up her scattered clothes. "I'll be ready in a minute," she said, heading for the door.

Only to have him reach out and slam it shut. "You can get dressed here. I'm not letting you out of my sight."

"If you expect me to get dressed, you're going to have to."

He simply leaned back against the door, folding his arms across his chest.

She made a low, growling noise. He didn't move. With a frustrated sigh she turned her back to him, reaching for her bra.

Putting it on while she was still wearing the tank top was tricky, but she managed, turning back around triumphantly when she finished. Only to find he wasn't even watching her—she could've ripped off her shirt and flashed him and he wouldn't have noticed. He was staring at his cell phone, reading a text message.

She yanked her jeans on over the boxers, pulled a long-sleeved T-shirt over her head and shoved the last of her things into the heavy backpack. He didn't move, still staring at the tiny screen.

Then he glanced up at her, almost as if he'd forgotten her existence.

"Trouble," he said.

People like Reno and Taka wouldn't use that

term lightly, and Jilly froze. "Is it my sister? Has something happened?"

He was texting back, his long, slender fingers flying over the keypad, ignoring her. He glanced up at her. His eyes were a deep rich brown—for some reason, she had thought they were green. "Are you ready? Where are your shoes?"

"In the entryway, of course." If he was surprised that she knew proper etiquette, he didn't show it. "Are you going to answer my question? What kind of trouble?"

"Read for yourself," he said, tossing the phone to her. He was lucky; she just managed to catch it. It wouldn't help either of them if it shattered on the hard floor. She looked down at the text message.

"Very funny," she said, resisting the impulse to throw the phone back at him. She placed it carefully in his outstretched hand. "I can't read *kanji*."

"I know." He shoved the phone in the pocket of his pants, making the leather pull against his crotch for a moment.

And what the hell was she doing, noticing? It had become clear quite quickly that Reno was the enemy, and the smartest thing she could do was to get away from him as soon as possible, or she probably *would* find herself on a plane back to L.A., and she wasn't going anywhere until she saw Summer. Of course, escaping from someone on their home turf was great in theory, but tricky in practice. She could try reason, though the man standing in front of her didn't look particularly reasonable. He looked annoyed, bored and impatient.

And to think she used to lie in her bed at her family's mansion in the Hollywood Hills and fantasize about him. Them. Together.

Her sister had warned her about Reno. And she had no doubt that she and Taka had done their best to keep her away from the punk black sheep of the family.

Big mistake on their part. Ten minutes in his presence and she was so over him. A little exposure therapy would have taken care of the problem long ago.

She took a deep, calming breath. "We're on the same side, you know. I just want to find my sister. Just let me talk to her."

"I don't know where they are. Perhaps my English isn't that good or maybe you just aren't listening. They're in hiding—people are out to kill them, and they'll use you to get to them. So you're going back to your safe life in Hollywood and leaving the professionals to take care of things."

"Professionals? You don't strike me as Committee material. Not if Taka and Peter are anything to go by."

The insult went right past him. "Stop stalling. We need to get the hell out of here."

"Not until you tell me what was on the cell phone."

For a moment he looked as if he'd toss her over his shoulder and haul her ass out of there. She'd like to see him try. They were close to the same height—five feet ten inches, and she wasn't built along the whipcord lines he was.

Maybe he thought better of using force. "Three Russian operatives arrived in Japan four days ago to kill Taka-san and his wife. They were forewarned and went into hiding. Five more Russians arrived at Narita airport several hours ago, and they're going to want to catch up with the first three."

"And?"

"And the first three are dead. Or close enough that it won't matter. The newcomers don't seem to know that their paycheck has dried up. As soon as they do they'll go on to their next job and we'll be safe. Unless they decide to take revenge for the loss of their friends. Whatever the case, we need to get the hell out of here before someone finds them."

"Them?"

"The first three Russians," he said impatiently. "Come on."

He moved away from his spot against the door, opening it. He turned off the light, plunging them into darkness once more, and he took her hand in an unbreakable grip. "Just stay with me and look straight ahead," he growled.

"Why did you turn off the lights? I thought we were safe."

"There are some things you're better off not seeing."

Enough was enough, Jilly decided, incensed. Reno was old-fashioned and sexist, the polar opposite of his cousin. "I can judge that for myself," she said, switching the light back on before he could stop her.

She saw the pool of blood first, then the body of the man.

His head was at a strange angle, and the blood was coming from his mouth and his ears and his slashed throat. Beyond him was another body, eyes wide-open and staring, lying spread-eagled in a pool of blood, dead, as well.

A moment later it was darkness again, and the room swung in dizzy circles as Reno picked her up and tossed her over his shoulder.

They were out in the night air moments later,

leaving the carnage behind them. He moved fast into the darkness, and he made it to the inside of the small park before he set her down.

She immediately threw up. She could still smell it—the blood, the stink of death that she'd never known before. Reno moved away, leaving her alone while she emptied her stomach of its meager contents. He must've known she was too much of a wuss to run.

She took a breath, forestalling the dry heaves that were threatening, and shoved her hair back from her sweat-damp face as a stray shudder swept her body.

He turned and tossed her sneakers to her. "You finished?"

She raised her head from her knees to look at him. "Did you do that?"

"You're still in one piece, aren't you? Of course I did. And it's your own fucking fault for turning the light on. I told you there were things you don't need to see."

"You killed them? Both of them?"

"Three of them. The other one was in the garden. Get over it. Taka is going to be pissed as hell that I even let you see that."

She swallowed. "Isn't he going to be more annoyed at finding three…bodies in his house?"

"It'll be cleaned up by the time it's safe for them to return. My grandfather will see to it." He came back to stand over her, holding out a hand to pull her to her feet, but she ignored it, scrambling up on her own. She still felt weak and shaky, but she wasn't about to let him see.

"Okay," she said. "Narita airport. The hell with jet lag."

"Change of plans. They're watching the airports. The message came from one of my grandfather's men, warning me. I'm going to have to keep you out of sight for a few days until I can get you out."

"You don't have to do anything. I'll check into one of the big tourist hotels and wait until you kill the other five." She didn't bother to hide the bitterness in her voice. "I can't imagine any place safer."

"I said you needed to be kept out of sight. What makes you think the center of Tokyo is out of sight? They'll be checking all the Western-style hotels, looking for you."

"They, whoever they are, don't even know I exist, much less that I've come to Japan."

"They know," he said, his voice as flat as his expression. "Come." He tossed her knapsack to her, and she caught it, almost dropping the heavy weight. "You'll need to put that on."

She didn't argue, shouldering it. "How far are we walking?"

"We're not walking." He vanished into the bushes, and for the first time she noticed the gleam of chrome through the greenery. A moment later he reappeared, pushing a huge, heavy-looking Harley-Davidson motorcycle.

Jilly looked at it with a sinking heart. It was difficult enough when the exotic, undeniably gorgeous creature of her fantasies had turned out to be an obnoxious bully. Of course he had to have a Harley, as well, completing the perfect bad-boy image. With the tattooed teardrops on his high cheekbones and spiky, waist-length, flame-colored hair and his long, leather-clad legs and pointy-toed cowboy boots, he was almost irresistible, despite his manners.

A Harley sealed the deal. He was all her adolescent fantasies come true.

And it was time to grow up.

# 3

Shit. Bloody shit. Holy motherfucker. Goddamn *gaijin* idiot bitch blundering into trouble. He needed to punch something or someone—he was wound up, furious, ready to explode.

She was plastered against him on the back of the motorcycle, and even through his leather jacket and her baggy sweatshirt he could feel her breasts. This was hell, seeing her for the first time in more than two years, when he'd done such a good job of forgetting about her, only to find her in men's underwear and no bra. He was still hard, making the motorcycle even more uncomfortable.

He had only one helmet, and the laws were strict. As long as he stayed in the territory controlled by his grandfather he'd be fine—the police would recognize the flame-red hair and give him a wide berth.

He didn't have the faintest goddamned idea

where to take her. His own apartment was probably being watched and Jilly Lovitz wasn't likely to fit in with the people he usually hung with. He could just imagine how Kyo would react to someone like Jilly. Kyo was a nasty little motherfucker who liked to torment *gaijin,* and Jilly would be fair game.

His job wasn't to protect her from people like Kyo. It was to keep her alive. Maybe a few hours with a maniacal *yakuza* would scare her into staying in her safe home and not go racing off unannounced to a country where she wasn't wanted.

He should take her to his grandfather's. It was the logical thing to do—drop her off and let Ojiisan deal with her. She'd be safe in his grandfather's fortress, with an armed guard of at least twenty men. If the Russians were foolish enough to attempt anything, his grandfather would see to their tidy disposal.

They were coming into a busier part of the city—all he needed to do was turn left and follow the street to his grandfather's compound. It didn't matter that he told the old man he'd take care of things. If anything Ojiisan would be pleased at his grandson's belated obedience.

It was the smart thing to do, the safe careful choice.

Who the hell was he kidding—he'd never been safe or careful in his life and he wasn't about to start now. The girl plastered against him felt warm, soft, and he deserved something for the aggravation she caused him.

He wasn't going to sleep with her—he valued his head too much to risk Taka's fury. It had been almost two years since Taka told him to keep away from his sister-in-law, but he had no doubt Taka still meant what he said.

No, he deserved something, just to taste, and he was going to take it. It would be worth a broken bone or two.

She had her head down—his body was shielding her from the wind. Her arms were tight around his waist. What would she do if he took one of those hands and put it between his legs?

Probably cause him to spin out. Right now, she was too shook up for him to even attempt anything. It would be better all around if he just put her on a plane back to California and forgot about her. Except that he hadn't really forgotten about her for the last two years—there was no reason things were going to be any different. Especially now that she was all grown up.

He turned right, heading away from his grandfather's compound. He needed to dump the

Harley—it was too conspicuous. He needed to find a salaryman's car, something cheap and practical and anonymous.

The very thought made him shudder. Maybe being conspicuous was the safest way to play. There'd be too many people watching for anyone to try a snatch and grab with his passenger.

Or was she his hostage? He wasn't quite sure.

In the meantime, he needed someplace safe and anonymous to spend what little was left of the night. There were traditional inns to the north— they would be off the grid and no one using modern technology would be able to find them.

And a *ryokan* was a definite buzz kill, with thin futons on the floor rather than a hotel room with a big, inviting bed to tempt him. It was the smartest thing to do. Too bad he didn't feel like being smart. He'd do it anyway.

He was coming down from the adrenaline rush. He didn't want to think about what he'd had to do back at Taka's house. It was a waste of time brooding about it. They were professionals, and he'd had no choice. Right now he was dead tired, and she must be just as jet-lagged as he was. They needed someplace safe so he could get a few hours' sleep. And figure out what his next move was.

\* \* \*

Jilly was beyond cold, beyond feeling as she clung to the only thing safe in a crazy world. She put her head against his black leather jacket, closing her eyes, breathing in the smell of the night.

She had no sense of time or space—it felt as if she were riding a dragon, clinging to the only thing solid and safe. A man who had just killed three people and didn't seem to notice.

Summer had never given her more than a brief outline of what happened when she first met Takashi O'Brien. People had died. People had shot at her while she escaped with Isobel Lambert.

But she'd never actually seen death. Never had to wrap her arms around someone who'd just dealt it.

She turned her face to breathe in the smell of leather. It was oddly comforting. She didn't know how long she been riding on the back of the motorcycle—it could have been one hour or five. Her body ached, her arms and her thighs were numb and she wanted him to stop this mad, hurtling pace and rest. She wanted to ride forever on the back of the dragon.

When he finally stopped, she almost fell—he caught her easily enough, with cool impersonal hands.

The street was dark, the building in front of them darker still. A row of small flags draped the entrance to the house, but she was in no shape to figure what they meant.

"Come on," he said, impatient, as she stared up at the building.

"Where are we?" She didn't recognize her own voice—it sounded as if she'd been screaming and she'd hardly said a word. She must be in shock, she thought.

"A *ryokan.*" He clearly wasn't about to explain further. And part of her was willing just to follow him, mindlessly.

She pulled herself together. "Why? Why here?"

"The people looking for us would track us down if we went to one of the big Western-style hotels. We can spend the rest of the night here, sleep and figure out what the fuck we're going to do."

"We?" she echoed.

"If they don't know I took care of the men in Taka's house, it won't take them long to find out. I don't think they're going to bother with revenge—mercenaries are too practical to kill for anything other than profit, and their paycheck has dried up. Once they realize there's nothing to be gained, they'll leave Japan and we'll be safe." He tried to take her arm, but she yanked free.

"I'm not going anywhere until you explain what the hell is going on. Who are these Russians? Why would they want to kill Taka? And who's paying them?" Her voice was stronger now, and she looked into his eyes, meeting his cool, assessing gaze head-on.

"I'm not going to stand out in the open and explain anything. Come with me willingly or I'll knock you out and carry you in."

"You and what army?"

His forehead wrinkled. "Army?" he echoed.

His English was so good she'd forgotten he might not know idioms. "I mean, I dare you," she said, fierce.

Big mistake. In the crazy hours she'd forgotten how he'd manhandled her out of Taka's house.

"If you say so," he said. She didn't see it coming, didn't see a move. Just a sudden and enveloping darkness, and she fell into it, willingly.

Everything hurt. Jilly's back, shoulders, butt, knees. She didn't want to open her eyes—the last time she'd opened her eyes, death and violence had followed. Maybe if she could ignore the pain, she could go back to sleep, in spite of the mercilessly bright light battering against her eyelids.

"Stop faking it. I know you're awake."

She knew that voice, knew the conflict it aroused inside her. The beautiful bad boy on the motorcycle. The psychotic bully who'd knocked her unconscious.

She opened her eyes. They were in a traditional Japanese room, *shoji* screens encasing them on two sides, thin mattresses on the floor. Reno was sitting on one wearing a light cotton robe decorated with blue crests. He'd taken a shower and his long hair hung loose around his shoulders, darker when it was wet, a deep, respectable auburn rather than the bright flame.

She wasn't sure what was making her madder—the fact that he had knocked her out, or that he'd had a shower when she would've killed for one. She sat up, realizing she'd been sleeping, if you could call it that, on one of the identical thin futons. No wonder her entire body felt stiff and ancient. A bed of nails wouldn't have been much worse.

And she looked down, not at the futon but at the neat pile of her clothes, next to the mattress. She was wearing a thin cotton robe, a *yukata*, a perfect match to the one Reno was wearing, and it probably looked just as ridiculous on a *gaijin* as it looked wonderful on him.

"Don't get excited," he said. "The owner undressed you for me and put the *yukata* on. I told her you were drunk and passed out."

Jilly didn't know whether to be relieved or angry. "I don't drink."

"I don't think she cared. You've got your choice. You can go to the women's baths or you can sit there and watch me dress."

"Where is the bath?"

The faint curve of his mouth was more a smirk than a smile. "Go out into the hallway and turn left. The women's bath is at the end of the hall. Don't make the mistake of turning right—you'd end up in the men's bath, and I don't think your foreign eyes could handle the shock of seeing a Japanese man naked."

She kept her mouth shut. If she denied it, he'd probably drop the robe just to prove his point and she really didn't want to see Reno naked.

She'd been trying not to look at him, but she could feel the color flood her face anyway. Ridiculous—she wasn't used to blushing, wasn't used to being coy. You couldn't grow up in Southern California, much less around a mother like Lianne, without learning to be unaffected by any kind of nudity.

It was just this one particular man, and it had less to do with reality and more to do with the stupid crush that had once taken up far too much of her time.

At least she'd accomplished one thing she'd set out to do. She'd gotten over any lingering fantasy about Reno. For that matter, the past twenty-four hours had been so nerve-racking that the embarrassingly wretched, fumbling, one-night stand she'd been running from had faded into nothingness.

Really, the crush on Reno had been her sister's fault, no matter how well meaning she'd been. If Summer hadn't kept them an ocean apart, she would've gotten over it quickly. It was the exotic mystery of him—familiarity, if it didn't breed contempt, at least bred a comforting degree of imperviousness.

But she still didn't want to see him naked.

She scooped up her clothes, heading for the sliding screen, just as he began to untie the belt of the *yukata*. "Asshole," she muttered under her breath, sliding the door closed behind her.

But his soft laugh carried anyway.

The narrow hall was deserted, as was the women's bathing room, and the large communal bath held nothing but steaming water. Just as well—she wasn't in the mood for an audience.

Stripping off the *yukata*, she sat down on a

low stool and began to wash herself. She'd been around her sister long enough to know the proper bath etiquette. Clean yourself before you got in the bath, and never bring soap with you.

The hot bath was glorious, enveloping her aching body in a liquid embrace. She wasn't sure what the rules were about ducking her head under, but she couldn't resist, feeling her short-cropped hair flow around her in the hot, hot water.

Maybe she'd just stay there until her skin got all wrinkled and pruney, and Reno gave up on his self-appointed mission to look out for her. He wouldn't come after her in the women's bath; she'd be temporarily safe from interruption, at least for a short, blessedly peaceful time.

Except now a quiet young Japanese woman entered, dressed in the same *yukata*.

*"Ohayo,"* Jilly said, wishing her good morning.

The woman looked startled, and whether it was from a *gaijin* speaking Japanese or the fact that a stranger spoke to her, Jilly couldn't be sure. She murmured an answering *"oha"* before she turned her back and began to wash her delicate body.

Making Jilly feel like a hulking giant. She was probably twice the size of the small, slender woman, and she had no more than a stubborn ten pounds too much by American standards. No wonder Reno was looking at her with nothing warmer than annoyance. She must look like a porker compared to what he was used to.

One thing was certain—she wasn't climbing out of the bath and exposing her body to the woman's curious eyes.

Unfortunately once in the water, the woman seemed to have no interest in leaving. She closed her eyes, leaned her perfect head back and let the water lap around her.

Jilly started to move toward the edge of the bath, and the woman's eyes opened, looking at her curiously. Jilly stayed put.

Not that Jilly could blame her. She'd probably never seen a woman who was almost six feet tall. But her curiosity was going to have to remain unsatisfied, because Jilly wasn't going anywhere with an audience. She'd spent most of her life around her exhibitionist mother, who had the best body money could buy, and in reaction she was almost obsessively modest. She didn't even want her mother's dog to see her naked.

She could hear voices out in the corridor, and a moment later the door slid open and a harried-looking woman began chiding her in very fast Japanese.

Jilly only knew every fourth word, but she had

no trouble understanding. She was supposed to get out of the bath—her brother was waiting for her.

At that point, an elderly gentleman poked his head in the door, clearly drawn by the noise, and Jilly sank down lower in the bath, willing them all to go away.

The woman, presumably the innkeeper, had to pause to take a breath. The other woman in the bath had sat up, curious and totally unconcerned with the audience.

A moment later the old gentleman was politely but firmly moved from the doorway, and Reno strode in, causing both Japanese women to shriek in protest. Apparently observing from the hall was kosher, but actually entering the inner sanctum was not.

"Go away," Jilly snapped.

"Get out of the bath." He crossed the small room, ignoring the restraining hands of the innkeeper, ignoring the young woman who slumped lower in the bath, towering over Jilly with an expression on his face that looked ancient. The look of a samurai about to behead his enemy.

She tried to move out of his way, but she underestimated him. He reached down into the water, caught her arms and hauled her out, stark naked and dripping wet.

The shrieks increased, joined by Jilly's, but Reno's sharp words silenced them all.

She tried to squirm out of his grasp, but he held tight, grabbing her discarded *yukata* and wrapping it around her like a blanket before he hustled her out of the room, past the dignified gentleman who was looking at her with unabashed enthusiasm.

Reno was muttering under his breath. He shoved her back in the room, accompanied by a terse "get dressed" and somehow managed to close the sliding paper screen door with the equivalent of a slam.

She yanked her clothes on quickly, knowing he was just as likely to come back in and watch her. A moment later she slid the door open again, expecting to meet his glowering face.

The hall was empty when she poked her head out, and she was wondering whether he'd decided to abandon her after all when she heard the voices. Men's voices, speaking lousy Japanese. With a Russian accent.

And then Reno was there, her shoes in his hand, and she had enough sense to simply go with him, down the hall, away from the voices, as silent as he was.

The day was winter bright, the sun brilliant overhead as he herded her away from the inn.

The motorcycle was nowhere in sight, a small gray sedan sitting in its place.

He started to hustle her into the driver's seat, but at that point, enough was enough.

"I'm not driving—"

He swore again, shoving her in. "We drive on the left," he said. "Left side of the road, driver's side on the right." He slammed the door shut behind her and moved around to climb into the driver's seat.

"Oh, like the English."

"The English drive like us," he snapped, his voice deep and arrogant.

He looked ridiculous—an exotic bird of paradise in a commuter car. "Fasten your seat belt," he said, not bothering to do his up.

"Where is the motorcycle?"

"I ditched it. Someone will find it sooner or later and return it to the rental company."

"Not in the U.S."

"We're not in the U.S., in case you haven't noticed. People don't steal lost property, they return it."

"How did you get this car?"

"I stole it."

Riding on the back of a motorcycle had been better—even if it was bright daylight, she still would have been able to bury her head against his back and not see a thing. Sitting in the front seat of the cramped little car, she had to watch everything—the horrific traffic, Reno's darting, bobbing driving style, more like a boxer's than a driver's, and to top everything off she was on the wrong side, feeling as if she were responsible for the car.

She tried closing her eyes, but that only made it worse. There was an annoying jingle sound behind her, like Santa's reindeer gone berserk, and her eyes flashed open again.

"What the hell is that noise?" she demanded.

"Look behind you."

She had expected to see a Japanese Good Humor Man on steroids, only to see a tiny object suction-cupped to the back window. It looked like a miniature portable shrine, accompanied by bells and a scrap of writing, and she unfastened her seat belt to snatch it off the window.

"It's a safe driving talisman," Reno said, just before she grabbed it, and made a sudden sharp right turn in front of ten cars coming directly at him. She fell against him, his hard, strong body, and she swiftly pushed away from him, sitting back in her seat and refastening the seat belt with shaking hands. With Reno's driving and

Tokyo traffic they were going to need all the luck they could get.

"Where are we going?"

"I'm taking you to Osaka. Kansai airport should be safer, and the sooner you get the hell out of Japan, the better. The Russians clearly haven't gotten word that their services are no longer required, and it's too much of a pain in the ass to keep you away from them."

"Why do they even want me?"

"They don't," he said in a flat tone. "You're just a means to an end. If they have you, Taka will have to come out of hiding. You're not important at all except for your relationship."

"Great to know," she said sarcastically. "And what makes you think they won't come after me at home? Though I don't suppose that would be your problem—as long as you hand me off it's no longer your business. And I still don't understand why you're the one who came after me in the first place when you clearly have a problem with me. Why didn't you just refuse?"

"I wasn't ordered. I insisted. You don't understand Japanese traditions—whether I like it or not you now belong to our family, and family is protected."

"Well, look at it this way. You send me back

and it'll be up to someone else to keep the bad guys away."

"Once they know there's no money, there'll be no incentive to come after you," he snapped.

"And when will that be? They seem to be slow learners."

He just looked at her. And then began swearing under his breath. At least she assumed it was swearing—she recognized the English obscenities and a few of the French, but her knowledge of Japanese curses was so far woefully small. Being around Reno, that was bound to improve.

"Sorry to be such a nuisance," she said, trying to sound abject and failing. She still hadn't gotten past him hauling her naked out of the bath. "But I don't think Osaka and sending me home without protection is a wise idea."

He only grunted, driving faster. He had an unfortunate tendency to make sudden, precipitous turns, and it almost seemed as if they were driving in circles. They probably were, just to make sure no one was following them. No matter what the reason, it was making her dizzy.

She closed her eyes, sliding down as well as she could in the small seat. "Wake me when we get there," she said. And proceeded to ignore him and everything else.

# 4

*Wake me when we get there*, Reno thought, gunning the motor. *Get where? I don't have a fucking clue where we're going. She was right—Osaka and an airplane home were out of the question.*

He glanced over at the girl beside him. He wasn't going to think about it. He wasn't going to remember what her long, pale body looked like, dripping wet, even if the image was burned into his eyeballs. He wasn't going to think about the way she smelled, of sandalwood soap and water. He most definitely wasn't going to think about the way she felt, her sleek wet skin, the softness beneath the enveloping *yukata*. He wasn't going to think about anything but getting rid of her as fast as he could.

She was right, of course. The Russians might not have been aware of her existence before, but now that they knew, there was a good chance they wouldn't simply forget about her once he got her out of Japan. They didn't seem to be easily discouraged, which didn't make sense. Any soldier-for-hire worth his salt wasn't going to fight for principle or revenge. They killed for money, and with Thomason's death the money had dried up. But they seemed to be ignoring that simple fact. So who else could be paying them? Feeding them information?

For some reason Jilly was still prime bait, and the last thing he was going to do was appoint himself her private bodyguard.

He was going to need help, whether he wanted to admit it or not. And it was going to have to come from his grandfather—Peter and the Committee just didn't have the resources right now.

His grandfather's compound in one of the industrial areas of Tokyo was an armed fortress—no one could get to her there. He pulled the cell phone from his pocket and began texting, one eye on the road, one hand on the steering wheel. It was a good thing Jilly had decided to close her eyes, otherwise she'd probably be screaming at him.

God only knew what he saw in her. She was too big—almost as tall as he was, and while her body was the kind that filled his wet dreams she wasn't his type. He despised American women. He had a grudging affection for his cousin Taka's American wife, but in general he didn't like them. At least, not anywhere but in bed.

And he wasn't going to fuck Taka's sister-in-law. Not if he wanted to keep his balls.

The cell phone vibrated in his hand, an almost instant response. *Keep away from the compound— it was too dangerous. I'll find Taka. Head for the summer cottage in the mountains and wait for word.*

He could do that. He was tired. He'd spent most of what was left of the night staring at her while she slept, watching the rise and fall of her breasts beneath the thin cotton.

He hadn't lied to her—he'd had the motherly innkeeper undress her. Once he'd carried her in, he hadn't touched her. It wasn't his fault if he'd been hoping she was a restless sleeper, tossing and turning so that the robe opened.

But she'd been utterly still, so still that for a while he'd wondered if he'd accidentally killed her, used a little too much pressure when he knocked her out.

Then Taka really would have killed him.

He'd been halfway across the small room on his knees, ready to touch her, just to make sure she was still alive, when she made a small sound, halfway between a sigh and a moan.

He froze, ready to jump her from the sheer sexuality of that sound, but instead he retreated back to his own futon, to sit and watch her as the morning light began to slip into the room. He was adept at self-control on the few occasions he chose to use it. This was one of those occasions. He wasn't going to touch her.

They were safe for the moment—he'd taken enough obscure detours to throw off a native, and the Russian mercenaries would be helpless in the complex road system that snaked through Tokyo. Once they were beyond the sprawling city he could relax, at least a little bit, while he figured out what the hell to do with her.

Maybe Ojiisan would get word to Taka and his troubles would be over. No way was Taka going to leave his wife's sister in Reno's uncharitable hands—they'd made sure Jilly and Reno had been kept a half a world away from each other since they'd met. He didn't think that was about to change. Not since Su-chan had laid down the law soon after she'd married Taka.

"I need you to do me a favor," she'd said.

He'd looked at her. Summer Hawthorne was fearless, devoted to her husband, and Taka would beat the shit out of him if he showed her any disrespect. At least, any more than he dished out to everyone with the exception of his austere grandfather.

"All right," he'd said, bowing slightly out of habit.

Summer didn't look convinced. "You probably won't like it."

"I try very hard not to do anything I don't want to do, but you saved my life, so I must owe you."

"I want you to keep out of California."

He said nothing for a moment, then, "My grandfather has a number of important businesses all along the West Coast of your country, including real estate investments in and around L.A. I go where he sends me, and since I'm bilingual I'm the best choice, particularly with Taka out of the picture."

"He could send someone else. And it's just the L.A. area I want you to keep away from."

"Why?"

"My sister."

"I don't remember your sister," he said, a lie. But Su-chan was too anxious to notice.

"You saw her at Peter and Genevieve's house. She's tall, kind of awkward, blond hair when she isn't dyeing it. Her name's Jilly."

"I remember," he conceded, not showing how well he remembered. "What about her?"

"She wants to come visit, and I don't want her here."

"And what does that have to do with me?"

"You're the reason I don't want her here." He didn't say anything, and she stumbled on. "She's got some silly adolescent crush on you. You've got to understand my sister has lived a very sheltered life. She's freakishly smart—she graduated from high school when she was fifteen, college when she was eighteen. She'd always been surrounded by people who were much older than she was, and she's never had the chance to develop normal relationships."

"And what does that have to do with me?"

Su-chan bit her lip. "She has a crush on you. I don't know what you said to her or what happened in England—I was a little preoccupied.…"

"You and Taka were all over each other—your sister and I could have been fucking in the garden and you wouldn't have noticed."

Summer turned pale. "Did you?"

"Fuck in the garden? Fuck at all? No. As a matter of fact, I don't think we even talked before I got hustled out of there."

Su-chan sighed. "You didn't need to. She took one look at you and lost all common sense. You shouldn't be surprised—you know you're catnip where women are concerned. They can't leave you alone."

"Su-chan, if your sister has fallen in love with me, then it's not my fault."

"She hasn't 'fallen in love,'" she said crossly. "She's got a crush, that's all."

"How do you even know that?"

"When she calls, she asks about you. She somehow managed to find a couple of pictures of you and has them as her computer wallpaper. Hell, she probably practices writing her name as Mrs. Jilly Reno."

"You're not talking about a twelve-year-old," he pointed out.

"Taka thinks I'm overreacting, too," Summer said. "I know what you're like, and I wouldn't think of trying to change you. I just need you to keep away from my sister until she grows out of this."

"No problem. I don't like American women and I don't like California." That wasn't strictly true—he'd always liked Los Angeles the few times he'd visited. "How long do you think it'll take her to get over me?"

"Don't sound so self-satisfied. Teenage crushes are usually short-lived."

"But your sister isn't a normal teenager, is she?" He still couldn't believe how young she'd been. He'd always had a preference for women at least a couple of years older than he was—more experience, less emotion. She was the oddest combination of young body, old soul. And he hadn't been able to take his eyes off her.

"She's twenty. And as long as you keep your distance, then everything will be all right. She's probably outgrown you by now, but I don't want to risk anything."

"I'm not going to hurt your sister, Su-chan."

"Reno, you hurt anyone who cares about you, and my sister is vulnerable. I don't want you breaking her heart."

"I promise I won't go anywhere near her. I don't want to have a lovesick child hanging all over me any more than you do."

She hadn't looked convinced, probably because Su-chan was a very smart woman, and she knew people. "You promise?"

He'd let out a sigh of resignation. "I promise. The last thing I want is someone thinking she's in love with me. I like my sex casual."

She still didn't look happy. "No sex with Jilly," she warned.

"No conversation, no getting within five thousand miles of her. You can trust me."

And Su-chan had had no choice but to do so.

But that was before Russian mercenaries had been sent to kill them and anyone who mattered to them. Summer might have preferred if someone else had come to Japan to save her sister's life, but in the end it was her life that mattered, and Summer wouldn't be picky about who helped her. Besides, Reno was making sure Jilly was so annoyed with him that she'd never want to see him again. They'd worry about the rest of it once the Russians realized they were chasing a ghost mission.

In the meantime, they needed to disappear. His grandfather's summerhouse in the Saitama Prefecture would be perfect. It would be closed for the season, but there'd still be staff on call, just in case his austere grandfather decided he wanted a steaming mineral bath. Saitama was known for its hot springs and their restorative effects—known to cure cancer, increase a man's virility and promote long life—and his grandfather's trips had become more frequent. Maybe he was going for a shot of virility, but he doubted it. His grandfather looked old and frail. The man who'd seemed indestructible was suddenly looking mortal.

And the last thing Reno needed right now was a surge of virility. Jilly Lovitz was providing enough of a challenge when he was determined to keep his hands off her. He didn't need more stimulation.

It didn't help the way she looked at him, when she thought he wouldn't notice. He could get her on her back without half trying. As far back as he could remember he could have any woman he wanted, and Jilly was just one more.

He didn't want this one, and not just because Su-chan had asked him not to. Jilly Lovitz came with too many problems, too much baggage. He needed to dump her, fast. He was counting on Ojiisan to get Taka out of hiding long enough to take over. Taka could keep her safe from Russian mercenaries and stray assassins. And him.

They followed the rail line north. He wasn't sure whether she slept or just pretended to get out of talking to him. He didn't give a shit. He just wanted to get rid of her.

He stopped at one of the train stations and ran in to get a couple of their justly famous bento boxes. Jilly didn't open her eyes when he returned, so he set the packages on the backseat and took off again.

Three hours later they were climbing the narrow, twisting road that led to his grandfather's summerhouse. She'd woken up long enough to devour the contents of the bento box, all without a word of complaint. He'd thought the raw eel might stop her, and he was half tempted to encourage her with the wasabi, but she seemed to know her way around Japanese food.

"Aren't you going to eat?" she asked.

"When we get there," he growled.

She was clearly unintimidated. "Get where? Or are we still driving in circles?"

He ignored her.

She poked him with her chopsticks. He was so astonished he almost veered off the narrow road.

"Don't do that!" he snapped.

"Don't annoy me," she replied in a sweet voice. "Where are we heading?"

"An *onsen* belonging to my grandfather. A traditional bathhouse," he explained when her forehead wrinkled in confusion.

"I think I've had enough of Japanese baths," she said in a dry voice.

Not that he had any reason to explain further. "It's closed for the winter, and it's up in the mountains. No one will be able to find us. We'll wait there until Ojiisan gets in touch with Taka." He glanced at her. She'd survived the wasabi—there was just a spot of it at the corner of her full mouth, and he had the sudden insane desire to lick it off. "You want to see your sister, right? That's why you came to Japan in the first place, isn't it?"

"I had a number of reasons," she said. "Seeing Summer was the main one, but I was planning on touring the country, doing a little research, taking care of some old business. At this point the research can wait—I just want to get home."

He couldn't blame her. She wasn't used to running for her life.

Though, she'd had to do it once before, when she'd been kidnapped by a lunatic cult. But that had been a blip in her safe little American world. Still, she was handling it well enough.

She was like her sister in many ways—fearless, strong, adventurous. Most of the women he slept with would have been babbling hysterically by now. But Jilly had merely endured, even as she passed the dead bodies and escaped hired killers.

Though there was no reason to compare her with the women he slept with. Because he wasn't going there. Not ever.

Night fell early, as they drove north, and the headlights speared weakly through the night as they climbed higher. The tiny commuter car wasn't made for steep inclines, and his booted foot was pressed all the way to the floor.

She hadn't said a word for the past few

hours—he could be grateful for that much. He didn't need some *gaijin* yammering at him, making idiot demands.

Not that he had any reason to think Summer's sister was demanding. She was bearable so far, and with any luck he'd get rid of her before she turned shrewish.

He glanced over at her. She was looking out the window, and her reflection was mirrored in the glass. Pretty. It would be foolish to deny it—Jilly Lovitz was pretty. She had big brown eyes—round, baby eyes with thick lashes. Her mouth was a little too big, but he liked it, even if he couldn't stop thinking of things she could do with that mouth. Her hair was short, curling as it dried, a blond color that he knew was entirely natural. He just wished he could forget that part.

He drove over the rise and started down the steep little road that led to the sheltered summerhouse below. There were no lights at the end of the road—a surprise. His grandfather had told him he'd have the caretaker open up the place for them. It was getting colder, and there was the smell of snow in the air.

He stopped the car in the middle of their descent, so abruptly it skidded for a moment, and stared at the elaborate house through the misty darkness.

"We're walking?" Jilly said, reaching for her seat belt.

"Something's wrong," he said. The road to the summerhouse was deliberately narrow, to keep the approach quiet and soothing, and he was damned if he could think of a place to turn around, even in this tiny car. He stared down at the bathhouse, then shoved the car into Reverse and began backing up the steep, winding road as fast as he could.

Lights flared on at the seemingly deserted house, and then he heard the pop, pop, pop of what could only be gunfire as the wheels spun. A moment later one shattered the windshield.

"Get down!"

Jilly was fumbling frantically with her seat belt, trying to refasten it, and he couldn't afford to give her even a moment of attention. "Forget about it," he snarled, pushing her down into the well of the car as he turned to guide the car back up the incline as fast as the damned thing would go.

He could see headlights of another car now, down at the house. They were coming after them, and whatever they were driving was bound to be faster than the anonymous piece of shit he'd stolen. If he didn't figure a way out of this, they were going to die.

She was crouched down, and all he could see was the top of her blond head. He swore under his breath as he backed the car up, the tires spinning on the dirt road, faster, as the lights in front of him were getting brighter.

"When I tell you to, I want you to jump out of the car, roll into the bushes and stay there."

"Do what?" Her voice was finally getting a panicky edge to it.

"I'll slow down. There's a curve up ahead, and we'll be out of sight for a few moments. You'll jump out of the car and hide in the woods until I come to get you."

"And what if it's not you who finds me?"

"Then I'll already be dead," he said. "And you'll be on your own."

"I don't want to leave you."

If he had the time he'd think about the odd tone in her voice, the way it hit his stomach. Maybe later. If there was a later. "You don't have a choice. If you don't jump I'm shoving you. Be ready."

They were almost at the curve. The car was gaining on them, fast, and it was going to be a close call. He rounded the curve, slammed the car into the turnaround, opened the passenger door and got ready to shove.

She was already out, diving into the bushes be-

fore he could touch her. He shoved the car into
Drive, spinning the wheels as he headed up the
winding road, going forward. A moment later the
headlights appeared behind him as they rounded
the corner, never slowing down. They didn't realize he'd dumped her.

The day he couldn't outdrive Russian mercenaries on his own turf was the day he deserved to
die. Even in this piece of shit he outclassed them.
He shoved his foot down harder on the accelera-
tor, the cheap tires spun, and he was gone, the
Russians trailing behind him.

# 5

Jilly scrambled into the bushes, flinging herself over a slight rise and then sliding down the other side into a narrow depression. She froze, barely breathing, as she heard the cars from up above. If they stopped she was screwed, if they kept going she was safe. Until Reno came and found her.

The sound of the car was heavier than the small car Reno had stolen, and she heard the heavy groan of the engine as it shifted into a lower gear. It sped up, the small amount of light fading, and she was suddenly alone. In a forest in Japan in the middle of winter, with nothing more than a sweat-shirt for warmth and thin sneakers on her feet.

She let out her pent-up breath, leaning back against the outcropping behind her, and closed her eyes. He'd come back for her. As soon as he lost the Russians, or whoever they were, he'd come back. He said he would. He might find her a pain in the butt, an inconvenience disturbing his perfect life, but she couldn't doubt his sense of responsibility. Could she?

At the very least, she had no doubt that Reno's cousin, Taka, could be a very scary man indeed if crossed, and he wouldn't like it if Reno abandoned her. All she had to do was wait.

Unless the Russians caught up with him. The stolen car was underpowered, and even if Reno seemed frighteningly efficient, he was hardly immortal. The people of the world her sister married into were living dangerous lives—she'd seen that firsthand. What if Reno wasn't able to outrun them?

They'd come after her. It was that simple, that finite. If he didn't lose them, come back for her, then she'd die. All because she'd run off to Japan without thinking it through. She'd just wanted to put the embarrassment of her one lousy night of sex behind her, one stupid mistake with an uncaring jock who looked just the slightest bit like someone who was turning out to be a walking nightmare. She wanted her sister, she wanted to immerse herself in the magic-strewn Heian period of ancient Japan. And she'd wanted to get over any lingering fantasies about Reno, the ultimate bad boy.

She'd accomplished that much, and the unpleasant night with a graduate student should seem more like a comedy than a tragedy. As for the rest of it, she wasn't ready to die because she'd been impulsive. If she was going to die, she wanted it to mean something.

She opened her eyes. It was cold—the scent of snow was on the air and ice was sinking into her bones. She'd spent most of her life in Southern California—her blood was too thin for winter in the mountains.

Was he coming back for her? What if he didn't? What if the Russians killed him? Was she going to wait here and let them find her and kill her? Or was she going to sit here and freeze to death?

Neither seemed particularly pleasant. If she hadn't jumped out of the car, he would have pushed her—she had no doubt about that. He was entirely ruthless and unsentimental—a punk samurai with loyalty to his cousin and not much else.

So why had she thought he was so deliciously romantic? He was unlike anyone she'd ever known. Edgy, absurd, exotic and beautiful, and every man or boy she'd met since she first saw him had always paled in comparison. Even Duke had been a quarter Chinese—probably why she'd chosen him in the first place.

She'd been an idiot, but then her experience with men was pretty pathetic. She'd always been the odd one out. It was no wonder she'd never had a real boyfriend. There'd been no prom, no parties, no group of girls to giggle with. On top of being freakishly smart, she was too tall. If she had to be so smart, couldn't she have at least looked small and helpless, instead of being a strapping almost-six-foot tall?

And the depressing truth was, she was likely to die a virgin. A twenty-year-old virgin with the mind of a scientist and the experience of a twelve-year-old. And the sappy romantic longings of an adolescent.

The worst mistake had been to try to remedy that particular problem. With another graduate student, albeit someone ten years older than she was. She'd had enough sense to keep her distance from the predatory professors, who seemed to take pride in going through the female population of their classes.

Duke had been just as big a mistake. She should have known that from his name. She'd waited too long to tell him she was a virgin, which he'd found both a turnoff and a joke, and even now she wasn't sure if his rough, fumbling attempt at intercourse had actually de-virginized her. She'd bled, and he'd spilled all over her, leaving her covered with blood and goo, and then he'd walked out, not even kissing her. And she'd been too stupid to realize the story would be halfway across campus by the next morning. It was no wonder she'd run.

Any lingering romantic fantasies should have been wiped out by the harsh reality of Reno. He wasn't the stuff of her daydreams, he was a man who killed when he had to. A man who clearly found her—a huge, gawky, inconvenient female—less than charming.

Maybe she'd rather freeze to death in the woods than face him again.

No, that was being melodramatic. At least he had no idea she'd once had a mad crush on him. One that was vanishing swiftly, the colder she got. She wrapped her arms around her body, trying to hug some heat into her, and tucked her hands in her armpits. If she started shivering, she wasn't going to stop. She gritted her teeth, tensing her body so she wouldn't shake. Cold, it was so damned cold. Where the hell was Reno?

Maybe she should try to make it out of the woods on her own. She'd made such a mess of her life she should probably want to die, but she wasn't that far gone yet. She had every intention of living a long, vigorous, probably celibate life.

They'd passed through several small towns on their way up the mountain—if she managed to reach civilization, she'd be able to find help. They wouldn't like that she had no money or identification—both those things were in her backpack in Reno's stolen car—but they'd probably help her anyway. And if worse came to worst, a Japanese prison was probably a lot warmer than a mountainside in winter, and her powerful father would be more than able to extricate her quickly. Ralph Lovitz was a force of nature, a self-made man, a billionaire and full of sheer protective rage where his family was concerned. He had more money than God, and he'd always make sure nothing bad happened to her. She'd be perfectly fine, she told herself.

The first flake of snow drifted down and settled on her nose. She'd lost feeling in her feet, her hands, her butt on the cold, hard ground. She'd given up the fight to keep from shivering, and she sat huddled in a ball, her arms around her knees, shaking with the cold. Snow began drifting down rapidly, covering everything, and the bright winter moon made the landscape look like a fairy-tale setting. A fairy tale of death.

\* \* \*

She was crying. Good thing Reno was either dead or had given up on her—he already found her annoying enough. If she kept crying, and that seemed more than likely, he'd probably want to strangle her himself.

She let out a tiny sob, followed by a hiccup. Tears never helped anything—her sister would have told her that. No, she wouldn't. Summer would put her arms around her and tell her everything would be all right.

But Summer had disappeared. Maybe she was dead, as well. Maybe Lianne Lovitz was going to lose both her daughters. And no one would ever find her body—she'd just freeze to death and maybe twenty years from now a hiker would come across her corpse....

She let out another sob. At least freezing to death didn't hurt. You just went to sleep; everything got numb and then you slept and then it was over.

But she didn't want it to be over. Where the hell was Reno? It didn't matter how much of an asshole he was, it didn't matter what a pain he thought she was, she wanted him to come back and save her. How could he have abandoned her like this?

He'd be back. The only reason he wouldn't be back was if he'd been killed. One man in a cheap car against an SUV-load of mercenaries who already held a grudge. She was an idiot to think he had a chance in hell of making it.

She should get to her feet. Try to walk out of here, but her feet were numb and she was shivering too badly to get to her feet. She needed to stop crying—the tears would be freezing to her face before long. She rubbed them away with her sleeve. He was dead, she was abandoned, and she didn't know which was worse.

"Are you crying?"

The voice was annoyed, impatient, and came from the hill below her, as Reno appeared from a thick stand of trees.

She didn't stop to think, she simply flew from her huddled spot and leapt on him, knocking him flat as she wept all over him.

"I thought you were dead!" she sobbed. "I thought they'd caught you and killed you and I was going to die alone in the woods."

He lay still beneath her for a moment, then pulled her arms away from his neck, pushing her up so he could look at her. "I'm hard to kill," he said. There was an odd expression in his eyes, one she couldn't read. But she could guess. Annoyance.

"Sorry," she said, scrambling to her feet, slipping a bit on the icy ground. He jumped up, effortlessly, catching her arm as she slid, holding her upright.

"Come on," he said after a long, awkward moment. "The truck's down below."

"The truck? Where'd you get a truck?"

"I stole it."

She sighed, the sound shaky as she pulled herself together. "You're lucky your grandfather's a gangster or they'd throw your ass in jail so fast. Unless stealing cars is considered a minor crime."

"I wouldn't call Ojiisan a gangster," he said, starting down the steep hill, one hand clasped on her hand. "And I'm not sure I'd call myself lucky. I think he's got a traitor in his organization. Your Russians have had inside information—there's no way they'd know about the summerhouse unless someone told them."

She skidded, and his hand tightened on her arm. She was going to have bruises, she thought. Unless her flesh was too frozen to show them. "You said he owned the place. Maybe they just made an educated guess. And they're not my Russians. They're after you now, too."

"I don't believe in educated guesses." He tugged at her. "Hurry up. We need to get out of here before the snow gets deeper."

"I'm t-t-trying," she said, unable to control her shivers.

He halted. "Idiot *gaijin,*" he muttered under his breath, stripping off his leather jacket. "You could have told me you were cold."

She didn't want to accept it, but he wasn't giving her any choice. She felt the warmth wrap around her, his body warmth, as he shoved her arms inside and pulled it tight. He was skinny, she had boobs, but at least he managed to zip it up, cursing the whole time. And even if she felt the accidental brush of his hand across her breast, he didn't notice.

"Aren't you cold?" she asked, her teeth still chattering as the warmth sank into her bones. He was only wearing a dark T-shirt, and somehow, in these dire circumstances, she managed to notice that for a skinny punk he certainly filled out the T-shirt well. She also saw the dragon tattoo snaking down his arm. How fitting.

"I'll survive," he said, starting the steep descent once more, dragging her after him.

The hike down seemed endless, but at least she'd stopped shivering. Her sneakers kept slipping in the thin layer of snow, but Reno, in his smooth-soled cowboy boots, seemed to be having no trouble at all. His bright red hair was a beacon in the moonlit night—probably keeping him warm, she thought grumpily. When they finally came out onto the deserted mountain road, the small, narrow delivery van was waiting.

"Thank God," she breathed, heading for the passenger door.

Only to have him catch her, hauling her back. "Right-hand drive," he reminded her, opening the door.

Now that they'd finally reached their destination, her muscles decided not to work. She tried to climb up into the van, but her legs refused to obey her, and her hands were too numb to haul herself in.

He picked her up effortlessly, which was a shock, and put her in the seat, closing the door before coming around the other side. He reached beneath the dashboard and the engine roared to life, the headlights spearing through the darkness down the long, narrow road ahead.

"Aren't you afraid the Russians are going to find us?" She fumbled with the seat belt, finally managing to fasten it.

"No."

"Why?"

He shot her a look. "You don't want to know."

"You killed them? How many people have you killed?" she demanded, shocked.

"Their car went off the road. I don't know whether they're dead, and I don't care. At least they're not a problem right now. And as for how many people I've killed, you don't want to know that, either."

She should feel sick. Horrified, stunned. But the horrible truth was, she felt fine. He killed. He killed to protect her. And some ancient, atavistic streak inside her wanted to preen and purr. She was one sick puppy.

To cover the silence she leaned forward, fiddling with the knobs. "Is there any way to turn up the heat?"

"Probably not. Stop bitching. I gave you my jacket."

"I didn't ask you to. And I'm not bitching. I'm just not used to winters."

"I forgot—you're a California girl." He made it sound one step removed from the village idiot.

She started to unzip the jacket. "Take your goddamn coat…"

His arm slammed out, stopping her. "Leave it on," he said. "I don't need it, and you do."

As a matter of fact, she wished he would put it back on. She could see him too well in the reflection of the dashboard lights, and his muscled arms were…disturbing.

*Get over him, Jilly,* she told herself sternly. *He thinks you're a pain in the ass.*

"Okay, I give up," she said. "Take me to the airport and I'll get the first plane out. I won't fight you."

"It wouldn't do you any good if you did fight me. You're getting out as soon as it's safe. Until I find out what's going on we're on our own, and I'm not going to let you walk into a trap."

"I'd be grateful you're looking out for me if I didn't think you were simply afraid of your cousin."

A faint smile curved his mouth. "I can hold my own against Taka. Remember, I grew up with him. But you're right, I don't want to piss him off unnecessarily. Besides, I like your sister."

"You do?" She was astonished. "My sister told me you hated all American women."

"There are exceptions." He didn't look at her this time, and his voice was cool. While she sincerely doubted she was one of the exceptions, she wasn't going to push it.

"So you're not taking me to the airport?"

"No."

Staying in Japan was hazardous to her health. Staying with Reno was asking for trouble. So why was she relieved? Because she'd gone out of her freaking mind, that's why.

"Why are you shaking your head?"

She jerked, startled. He must have been watching her. How often had he watched her when she hadn't realized it? And what had she given away?

"Just disbelief about this stupid situation," she said in all honesty. He wouldn't know that the stupidity was her reaction to him.

"You walked into it. You have no one to blame but yourself."

"Are you always this sympathetic?"

To her surprise he laughed. She wasn't sure if she'd ever heard him laugh before. She certainly hadn't seen him smile. "Are you always such a pussy?" he said.

She almost choked. "Believe it or not, I'm not used to running for my life."

"You managed once before."

"Isobel was a lot nicer."

"True enough. I'm not very nice."

"I noticed," she grumbled.

He laughed again. If she didn't know better she'd think he was enjoying this. But he couldn't be. He was saddled with a major irritation, and they were on the run for their lives. He could hardly be having a good time.

She settled back into her seat, folding her arms across her chest. Hugging the jacket around her, as if it were his arms around her, protecting her. At least he wouldn't realize what she was doing.

Maybe, when she finally got on a plane back to California, he'd let her keep the jacket. It probably had American female cooties on it. Maybe it would remind her of what an idiot she'd been.

Or maybe it would remind her of how his warm, hard body had felt beneath hers when she'd knocked him over in hysterical relief.

Even without the jacket she was going to have a hard time forgetting.

She needed to get laid. It was that simple, and it was only her ridiculously semivirginal state that was making her crazy. Obsessed with Reno. She needed to get back to California, choose the first nice, good-looking man she could find and get it over with. Someone with more discretion, patience and sympathy than the wretched Duke. And then she'd be completely immune.

Because there was no room in her life for a Yakuza punk samurai.

Or to be honest, there was no room in his life for her. And the sooner she accepted that fact the better off she'd be.

She hugged herself anyway, snuggling deeper into the leather. If that was the only kind of embrace she was going to get she might as well enjoy it. It was going to be over soon enough.

The crazy, fucked-up thing was, he was enjoying himself. On the run for his life, with a *gaijin* tagging along, and he was feeling more alive than he had in a long time. Taka would kill him.

Reno looked over at her. She was huddled into his jacket, her face turned away, and he knew a moment's regret. He would have much rather been the one to wrap around her, but he had too much regard for his life to risk Taka's wrath. He was going to keep her in one piece, unmolested, no matter how tempting she was. It wasn't as if there weren't a thousand other women in the world.

Besides, even worse than Taka, he didn't want to upset Su-chan. Women were like that—able to make you feel like a total shit with just a look, and he'd made a promise. He'd prefer it if Taka took a swing at him.

No, things would be much better all around if he just left her alone. Taka and Su-chan would be happier, Grandfather would be happier, he and Jilly would be happier. If she'd just stop looking at him when she thought he didn't notice.

If he could just stop thinking about the erotic possibilities of her mouth and her long, curved body.

He needed to concentrate on the business at hand. Who had told the Russians where to find them? Someone close to his grandfather, someone the old man trusted, and the old man didn't trust many people.

At least the Russians were taken care of, in a twisted heap of metal at the bottom of a cliff, and instinct told him that was the last of them.

Unless someone decided to take the two of them out for the fun of it, and mercenaries kept business and pleasure far apart. If they kept coming it meant that someone else was paying the bills.

He glanced over at her. No one was getting to her, no one was going to hurt her. He wasn't sure why he felt so strongly about an irritating stranger, but he did. No one was going to hurt her.

Not even him.

# 6

Takashi O'Brien stood on the narrow porch of the old inn, staring out at the Pacific Ocean. It was off-season on the island of Hokkaido, and most of the places were closed for the winter. No one knew that he and Su-chan were hidden up here in a place that had once belonged to his grandfather. They'd arrived at the small inlet by boat, with enough food to keep them going until they heard it was safe to come back. But Taka was getting edgy.

"Is something wrong?" He heard his wife's sleepy voice behind him. He turned to look at her—she was wrapped in a duvet, her long hair in her eyes, her mouth as delicious as always.

He went to her, pulling her into his arms, keeping the duvet wrapped tight around her naked body so the cold winter wind wouldn't bite into her. "I should have heard something by now."

"But we don't get cell-phone service out here. At least, my phone didn't work."

"Cell phones don't work. My PDA works on a different frequency. Peter won't use it until he knows it's safe, and there's no word."

She leaned back against him, and he could feel her warmth sink into his bones. It was easy enough to stop thinking and lose himself in her, but he'd let things go on for long enough. "You think they haven't been able to stop the Russians?" she asked.

"It should have been an easy job. My great-uncle's organization is very efficient—there was no need for anyone else to be involved. But it should have been dealt with days ago. Something's wrong. They shouldn't keep on coming."

"Are we going back, then?"

"I'm going back. You're staying here where it's safe. There's more than enough firewood, and the food will last long enough if you ration your Diet Coke habit." He could feel her stiffen in his arms, and he kissed the top of her head. "Trust me."

"Like hell," she said sweetly, pulling away from him. "You know you can't make me stay here."

"You know I can."

She just looked at him. He'd seen that look before, and it always meant trouble. It was a good thing he was going to be out of reach for the next few days. She'd build up a good head of steam, probably come at him with a knife, and then there'd be mind-fucking sex.

"Let's get our things," he said in his most resigned voice.

"I'm glad you're learning," she shot back, turning and heading into the empty inn. Dropping the duvet on the floor as she headed to the bedroom.

He picked it up, following her, wondering if there was enough time for sex to lull her into a false state of security. Probably not. Once on alert, he didn't dare waste time.

She went into the bedroom, he tossed the duvet after her, then slammed and locked the door. If he moved fast, she wouldn't realize there was a way out the back of the room, smashing through the paper screens.

He could still hear her yelling as he ran out of the building, down onto the beach and the boat they'd hidden. He was well out into the water when she finally appeared on the beach, stark naked, screaming at him. For a moment he was afraid she'd try to swim after him, but even in her fury she had enough sense not to jump into a winter ocean.

"I'll be back as soon as it's safe," he shouted to her, but she was too busy screaming curses at him to hear. It didn't matter. All that mattered was making sure no one could get to her. He'd been counting on his great-uncle to take care of things. Clearly he was going to have to do it himself.

And then he was going to have to spend a lot of time making it up to Summer.

"You sadistic son-of-a-bitch asshole!" she shrieked. "Get your scrawny butt back here!"

But he simply gunned the motor, loud enough to drown her out, looked forward and sped away, as her cries of anger disappeared into the foggy morning.

Reno drove fast, as he always did. If the police stopped him, it might be the best thing—they'd take both of them into custody and no stray mercenary would be able to get within a hundred feet of them. Of course, that would mean his grandfather would have to pull a few strings to get them out, but that would be child's play to a man like his grandfather.

Unless, of course, he delegated the job to whoever had ratted them out.

No, maybe the police weren't the answer. He hated to admit weakness, but he was tired and hungry, and more than anything, he needed a few hours of sleep before he could figure out what the fuck he was going to do.

Heading back toward Tokyo was a no-brainer—whether or not he was going to stop or keep on straight to Osaka remained to be seen. He'd need to ditch the delivery truck and find something with a little more power. He could buy something, but that would leave a paper trail, and right now he and Jilly needed to disappear. Ojiisan was going to have to make a lot of amends by the time Reno was ready to head back to England.

If he was going back. He couldn't get rid of the feeling that if he'd stayed in Japan his grandfather wouldn't be nurturing a traitor in his midst. Not that the old man had gotten weak. He'd be a powerhouse until he died, but lately he'd been passing on a lot of his power to his subordinates. The business had changed, he'd told Reno. Where there'd once been a code of honor, now there were just hoodlums and drug dealers. Ojiisan had always steered clear of the drug trade. He'd made a good enough living from the more respectable business of gambling and protection. He dabbled in counterfeit designer goods, as well, but never enough to disturb the police, who turned a politely blind eye to him and his business.

But the heads of Yakuza families didn't retire. The *oyabun* retained their power until they died, and were mourned by their *kobun,* their loyal soldiers. But one of his grandfather's soldiers wasn't so loyal, and that could spread among the younger men who wanted the kind of money drugs and weapons could bring in. Grandfather was right—there was no honor left.

He glanced over at her. She was staring out into the darkness, and in the darkness he couldn't see her clearly. It didn't matter—what she was thinking made no difference to him. His way was clear. In the meantime he was going to have to resort to drastic measures. And he didn't think his unwilling hostage was going to like it one tiny bit.

She was doing her best to ignore him as he sped through the night, but when he pulled out his cell phone and started pushing buttons, she almost shrieked.

"Is that legal? To talk on the phone while you drive?" she demanded, clutching the seat.

He glanced over at her. "I'm driving a stolen car, Ji-chan. I think the cell phone is the least of my worries." And he began speaking into the phone in rapid Japanese.

Jilly wasn't sure what was more horrifying, the way he was driving, or what he was saying. The driving would kill her more quickly, probably in the next couple of minutes, so she decided not to argue with him while he was still on the phone. She waited until he'd snapped it closed and shoved it back into his pocket before speaking.

"I'm *dead?*"

He jerked, startled, and stared at her. "You speak Japanese?" He made it sound as if she were a child molester.

"A little. You told whoever you were talking to that I was dead. That I'd died when my car went over the side of the mountain."

"Shit," he said, clearly annoyed. "And that was my grandfather. He's not happy that I failed to protect a member of the family. Which you are, by default, whether I like it or not. And you don't want to mess with my grandfather when he's not happy."

"You don't trust your grandfather with the truth? Unless, of course, that *was* the truth, just a bit premature, and you're planning to kill me."

"I'm tempted, just to shut you up, but Taka wouldn't like it, and disposing of your body would be a pain," he said.

"Are you sure? I thought you said your grandfather's men would wipe out all trace of your earlier bloodbath in Taka and Summer's house. Disposing of one small American shouldn't be that much of a challenge."

"Small?" he echoed derisively. "You're as tall

as I am. And yes, they could dump you. But I have absolutely no interest in killing you. That's more Taka's style. I just want to get rid of you. Unless of course, you'd rather I strangle you. You could probably talk me into it."

"You can strangle me if you want, as long as you feed me first. At this point food is more important than a long life."

"Hold on." Those weren't words to inspire her with confidence, and his previously dangerous speed suddenly became suicidal as he bobbed and darted between the heavy traffic, narrowly missing pedestrians and cyclists as he clipped a curb and ran right over another.

"Where are we?" Jilly lifted her head to peer out into the neon-bright night.

Reno didn't answer, of course. Why should she have expected him to? She'd spent the past two days asking him questions that he'd ignored. Why should it be any different? "If you don't answer me, I'll stab you with a chopstick again," she warned him.

He glanced at her. "You don't have any."

"Point taken. I'm starving. Find me chopsticks and food to go with them and tell me what the plan is."

"We're going to a love hotel."

"Right," she drawled. "Right after hell freezes over."

"Don't jump to any conclusions. They're anonymous—they have them all over Tokyo. You check in by machine—no witnesses. You'll like it—there are theme rooms. Pirates and samurai and slave girls. Just the kind of fantasy young women like."

"I have no deep-seated fantasy to be a slave girl," she snapped. "And I hate to tell you, but you're no Johnny Depp."

"That leaves samurai," he said. "You don't get a choice."

"Do they have two beds?"

"In a love hotel? Not likely. Don't worry— they're like a family theme park of sex. Everything clean and pretend."

"I'm not having sex with you, even pretend sex."

"I don't remember that I asked you for sex. If I'd wanted it, we would have already done it."

At some point she really was going to hit him. She already knew perfectly well that he didn't find her to be anything more than a pain in the butt. He didn't need to embarrass her, as well.

"No love hotel," she said flatly, staying on point. "You'll have to knock me out and…" She let the words trail off as she remembered he'd already done just that. "No love hotel," she said.

"It's that or a capsule hotel."

She brightened. "Oh, cool! I've seen those on TV."

"You won't like that much better."

"A capsule hotel sounds perfect."

"And you think I'm going to do what you want?"

"I'm a lot less trouble if you do."

He smiled. Just when she was thinking he never smiled, he did, and she almost wished he hadn't. It was a smirk, as if he'd gotten exactly what he'd wanted and knew she wasn't about to back down.

And she wasn't. She might have to spend the night with him, as she'd had to spend every minute since he first walked into the back bedroom at Summer's house, but she didn't have to spend it in a place designed for illicit sex. She'd seen capsule hotels on TV—they were strictly utilitarian, for people who needed to sleep and nothing else before they went back to work the next day.

"No more arguments?" Reno said, his voice silky.

Why did she feel she'd walked into a trap? "No more arguments. As long as it's not a love hotel I won't put up a fuss."

"You Americans are so puritanical," he said.

"It's much better to be practical about these things. Sex is recreational, marriage is a business matter."

"And what is love?"

"Doesn't exist."

She just looked at him. "What about Taka and Summer? Don't you think they're in love?"

"Su-chan is American, Taka is half."

"Meaning only *gaijin* fall in love?"

"Meaning only *gaijin* are fool enough to pay any attention. The best thing to do if you start thinking such things is to lie down and wait for it to pass. It always does."

She stared at him. "You speak from your great experience at falling in love?"

"I've avoided it. It's a weakness and a waste of time, if it even exists. I'm better off without it." He pulled the car to a stop. The street was darker than most of Tokyo's neon-lit brilliance, and he cut the engine, turning to look at her. "So you can stop looking at me like that when you think I don't know. I'll go to bed with you if that's what you want, but that's all you're getting."

She'd never hit another human being in her entire life. She punched him, hard, so fast and instinctive that he didn't have time to stop her, so fast that she didn't realize what she'd done until it was too late. She'd hit him hard—her knuckles had slammed against bone and flesh and it hurt.

He didn't move. "I guess that's a no," he said.

She'd been about to apologize, but the words died in her mouth. "Are you trying to make me hate you?" she said instead. She should apologize; she didn't believe in hitting people. But he'd needed a whack upside his head, big-time.

His answer surprised her. "Maybe." He opened the car door. "Stay put. I'm going to find us a place to stay. Just lock the doors and keep down."

He closed the door quietly and started down the empty street, a lone, wiry figure in the deserted night. She opened her door, suddenly nervous. "Are you coming back for me?" she called out.

He turned and grinned at her, a flash of white in the darkness. "Don't worry, Ji-chan. I'll let you know when I decide to feed you to the sharks. Lock the door."

She sank back in the seat, locking the door as ordered, pulling his jacket around her. He must be cold, he must be sick of her. She'd punched him. She still couldn't believe she'd done such a thing. The last person she'd hit had been Tommy Hepburn when he'd taken her Tonka truck in first grade. She'd hit Reno, and while a part of her was horrified, part of her was glad she'd done it.

Her hand hurt. She could still feel the bone and flesh in his cold, pretty face. There was no violence in her—she was a pacifist in every sense of the word. And she wanted to hit him again.

She'd better think twice about doing it again. He wasn't the kind of man to let someone get away with it twice.

Maybe he knew he'd deserved it. Maybe he just didn't care. Maybe he was lying and never coming back, leaving her on her own in a strange city. She could handle it. As long as he wasn't dead, she could just as easily abandon him as he abandon her.

And she would. If he wasn't back in half an hour. Not that she had any way of telling time; it was after midnight, but then, her sense of time was all screwed up. Days were blending together—had she first landed yesterday or the day before? She hadn't the faintest idea of the date. She'd gone backward in time, and the snatched hours of sleep, the constant movement on top of normal jet lag, had put her in an altered state of consciousness.

She should give him back his jacket. He must be cold. It wasn't snowing in the city, but it was still midwinter and he was wearing nothing more than a skin-tight T-shirt.

She stayed put. Either he'd come back or he wouldn't. At that point she was too tired to worry about it. She slid down and closed her eyes, practicing her deep breathing. *Good air in, bad air out, shut out all those scary thoughts....*

Someone loomed up outside her window, and she let out a small scream as he rapped at the window. He'd come back for her. Whoopee.

"Come on," he said when she opened the door. "We're going the rest of the way on foot."

"What about the truck?"

"Someone will find it and return it."

"Don't you think you ought to wipe it?"

"Wipe it?"

"Make sure your fingerprints aren't all over it," she elaborated. "You don't want the police matching you with car theft."

"They can't. My fingerprints have never been taken."

"They don't fingerprint you here when they arrest you?"

"I've never been arrested."

She climbed down out of the truck, holding on in case her legs were still unsteady. She didn't want him touching her if she could help it. Signs of weakness were disastrous. "I'm disappointed," she said. "I thought you were the quintessential bad boy. You're just a poseur."

She didn't manage to rile him. "No, I'm good at not getting caught." He pulled a cap from his back pocket. "Put this on and keep your head down. I don't think anyone will see you, but I believe in being careful. I need to sleep, and I don't want to have to find another place you'll approve of."

She took the hat, a slightly grubby baseball-style hat with a Hello Kitty samurai in pink camo, and put it on her head. "Don't you want your jacket? You must be cold."

He didn't answer, reaching out and tucking her hair beneath the cap. The touch of his hand on her head was startling—he was surprisingly gentle as he pushed the hair up under the cap. "Follow me and don't say anything. If anyone sees us, they'll just assume we're a couple of *doseiaisha* out for a good time."

"A couple of what?"

"Gay men. Though they'd be more likely to go to a love hotel. And they'd be more comfortable."

"Why do they…?"

"Capsule hotels are only for men."

"Great," she said. "So not only do I have to stay

with you, I have to become a cross-dresser, as well."

"It's a good thing no one will look closely—you'd never pass. You're going to have to keep from talking, which I know is almost impossible for you. No one was around when I checked in, but you never can tell who might be up and about. Most people who spend the night here are salary-men who are too drunk to make it home, and they sleep soundly, but I'll need to guard the toilet if you need to use it."

"I need to use it," she said, her voice grim.

"Then do what I tell you."

She was having to spend far too much time doing what he told her to do, but now was no time for a mutiny. She wasn't used to being ordered around—she'd been living on her own in an adult world for so many years because of her freakish mind, and she'd never liked being told what to do.

The building was square and anonymous, and while she'd managed to become conversational in Japanese in record time, she'd barely attempted to learn *kanji*. That would take years of study, even for her usually lightning-fast brain. They were in luck—the only person they passed head-ing down the narrow hallway was someone so blind drunk she could have been wearing a prom dress and he wouldn't have noticed.

It looked like some science-fiction beehive. Reno stopped before one column of capsules and slid the door up, exposing a small, narrow bed. There was a light overhead, a small shelf and what looked like a TV screen set into the wall.

"All the comforts of home," she said.

"Climb in."

Not that she had any choice. She could hear the faint snores from the capsules surrounding hers, but that didn't mean they wouldn't wake up. She climbed up into the capsule, stretching out.

A moment later he followed her.

"What are you doing?" she shrieked. Or tried to. He slammed his hand over her mouth to silence her, and his face was next to hers, his body plastered full-length against hers in the tiny space.

"You didn't think I was going to let you go anywhere alone, did you? You would have had more room in a love hotel, but you were too squeamish, so this is what you get, with me included. At least it's too small to do much more than sleep, even if you're feeling kinky. And you don't strike me as the kinky sort."

There was nothing she could say. For one thing, his hand still covered her mouth, silencing her. For another, she felt assaulted, overwhelmed by his presence in the tiny capsule, his long legs against hers, his chest too close, his mouth…his mouth… "Are you going to behave?" he asked, his voice silken.

After a moment she nodded, glaring at him, and he moved his hand. "Smart girl," he said.

She wasn't feeling particularly smart at that moment. She was feeling trapped, claustrophobic, hot and turned on, much as she hated to admit it. And there wasn't a damned thing she could do about it.

"You can take off my jacket now," he said.

"I'm not taking anything else off."

He ignored her. She tried to move far enough away from him to reach the zipper, but the plastic wall was right there, he was crammed in front of her, and in order to get her hand up she would have to jab him with her elbow.

Which seemed like a good idea. He must have been expecting it, because he didn't flinch, annoying her further. She unzipped the jacket, trying to wiggle out of it, but wiggling against Reno's hard, hot body was a big mistake, and she froze, the jacket half on and half off.

He put his hands on her. Or course he would, pushing the jacket down her arms and off her, tossing it toward their feet. Before she realized what he was doing he'd caught the hem of her sweatshirt and began pulling that off, too, and fighting it would only bring him closer. At this point he was going to do what he wanted—skinny though he was, he seemed huge in the narrow plastic coffin and far too strong. The space was made for an average-size Japanese man, not for two people almost six feet tall.

She let the sweatshirt go the way of the jacket, waiting for him to just try touching the fly of her jeans, but he seemed to have stripped her enough. Another disheartening reminder of just how resistible she was.

He managed to sit up in the cramped space, barely, and looked at her. "Do you need to use the toilet? I'll stand guard for you."

It wasn't as if she could tell him no. She nodded, and he slid out of the capsule with annoying grace, holding up a hand to stop her while he checked the corridor. Then he nodded, and she slid after him.

The toilet room was neat and utilitarian, with dividers between each urinal. Japanese men must be more modest than Western men. And she was not going to think about that.

She slipped into the stall and shut the door behind her, doing her business quickly. Listening with annoyance as Reno calmly did the same in the outer room.

He was leaning in the open doorway, waiting for her when she finally emerged. He gave her enough time to wash her hands before he hustled her back to the capsule, and to her relief he didn't immediately follow her into the cramped space.

"I'll be right back," he said, pulling the shade down after her.

She let out her pent-up breath. Maybe he wasn't really planning to sleep with her—it would be just like him to torment her like that when he'd already secured his own capsule. Asshole. She leaned back against the plastic wall, closing her eyes, trying to make the stress wash away from her. It encased her like a straightjacket.

The door slid up again, and Reno tossed something toward her. A thin cotton outfit that looked like a cross between surgeon's scrubs and baby doll pajamas. "Put it on."

He didn't give her time to argue, sliding the door down again. She considered arguing, then began unbuttoning her shirt.

By the time he came back she was dressed in the dark blue pajamas, her clothes neatly folded with her sneakers resting on top of them. She was half afraid he'd be wearing the same thing, as he had in the *ryokan,* but he was still in his T-shirt and jeans.

He vaulted into the capsule, graceful and efficient, and slid the screen closed behind him. In the intervening minutes he hadn't gotten any smaller—he filled the narrow space. He stretched out, taking up far too much room as she tried to make herself as small as possible in the far corner.

"You may as well lie down, Jilly. You're not getting out of here past me, and I intend to sleep until they turf us out in the morning. You're just going to be uncomfortable sitting like that."

"I'm fine," she said in a frosty voice.

"I'm not." With an economy of motion he pulled her down beside him, crammed next to him in the narrow space, and then reached up and turned off the overhead light, plunging the space into darkness.

They were on their sides, face-to-face, and she realized belatedly that she should have left her bra on. Left all her clothes on, and borrowed a suit of armor, as well. She was lying plastered up against him, her legs almost as long as his, hip to hip, breast to chest, faces too damned close.

"Go to sleep," he said, his voice cool and bored. She tried to move back, but his arm snaked around her, holding her there.

"You first," she snapped.

It was too dark to see him, but she had the uncanny feeling that he smiled. Not the unpleasant smirk, not the mockery. A genuine smile.

"If you want," he said, and almost instantly she could feel his body relax, the tension and alertness vanish, as his breathing slowed, even his heart rate steadied.

Whereas she was still wired.

She moved, and his arm immediately tightened. "Stop fighting it," he murmured.

*Stop fighting what?* she thought miserably. There's nothing she wanted more than sleep, but that wasn't coming anytime soon, no matter how freaking tired she was. Stop fighting his control over her? That was more likely. The more he tried to make her do what he wanted, the more she resisted. If it had been Taka, she wouldn't have argued, but Reno brought out her rebellious streak.

Or stop fighting her feelings? That wasn't about to happen, and it wouldn't do her any good if it did. So she'd spent two years in L.A. fantasizing about him. She'd spent the two years before that fantasizing about Johnny Depp and she'd gotten over it. Within an hour of being in Reno's company she'd moved miles past her adolescent crush as ugly reality set in.

Unfortunately while her conscious mind had seen the light, her body and her emotions weren't quite so quick. He was utterly still, too damned close to her, and she wanted to close the inch or two that separated them, press her body up against his and burrow against him. She wanted to see what kissing him would be like—putting her mouth on his. He had the most beautiful mouth she'd ever seen in a man, with rich, full lips. It didn't matter that everything that came out of that mouth annoyed her—it was still luscious.

It had to be the insanity of the past few days. She'd seen death, feared for her life. It was no wonder she was disoriented and clinging to the only semifamiliar thing in this alien world. For someone so dangerous he was still the only safety she knew, and it was probably nothing more than animal instinct that made her want to mate with him.

What the hell? Mate with him? She was out of her fucking mind. And if she didn't get the hell away from him, back to the safety of L.A. and minor inconveniences like a broken heart and shattered pride and a future with nothing but calm celibacy to keep her going, then she was really going to lose it.

At least he viewed her with as much interest as her single, lousy lover had—he might not know what a fool she was as far as he was concerned, but he was rejecting her just as thoroughly as Duke had. In fact, she couldn't even call it a one-night stand—it was more like a half-a-night stand, or even half-an-hour, and the very thought of it was….

A second later Reno moved, from what seemed like a sound sleep to a pantherlike speed, and she was lying beneath him, pinned, and in the darkness she could see his eyes glittering, staring down at her.

And for a moment the world seemed to fall away, as his mouth lowered toward hers.

# 7

She stared up at him, holding her breath, waiting, waiting for his head to move lower, for his full, rich mouth to touch hers, and she'd let go, she knew she would, just let herself sink into the thin mattress beneath her, into the hard bone and flesh pushing down on her, just let go and take him....

"Go to sleep," he said. His voice was cool, emotionless, and his body was hot and hard. Definitely hard, she realized with shock. Yet he'd said he didn't want her, didn't care....

"Don't jump to conclusions," Reno said, clearly reading her mind. "I can't lie on top of a beautiful woman without getting a hard-on, but it's nothing personal. Unless you want it to be."

She wanted it to be. She didn't want to think, didn't want to talk, didn't want to fight anymore. In fact, she didn't want to do anything but lose herself in the strange and seductive man pressed against her. He'd said she was beautiful.

And he wasn't even going to kiss her. "I don't want it to be."

"Now, that's a lie," he said. She expected him to mock her, but there was an oddly gentle note in his voice. "But we'll wait until you can be truthful. In the meantime, go to sleep."

"I'm trying," she said. "I don't have the control over my body that you have." She realized how her words sounded, and quickly amended, "I mean, over your own body."

His eyes were glittering in the darkness. "You were right the first time. I can take care of your little problem."

"I don't feel like being knocked unconscious again, thank you very much."

"That wasn't what I had in mind." He pushed his hand between their sandwiched bodies, between her legs, and she shrieked, trying to buck him off.

He slapped his other hand over her mouth, silencing her, and leaned down, whispering in her ear. "Hush. We don't want anyone to know what we're doing."

She tried to shake her head, but he was holding her head immobile. He put one leg between hers, forcing them apart, giving him access. And he was touching her, through the thin cotton cloth, touching her as if he did, indeed, know her body better than she did, and she arched beneath him.

"I'd suggest you do this for yourself but I think you'd probably hit me again," he whispered. "You're too tense, and this is the only way to relax so you can sleep. Think of it as a medical procedure."

She tried to bite his hand, but he was way ahead of her. "Close your eyes, Ji-chan, and let it go. The sooner you do, the sooner you'll come."

No one had ever touched her like that. He was right, she could have taken care of it herself, but his touch, through the rapidly dampening cloth, was something so powerful she didn't think there was any way to fight it. She knew her own body and she wasn't squeamish. She could bring herself to orgasm easily enough, but it had never felt like this, with a man's hands on her, his body, his heat overwhelming her in the tiny capsule, his breath rasping in her ear. And not just any man, but Reno touching her.

She was already way past arousal, the sensations sweeping through her body. Trying to squirm away from him only made it stronger. She felt the first little climax twist her body, and she fell back, panting slightly as he lifted his hand from her mouth.

"There," she said in a hoarse whisper. "You took care of it. I came. Now leave me alone."

His soft laugh filled the darkness. "You call that an orgasm? American men must be terrible lovers."

The second wave hit her harder, and she could barely hold back the cry that filled her throat. How did he know how to touch her, how hard, how gently, with those long, slender fingers of his? She jerked again as another powerful climax swept over her.

And then there was no more fighting it. It was building, building, to a black place that she'd never been before, beyond arousal, beyond orgasm, beyond life and death, ready to dive over into the darkness. She reached up for him, blindly, trying to bring his face to hers, wanting his mouth, but he was suddenly rough, and she shattered, slamming her face against his shoulder to muffle her own cry, her body convulsing, shivering, dying.

And then she fell back, limp. Her face was wet, and she realized she was crying. She couldn't catch her breath—her hoarse panting filled the tiny capsule.

He rolled off her, no longer holding her down. "That was an improvement," he said in a matter-of-fact voice. "It will have to do for now. You have a lot to learn about sex, don't you?"

She was beyond words. She couldn't even turn her back on him, not without pressing up against him. The shivers were slowly fading, even as a stray convulsion rippled through her body. She wanted to disappear, to die, to pretend that nothing had ever happened.

She jerked when she felt his hand on her face. It was oddly gentle. "Close your eyes and sleep, baby," he whispered with surprising tenderness as his fingers drifted over her eyelids. "You can hit me tomorrow. Sleep now."

And she did.

Shit. Ji-chan was crying. He hated it when women cried. Even if it was just a physical response to great sex, he hated it. And it wasn't just the power of her climax that brought the tears.

Shit. If he'd been dumb enough to do something like that, he could have stripped off his own jeans and gotten off as well, and now he was lying here with a hard-on that was probably going to kill him, and then who would look after Jilly, keep her safe?

No one ever died from an unsatisfied erection—he should know. He'd probably been hard from age twelve till he finally got laid at age fourteen, and he'd survived well enough.

Her breathing was deep and even now—she was sound asleep. Now he was the one who was wide-awake. Thinking about the feel of her beneath the thin cotton, the dampness, was making him even harder.

Reno slid his hand down inside his jeans, rearranging things to be more comfortable. He could always jerk off—she'd probably sleep through it, and even if she didn't, he wasn't asking her to take care of it. But he wasn't going to. Like a twelve-year-old kid, he wanted to keep his erection, and think about her. As soon as he got her out of Japan and into safe hands, he'd expend all that energy on someone willing. Despite his taunts, he had no intention of actually fucking her. He could wait for someone who didn't come with strings attached.

He closed his eyes. He didn't have the faintest idea what the hell he was going to do tomorrow. Or today, actually. He was going to have to get to his grandfather without going through the usual channels, which would be tricky. He was far too recognizable among the members of his grandfather's cell, and he had no idea who was gunning for him. Matsumoto-san had always hated him, as had Tomatsu-san. And then there was the new guy, Hitomi-san. He was an unknown—he couldn't ever remember Ojiisan bringing anyone new into the organization without telling his grandson and heir.

The problem was he needed to find a place to stash Ji-chan before he went looking. And he couldn't think of any place safe enough, anyone safe enough to leave her with.

He'd figure it out in the morning. His erection wasn't going away, but he could control his mind. He needed sleep, and for now they were safe inside their little bubble. He moved, just slightly, closing the few inches she'd managed to put between them, so that their bodies were touching, shoulder to thigh. And only then did he let himself sleep.

Jilly awoke in stages, drifting through the seven layers of bliss before she realized exactly where she was. Lying on her back in the narrow bed of a capsule hotel, with Reno's body sprawled across hers. And then she remembered what had happened just before she fell asleep, and she shoved at him, hard, so that he fell back with a grunt, his eyes flying open.

"Asshole," she said, scrambling away from him as best she could in the tiny space.

He reached to the wall and switched on the light, momentarily blinding her. When she opened her eyes again he was looking at her. And there was nothing she could do about it.

"Shouldn't we be getting out of here?" she said, determined to remain cool.

"Soon. The salarymen are all getting ready to go, and you're not supposed to be in here."

"You're going to tell me no one ever sneaks a woman in here?"

"The only reason to bring a woman in here is for sex, and there are more comfortable places. In case you didn't notice."

She was lucky—this time she could control her instinctive blush. And now that she was fully awake, she had the sudden, extremely uncomfortable image of having sex in that confined space, Reno on top of her, naked, hot, deliciously…

She blinked. She didn't even know what she was imagining—it had nothing to do with romance novels and more to do with exercise, if Reno was to be believed. As for her, she'd be better off not finding out. At least, not while she was in Japan and with this particular man, no matter how tempting he was.

"So we wait?" Even crammed against the far corner of the space she felt overwhelmed.

"You wait. I have things to do." He pushed the screen up, sliding out of the capsule.

"Are you coming back?" The words came out before she realized what she was saying, how needy she sounded. Of course she was needy. She was alone in a strange country with people trying to kill her. It was nothing personal when it came to Reno. Not that he'd believe it. Not when she wasn't sure whether even she'd believe it.

"Don't I always?" He slid the door down without waiting for her answer, and she took a deep breath.

There was a small mirror set into the molded plastic wall, and she forced herself to look at the stranger who stared back at her. Her short streaked hair was a tangled mess, her eyes were dark and shadowed, her mouth pale. Whether it was the lack of sleep, or stress, or a combination of the two, she looked as if she'd been run over by a truck. She needed a shower, a toothbrush, clean clothes, and none of those things were in the foreseeable future.

At least she could make sure he fed her. She'd be much better able to deal with him once she got food. Last night, if she was even going to think about it—and she wasn't—was simply an aberration brought on by exhaustion and hunger. Besides, it wasn't as if he'd given her any say in the matter. Was it rape when someone forced an orgasm on you? Maybe. Maybe she could ask Taka to kick his butt. Except she couldn't see herself explaining to her formidable brother-in-law what had gone on in the capsule hotel.

A cool, silent dignity was the best tack. She hadn't been able to stop him the night before, any more than she'd been able to stop her own response. And what a response it had been. She'd never felt anything like that, anything as bone-shakingly powerful. If she'd known that was what could happen with a man, she would have gotten rid of her virginity years ago.

Except that she'd been trying for quite a while now. She'd simply spent too much time as jail bait during college. No one was interested in someone her age, even if she was convinced she was an old soul. No one got close enough to find out.

Reno had. Way too close. She was going to have to do everything she could to put distance between them. Which was just about impossible, given their present circumstances. Maybe he'd come back with a foolproof escape for her, and she'd never have to see him again—except at the occasional family occasions that she couldn't avoid, which would be just fine with her. Time would make things better. In five years she'd be able to look him in the eye without feeling oddly vulnerable. Hell, maybe it would only take five days.

In the meantime, she had no choice but to put her clothes back on, the clothes she'd worn for too long. She managed to finger-comb her hair into some kind of order, though it was a little too punk for her peace of mind. Not that she'd ever minded looking punk; in fact, the cut had been designed for that effect. But right now Reno was punk enough for both of them. And she waited.

Of all the crimes and transgressions Reno had committed since he'd first appeared in her bedroom, returning to the claustrophobic capsule in clean clothes, damp hair and a freshly shaved face was the absolute worst. If she'd been on the fence before, she'd gone fully over to the other side now. She wanted him dead.

"Don't look at me like that," he said, reading her mind. She needed to remember he had the odd ability to do that. It wasn't making life any easier. "I couldn't very well sneak you into the bath. I'm taking you someplace safe where you can shower and change your clothes." He pulled a cloth out of his pocket and tied it around his head, obscuring the flame bright color. "Come on. The car's waiting."

"Let me guess—you stole another car."

"I couldn't very well buy it. Just keep your head down and don't wiggle your hips."

"I don't wiggle my hips!" she said, incensed.

"Yes, you do. You don't walk like a man. You've got hips like a porn star, and men are always watching them."

She didn't know whether to be annoyed or perversely flattered. Annoyed was easier. "Maybe they'll just think you brought your femme boyfriend in."

"You don't walk like a *gei,* you walk like a sex bomb."

"Oh, fuck you," she said, irritated.

"Taka wouldn't like it."

"Fuck Taka."

"Su-chan wouldn't like it."

She gave up. "You know, things would be a lot easier if you stopped trying to make me furious."

"Easier for whom? Besides, it doesn't require much effort on my part."

She looked at him. "No, that's true. You're just naturally infuriating."

"Remember that. Keep your head down, keep quiet and do what I say."

"Asshole," she muttered. And she slid out from the capsule, ready for one more day on the run.

# 8

The car he stole this time could have been a twin to their first venture into Grand Theft Auto, Jilly thought, assuming he didn't make a habit of it. It was an anonymous little gray sedan, and this time she didn't make the mistake of heading for the right side.

It was a cold, gray day, and she was reduced to her sweatshirt again; he'd commandeered the leather jacket, but she was damned if she was going to shiver. Her backpack was sitting on the backseat, full of clean underwear and textbooks, and she didn't know whether to be pissed that he hadn't brought it in or relieved that it hadn't been lost. She decided "pissed" was her default, and she leaned back against the seat, her arms folded across her chest, as he took off into the traffic at a nightmare speed.

Jilly had been raised on L.A. freeways, but occasionally cowardice was the only option. She squealed, shut her eyes and slid down where she sat, clutching the cloth seat with both hands and holding her breath. She considered praying, but she was too busy holding on as he sped through the crowded streets, clipped corners, zipped down back alleys that were barely wide enough for the small car. All she could do was wait it out, knowing she was going to die in a twisted pile of metal and flames, but at least he'd go with her, the son of a bitch, and—

He stopped so fast that her body hurtled toward the window, the seat belt and Reno's outstretched arm catching her before she made contact. "We're here," he said.

"Here, where?" They had parked outside of a huge warehouse-type building, surrounded by a high stone wall. It looked about as welcoming as a maximum-security prison.

"I decided it was time for you to meet my grandfather."

She just looked at him. "Doesn't he think I'm dead?"

"Ojiisan is adaptable. You have to be in his line of work."

"He won't mind that you lied to him?"

"He's not going to be pleased with me, but then,

he considered me a total disgrace to have let you die in the first place. I imagine finding you still alive will take care of some of his displeasure."

"Oh, I don't know. I'm kind of hoping he'll kick your butt," Jilly said cheerfully.

"If anyone could, it would be my grandfather," he said glumly. "He won't let anyone get to you, though. I'm putting you in his hands while I find out what the fuck is going on."

Suddenly she didn't feel like needling him. "You're leaving me?" There was no anxiety in her voice—she could be proud of that.

"Your prayers have been answered. I dump you with Ojiisan and you never have to see me again. He'll make arrangements for you to get home."

"Just like that?"

"Just like that." He must have finally noticed something in her tone of voice, because he looked at her more closely. "Don't tell me you aren't as happy to get rid of me as I am to get rid of you, because I won't believe you. I think we've had about as much of each other as we can stand."

The stupid idiot didn't even realize that his casual words were like a blow. If she didn't have to struggle so hard to be unaffected by them, she would have kicked him in the shins. Or burst into tears, neither of which was an option.

"Of course," she said, her voice cool. "I'm just wondering why you didn't take me here before and make life a lot easier."

"Ojiisan has a traitor in his organization. I don't know who, I don't know why."

"And you don't think this so-called traitor will decide to get rid of me?"

"There's no reason. You don't matter—the only reason anyone was after you was to lure Taka into the open. Once you're inside the compound, there will be dozens of men to look out for you. One traitor—even a handful of them—won't get past the protection my grandfather can set up."

"You know," she said in a conversational tone, "if you tell me I don't matter one more time, I'm going to…to…" She struggled, trying to think of something dire enough to threaten him with. "I'm going to cry," she said triumphantly.

And he did look rattled at the thought. "You matter to Summer," he said. "And I'm sure you matter to all your friends and lovers back in California. You just don't matter to me."

A gun, she thought. If she had a gun she'd shoot him. As it was, all she could do was summon up her sweetest smile. "Ditto," she said.

"Ditto?" he echoed, his forehead wrinkling. He was wearing sunglasses again, hiding his eyes from her, hiding his expression. She considered yanking them off his face, throwing them on the ground and stomping on them.

"Meaning, I feel the exact same way," she said. "Take me to your grandfather so we can get this over with."

For once he was smart enough to keep his mouth shut.

The walls looked old, solid, not the sort of protection a modern building deserved. Reno pushed through one of the huge doors, past two men waiting silently, with shiny dark gray suits and unsmiling faces. "Where's the *oyabun?*" he asked in Japanese. The reply was a little too fast, with a heavy accent that she couldn't quite get, but apparently Reno understood, and he took her arm, pulling her toward the huge, anonymous building.

She tried to yank her arm free, but his grip tightened, hard enough to leave bruises. "Don't fight me, Jilly," he said in a barely audible voice. "This isn't like anyplace you're used to. Until my grandfather takes responsibility, you'd better stay as close to me as possible."

"You don't have to hold my hand," she snapped, equally quiet.

"Yes, I do. Get over it."

There were eyes watching her, both seen and

unseen. Male eyes, blank and unreadable, as they passed group after group of well-dressed men with carefully arranged black hair. The *yakuza* army, and not a punkster among them, she thought. No wonder Reno went to such extremes.

He stopped before a pair of black-lacquered inner doors at the end of one long hallway, and Jilly had just time enough to notice the beauty and antiquity of them, clearly taken from some much older and more historic building, when they swung open, and a massive man stood waiting, blocking the entrance with his arms crossed.

"That's your grandfather?" she whispered, astonished. She could see how such a huge creature could inspire panic, though Reno didn't appear to be cowering.

"Kobayashi-san," he said, lowering his head slightly in greeting. *Okay, not Grandpa, then.* Whoever it was, he didn't look too happy to see them.

But Kobayashi's own bow was lower, signifying respect. "Your grandfather is tired, young master. He wasn't expecting you. Or the *gaijin*," he added, with a pointed look in her direction. His Japanese was slow and sonorous, and she got every word of it.

"My grandfather will welcome me," Reno replied with the same stilted courtesy, and the huge man moved out of the way, revealing the room behind him.

If Jilly had been in a more frivolous mood, she would have giggled. It looked like a throne room—a long approach, with a stately ruler seated at the far end, waiting for their humble approach. Except that nothing was amusing her at this point.

Reno kept her hand in his as they moved closer, and for the first time she got a good look at the notorious *oyabun,* the head of the family.

He was tiny. Old and frail, with wisps of white hair on a bald, freckled skull. Thin lips, eyes almost hidden beneath the crepey wrinkles. His suit was white, silk, exquisite. And his voice, when he spoke, was surprisingly strong.

"What have you brought me, Grandson? Back from the dead, is she?"

Reno bowed, so low his thick braid of hair brushed the ground, and he yanked her down with him. "We need your help, Ojiisan."

"I could have told you that," the old man said. "What took you so long to come to that conclusion?" He spoke English, slow, deliberate, and Reno switched to that language, as well.

"She should be safe at this point. The second

group of Russians met with an accident, and it seems unlikely that anyone else will come after her. But just to be certain I thought she would be safest under your protection while I made a few inquiries."

"My people can make the inquiries. Don't tell me you think your sources are more informed than mine."

Reno had risen by now, and he met his grandfather's sharp gaze with an innocent expression that fooled no one. "The Committee can get information...."

"The Committee is a group of overgrown children playing games," the old man said. "I know what's going on in my own country."

"Did you know that you have a traitor in your midst?"

The room was empty—even the huge Kobayashi had disappeared, and at Reno's simple words the old man froze. "I should have you killed for saying that," he said, and Jilly held her breath.

And then Reno laughed. "Ojiisan, you're terrifying the *gaijin*. She doesn't know that you couldn't even spank me when I was growing up."

"It would have been better if I had," the old man said. He turned his impenetrable gaze on Jilly, and she felt herself caught by those dark eyes. "Has my grandson taken good care of you? Has he been polite? I may not beat him, but his cousin, Takashi, will have no hesitation."

"He saved my life," she said. "Twice. I can't say much for his manners, though."

The *oyabun* gave a short bark of laughter. "I suppose that's more important. Would you excuse us while we talk? Kobayashi will take care of you. Has my grandson fed you?"

"Not recently," Reno said. "She's been complaining all morning. She wants a shower and a chance to change her clothes."

"We can see to that," the man said before Jilly could protest. A moment later Kobayashi appeared, surprisingly graceful and silent for such a large man. "Take Lovitz-san to the red room and bring her anything she needs. And make certain no one interrupts my talk with my nephew." He had switched back to Japanese, presumably for Kobayashi's sake.

The big man bowed low, and Jilly had no choice but to follow him. Their discussion had nothing to do with her, and Reno had already dismissed her from his mind. He was dumping her here, and she was just as glad to get rid of him. She hadn't been able to look him in the eye after the dark, tumbled moments of the night before, and now she wouldn't have to. She was safe inside this fortress—no one would dare contravene that scary little old man. If he truly had a traitor in his midst, then Jilly could only feel sorry for him. Ojiisan was no match for a dozen bad guys, and he had Reno to back him up.

As for her, she could just forget about Reno. He was done with her, and if she never saw him again, it would be too soon. Too bad Taka couldn't beat the crap out of him for no reason. Maybe he'd do it as a personal favor.

The food was divine. Miso soup, an egg dish mercifully free of tentacles and green tea. By the time she'd devoured everything, she was feeling almost human. Kobayashi had brought her backpack, and he'd shown her the bathroom connected to the room, his English brief but adequate. There was no mistaking his orders. She was to stay put until someone came and got her.

Which was fine as far as she was concerned. It would mean she was less likely to see the red-haired, tattooed skunk….

The shower felt so good she almost cried. There was a soaking tub, as well, but she decided to avoid that, remembering far too vividly what had happened the last time she'd lingered in a tub. Not that Reno gave a damn—he wasn't going to come striding in here and pull her out. She'd been dismissed. *Asshole.*

She pulled on her clean clothes, wishing for some reason that she'd brought a dress with her. Ojiisan was formal enough that she had the irrational urge to be on her best behavior, silly as it was. He'd have to take her as she was. He'd gotten used to Summer, and Summer was as free from vanity as Jilly was.

The bed in the room was Western-style, and she stretched out on it, bored. There was nothing to read in the room that wasn't in *kanji,* no TV, no radio. Just her and her thoughts, and at the moment they weren't the best company. She slept for a little while, just out of sheer boredom, and when she awoke the room was in dusk-laden shadows, and she was tired of being dutiful. She needed to find Kobayashi, anyone, and find out when she was going to go home.

She half expected the door to be locked, but it opened easily enough, and the hall was deserted. She considered calling out, then decided she didn't want to disturb any of the brutal-looking gangsters under Ojiisan's iron rule. Particularly if, as Reno said, they weren't as obedient as they were supposed to be.

She couldn't remember where Ojiisan's throne

room, as she thought of it, was, but she was bound to run into it sooner or later. She was wearing her sneakers, when she knew she shouldn't, but somehow wandering around this place in her socks made her feel just a little too vulnerable. Which was silly—she was under the protection of Ojiisan now. No one would dare touch her.

She heard the murmur of voices, and like a fool she went in that direction, looking for someone, anyone, who could answer her questions.

She saw the flash of light first, followed by a strange, popping noise. And then a thud, followed by a short, sharp word.

She knew what that noise, that flash, was, and she should have run. Instead she was frozen, telling herself she was imagining things, telling herself no one had just been shot. It was impossible—these things didn't happen.

But in her new, crazy, mixed-up life on the run they happened far too often. She moved quietly, cursing even the soft squeak of her sneakers, as she crept up to the open door, telling herself it would be nothing, knowing it would be nothing.

The man lay in a pool of blood on the floor, the hole in his forehead mute testimony to what had happened. She couldn't see the shooter, and she backed away, cold with fear, her stomach churning. There was a sound from the room, from someone just out of sight, and her nerve finally left her, and she ran down the hall, not caring how much noise she made, not knowing where she was going.

She felt something brush past her, the strange popping noise from behind her, and she realized with shock that someone was shooting at her, and if she didn't get out fast, she was going to be as dead as Reno had said she was. Who was trying to kill her? Maybe it was Reno himself, but she didn't dare slow down, didn't dare look behind her, afraid of who she might see.

She came to a corner and skidded around it, momentarily putting herself outside the line of fire. This hall was darker, and someone was coming toward her, and this time she knew she'd have no way of escaping. She was going to die, and Taka was going to be seriously annoyed, not to mention Summer, who would make his life miserable, and what the hell was she doing, thinking things like that when she was running for her life...?

He came out of nowhere, and she tried to fight him, blind with fear, but he simply wrapped his arms around her, imprisoning her against his body, and pulled her into darkness.

She whimpered in fear. Then she heard

Reno's voice in her ear, and it was the best sound in the world. "Be quiet, you idiot, or you'll get us both killed."

And at that moment Jilly Lovitz knew she was in love.

# 9

It was pitch-black, wherever they were, a tight, enclosed place, and Jilly was crammed up against him, his arms imprisoning her. She could feel her heart slamming against her chest as she tried to catch her breath. His heart was racing, too, which wasn't much of a comfort.

"Where are we?" she mouthed in a trace above a whisper.

She was half expecting him to slam his hand across her mouth, but instead he answered. "Janitor's closet," he whispered. "I don't think he saw us go in."

"Who?"

"Hitomi-san. Why the hell was he trying to kill you? Not that I blame him—you're enough to drive anyone to murder, but he must have had a reason."

"He killed someone. Or somebody did. I walked in on it."

"Holy motherfucker," Reno said. "You have great timing. Did you see the man who did it?"

"I didn't see anything," she said irritably. "And this is a gangster hideout, for God's sake. Don't people kill one another all the time?"

"No."

There was no noise from beyond the door, and now she could smell cleaning supplies. "It's a good thing I'm not claustrophobic," she whispered. "I could be having hysterics right now."

"No, you couldn't." Even in a whisper his flat statement was chilling. "I need to get you out of here."

Relief flooded her. "Yes, you do."

"Stay put." He released her, but the space was so small she was still crammed up against him. "I don't know how long this will take me. Whatever you do, don't move, don't make a sound."

She would have liked to protest. She would have liked to wrap her arms around him and haul him back. He was the only safety she knew, and he was abandoning her.

"Sure," she said, her whisper the epitome of calm while her mind was screaming. "Take your time."

She couldn't see him in the darkness. But somehow she knew he smiled. Not the smirk that he usually offered, but a real smile. "I won't abandon you, Ji-chan," he said. And a moment later he was gone, the momentary sliver of light from the darkened corridor blinding her as he slipped out of the tiny closet.

Ji-chan? He called her Ji-chan? That was an affectionate term, and as far as she could tell he found her nothing more than terminally annoying. Why had he said that?

She was shaking, she realized belatedly. Her legs were trembling, her heart was racing, and she leaned against the door, pressing her forehead against the cool metal, forcing herself to take slow, deep breaths. He'd come back for her. Whether he wanted to or not. It had nothing to do with her, or any feelings he might have for her. He'd taken her on as his responsibility and he wouldn't abandon her. But why in the world had he called her Ji-chan?

It was cold in the closet. It was midwinter, and she hadn't bothered with a sweatshirt when she'd left her room. Clearly the Japanese were not strong proponents of central heating, at least not in their gangland warehouses. The ice was seeping into her bones, making it even harder for her to stay calm. If she wasn't shaking apart from fear, she was trembling from the cold, and either way she was going to start knocking things over if she didn't pull herself together. *Serves me right for growing up in Southern California,* she told herself. She'd never complain about the heat again.

She lost track of time. Maybe Reno had dumped her after all. Gangland-style killings couldn't be that unusual—this was the *yakuza,* for God's sake. She was hardly naive when it came to organized crime. After all, she'd watched *The Sopranos.* Maybe she'd overreacted.

But then, why had someone, presumably the mysterious Hitomi-san, chased her, shot at her? And why bother? She hadn't seen the shooter—it wasn't as if she could identify anyone.

There wasn't enough room to sit—when she tried to push back from the door the wall was right behind her. Reno was just lucky the two of them had managed to squeeze in there when he'd yanked her into the tiny space. And it had only worked with her body absolutely plastered up against him, every inch of her pressed against his hard, hard body.

At least that thought was making her hot. All she had to do was keep remembering embarrassing moments and she'd keep from freezing to death. Fortunately or unfortunately she had a dozen of them, the worst being in the capsule with his cool, impersonal hands making her come her brains out.

No, maybe remembering wasn't a good idea. Because not only was it making her skin warm, she was getting turned on, and that was one place she definitely didn't want to go. Reno was out of her league, and it was a good thing. She had a hard-enough time dealing with the average American male. A wild card like Reno was more than she could handle.

Of course he'd take that moment to open the closet door, just as her face was flushed and her body tingling. Fortunately he was too intent on getting out of there to notice.

"Don't say anything, don't move unless I tell you to," he said in a low voice. "If you do, you'll get us both killed."

She wasn't about to come up with an argument. While the hallway was marginally lighter than the pitch-black closet, it was still almost impenetrable, and the only safety was the man in front of her, leading the way.

They passed one man on their trip through the maze of underground tunnels, and Reno moved so fast he was simply a blur in the darkness, and the man collapsed, unconscious, as Reno took her hand, pulling her deeper into the bowels of the building.

At first she didn't realize when they emerged

into the evening air—the cold that penetrated the old cement building was the same inside as out, and night had fallen. To her amazement they were outside the high walls of the cement-block compound that housed Ojiisan's headquarters, on a dark and deserted side street. "Now's the time to run, Jilly," Reno said, and took off, dragging her along behind him.

It was a good thing she had long legs—if she'd been short, she never would have kept up with him, and chances were he'd either abandon her and drag her limp body in the dirt if she fell. She was in decent shape—she ran three times a week and didn't smoke, but she wasn't used to a flat-out sprint, and her chest was burning, her heart banging against her rib cage. Reno, goddamn him, seemed barely touched by the fast pace. He was probably running fast so she couldn't argue with him.

It didn't matter—there was no way she was going to fall behind or complain. If he could do it, then so could she. And the faster she ran, the more the scene retreated, the dead man, all the dead men that she'd seen in the past few days.

And then, just as suddenly, he stopped, catching her as she hurtled forward, pushing back against a building and holding her there while she struggled to catch her breath.

He wasn't even winded. "We'll get a taxi from here," he said. "As soon as you stop sounding like an eighty-year-old man."

"Go...to...hell," she gasped, struggling for breath. They were on a side street, but the streetlights were on, and neon beckoned from around the corner. He just stood there, waiting while she brought her breathing under control. She shoved her sweat-damp hair away from her face with a shaking hand—at this rate she was going to get pneumonia and she didn't care. She just wanted this all to end.

A moment later he took her hand, pulled her arm through his in a perfect parody of young lovers, and walked her into the neon, into the crowded streets of Tokyo.

It wasn't until he'd gotten her ensconced in the backseat of a taxi that she noticed he'd covered his distinctive hair with a black kerchief emblazoned with *kanji*, and he'd tucked his bright red braid beneath the leather jacket. Except for his height, he could be any Tokyo hipster in shades, but there was no disguising Jilly. There weren't that many almost six feet tall *gaijin* women around, and there wasn't a damned thing she could do about it.

She waited until Reno gave instructions, so detailed she couldn't follow, and then she spoke.

"What next?" Her voice was hoarse from running.

He didn't bother to look at her—he was busy watching out the back, probably looking for signs of pursuit. "Train station," he said. "We're taking the train to Osaka and I'm putting you on a plane at Kansai Airport." He glanced at her then, just briefly. "You'll be safe enough."

"Why don't you just let me go on my own? You don't need to take the train—we're probably better off separated."

"You'll stand out wherever you are in Japan, and it won't take them long to find you," Reno said in a flat voice. "You saw something you weren't supposed to see, and they don't want you to have a chance to tell anyone."

She wanted to argue with his reasoning, but she couldn't. Instead she tried another tack. "Who are 'they'? And tell them what? What the hell is going on?" she demanded.

"If I knew, I'd probably tell you," he said, not the most comforting words she could have heard. "The Russians who were after you were simply trying to lure Taka out of hiding, but someone was telling them where we were going. If I'd realized how complicated things were, I would have stashed you somewhere while I warned my grandfather, but there aren't that many safe places out of reach of my grandfather's men. I should have known you'd get in trouble wherever I took you."

"It's not my fault someone was murdered," she shot back.

"It was your fault you were wandering around places you shouldn't have been. Why didn't you just stay in your room?"

"And then what? You would have gone off and your grandfather would have sent me back home and we all would have lived happily ever after? Except for the dead man."

He sighed. "Just do what I tell you from now on. Something is going on with my grandfather's family, and Hitomi-san is part of it. I tried to warn Ojiisan, but he simply told me not to worry, that he had it all under control. Right now there's nothing I can do to help him. I have to take care of you."

He sounded as disgruntled as she felt. "No, you don't," she said. "I can take care of myself."

His derisive laugh was annoying enough that she was tempted to kick him, but she'd seen enough violence in the past two days to last her her entire life, no matter how obnoxious he was. "You're as pathetic as a kitten," he said. "If your family had any sense they wouldn't let you out without a keeper."

The taxi was pulling up to a large, Victorian-looking building, and Reno spoke to him so rapidly Jilly could only get a few words. He shoved a fistful of yen into the driver's requisite white-gloved hand and dragged Jilly out the door.

It must be rush hour, she thought dazedly as he politely pushed his way through waves of people…though almost every hour seemed to be rush hour in Tokyo. "Keep your head down," he muttered, "and try to slump. We're trying to blend in here."

"Fat chance," she said, slumping anyway. Her streaky blond hair shouldn't be that much of a giveaway—it seemed like half the younger population had dyed their hair varying shades of blond and orange. Her height and her walk were two things she couldn't change. She kept her face down, slumped her shoulders and scuttled along behind Reno as best she could. She'd never been able to disappear in a crowd, and in a homogeneous society like Japan she was doomed from the start.

Not that Reno was doing that great a job, either, she thought critically, ducking behind him as he used a ticketing machine. Sunglasses after dark tended to draw attention, as well as his height. But even worse was the way he carried himself. Like a lord of the universe, a prince of fucking darkness. People moved out of his way automatically, and the hidden hair and tattoos were little help. If someone was looking for them, they'd be too damned easy to find.

"Oh, shit."

Reno whirled around, the tickets in one hand. "What?"

"I think they found us."

Kobayashi was hard to miss, the crowds parting around him like the Red Sea, and the two men with him, though tiny compared to Kobayashi, looked extremely lethal.

Reno froze. "Listen to me, Jilly, and do absolutely everything I tell you. No deviations, no thinking for yourself. When I give you the word, I want you to run to the left, as fast as you can. Push people over if you need to, just get the fuck out of here. Then get a taxi and have it take you to Narita."

"I don't have enough money...."

He shoved a wad of yen in her hand. "Get the first plane out, anywhere. Trust me."

"I don't..."

"Now!" he said, and shoved her, so hard she

almost fell, as Kobayashi loomed over them, reaching out a meaty arm to grab her.

She spun out of his way, knocking people aside, sprinting through the terminal. She could hear the noise behind her, the shouts, but she didn't stop, she just kept running as the crowd swallowed her up.

There was no mistaking the sign for the ladies' toilet, and she didn't even hesitate, running inside as she shoved the wad of yen into her jeans. The room was almost empty—two of the eight stalls were in use, and she ducked inside one, locking it, trying to catch her breath. And then she turned, to look at the ceramic hole in the floor with utter despair. There was no way she could use that while she was wearing jeans. She was just going to have to wait.

Wait to pee. Wait to catch her breath. Wait to see whether they were going to find her in the ladies' room, whether Reno was now a pulverized spot on the floor of the terminal, whether she was going die in the next few minutes.

One thing was certain. She wasn't getting a taxi to Narita airport without finding out that Reno was still alive. It was that simple.

And he'd probably kill her when he found out she didn't go.

Too bad. She'd had enough of running for her life, and she wasn't running out on Reno, no matter how much he wanted to get rid of her. She was in it for the long haul.

And he was about to find out just how tenacious she could be.

# *10*

Takashi O'Brien had his choice of two options. He could either go back to the tiny island off Hokkaido, find his furious wife and tell her that the one person she loved most in this world, besides him, had been murdered. Or he could find out what the hell had happened to his sister-in-law, and why Reno hadn't been able to keep her alive.

He was used to lying, used to living in a shadow world. He just wasn't used to lying to Summer anymore.

Something was up with his great-uncle, as well. Usually he could go to the old man to find out what was happening, but his instincts, which had saved his life countless times, told him to keep away. The office in London didn't know shit, except that Jilly had been killed, and until he found out who, and why, and how and made them pay, he couldn't face his wife with the truth.

In the meantime, all he could do was keep his head down, and find the man who should have been trusted to keep her safe. Reno. And then beat the hell out of him.

Jilly waited as long as she possibly could. People came and went, the baby-light voices of young Japanese women filling the tiled room and then leaving it in silence again. There was no sound of chaos from the main part of the terminal—whatever had gone down out there was over and done with. And she couldn't spend the rest of her life in a Japanese toilet.

She emerged from the stall, cautiously, but the room was finally empty. She was planning to open the main door just a crack, to see whether it looked safe, but just the moment she reached it, it slammed open as a group of chattering women pushed inside. They stopped talking when they saw her, an uneasy silence in the room.

"*Sumimasen,*" she murmured, slipping past them.

She'd been in the bathroom for at least a couple of hours. Unfortunately it looked as if it wasn't always rush hour in Tokyo. The main hall of the train station was almost empty, just a few random people at the vending machines.

The first place she looked was where she had last seen Reno, with Kobayashi looming down on him. The center of the hall was empty, and there was no blood on the floor. That proved nothing—the Japanese would clean everything quickly so there'd be no trace to offend the travelers. For all she knew Reno was in pieces somewhere, never to be found again….

"What the fuck are you doing here?"

She couldn't help it. She flung her arms around him, holding him so tight it was a wonder he could breathe. Oddly enough he didn't complain, he just stood there, putting up with it.

She finally let go, pulling back. He looked in reasonably good shape—a cut across one cheekbone, just under the teardrops, and he'd lost his sunglasses, but he was in one, glorious, bad-boy piece.

"Never mind," he said in a resigned voice. "I knew you weren't going to do what I told you to. Let's get out of here."

"We're going to Osaka?" Her voice sounded husky with unshed tears, and she quickly cleared her throat.

He shook his head. "No. They'll be watching the trains now. We're not going anywhere. But you're going to have to do what I tell you or I'll tie you up and put you there."

"Promises, promises," she said, feeling absurdly lighthearted. It didn't matter that he was a son of a bitch who found her a royal pain in the ass. He was alive, and she was staying with him. At least for now.

He just looked at her, and then suddenly she thought better of being playful. *Better not pull the lion's tail.* Reno was just a little too dangerous, even to her. She needed to remember who he was and what he was capable of.

"Did you kill them?" she said.

Reno didn't answer at first. "Who do you mean?" he said finally. "Kobayashi and his buddies? No. I just caused enough of a distraction to get the hell out of here. You're lucky I didn't trust you, or you'd be stuck here alone."

"I count my blessings," she muttered.

"You can count them later. Let's get out of here before someone else decides to come looking." He held out his hand, and she took it. Strange, the warmth and strength of it, his long fingers wrapping around hers. He didn't seem to notice.

He stole another car, of course. This time she watched him do it, aghast at how easy he made it seem, and a few minutes later they were careening through the nighttime traffic at horrifying speeds, and all she could do was hold on, since the seat belt wasn't working.

"Where are we going?" she managed to ask as he rounded one corner on what seemed like two wheels.

"I'm taking you to a friend's apartment where you can shower, change your clothes and sleep in a decent bed while I go talk to my grandfather again. He needs to know that Kobayashi is in on it. Maybe this time he won't treat me like an idiot. Though, knowing my grandfather, I'm not going to hold out hope."

"And what's your friend going to think?"

"He won't be there. It's the safest place I can think of—the only person who knows of its existence is Taka." He sped up, narrowly missing a small delivery truck, and took another sharp right. She closed her eyes and prayed, not opening them till he slammed to an abrupt stop.

She staggered out of the car, sank to her knees on the sidewalk and flung her arms out, crying, "Land!"

Reno was not amused, coming up behind her and hauling her up. "I know how to drive."

"You and Dale Earnhardt."

"Who's Dale Earnhardt?"

"Race-car driver. Died in a car crash," she said.

She looked up at the plain, blocklike building. There was a row of narrow balconies along one side, and futons were hanging over many of them.

"I'm going to try to find out where the hell Taka is. Things are in too big a mess right now— I don't know who can be trusted. As soon as I do, I'll dump you."

"Lovely," she muttered. "And I'll appreciate being dumped. Are we going to stand here trading insults?"

"No. You go first. Just in case someone's figured out about this place. Who the hell knows— maybe there are more Russians on the way."

"You sure you want me to be on the front line of fire? I thought you were supposed to protect me?"

"I'm beginning to think it's more trouble than it's worth."

She pushed open the door, faced with a long flight of narrow stairs running along the outside of the building. "Three flights up," Reno said. "No elevator."

She wisely kept her thoughts to herself, trudging up the stairs. He was right behind her, and if he'd been interested, he could be watching her ass, but he wasn't interested.

She was only slightly out of breath when they reached the third floor. At this point he pushed past her, his body brushing hers, and she felt her pulse quicken, the blood rushing to places it had no business rushing. At least she could manage her poker face.

He unlocked the anonymous white door at the end of the corridor, kicking off his cowboy boots with more ease than she would have thought, and stepped inside, holding the door open for her.

Her sneakers were a little trickier, but she got them off and put them on the small platform before stepping inside. The apartment smelled musty, closed up, as if no one had been there for months, and Reno quickly strode across the small space, pushing open the door to the narrow balcony, letting in the cold winter air while Jilly looked around her.

Somewhere she'd gotten the impression that Tokyo apartments were small and crammed with possessions. This particular one was certainly small, but it had a Zen-like simplicity. There was a futon couch on one wall, a computer on the other. Bookshelves neatly organized, every space used, what looked like diplomas framed and hung on the walls. One was in French, from the Sorbonne, given to Hiromasa Shinoda, summa cum laude, from the school of engineering.

"Your friend is an engineer?" she said. "I thought you'd only know biker gangs and gangsters."

"And secret agents," he added. "Masa was a childhood friend and a wonk. We live very different lives, but we still share certain things."

"Where is he? Isn't he going to mind that we're taking over his apartment?"

"He's out of the country. Besides, I had a key, didn't I? He knows I come here."

"But why? Don't you have your own apartment?"

"I do. Obviously the people who are working against my grandfather would know exactly where it is. This is where I go when I want to disappear." He headed toward the small kitchen alcove, looking through the packaged foods. "We've got dried octopus here if you're hungry."

"Tentacles," Jilly said glumly. "I don't eat tentacles." She wasn't going into the tiny kitchen with him—it would put her too close and she was feeling too skittish. "I'm sure I can find something."

"Are you trying to get rid of me?"

"You said you were going out to talk to your grandfather again. If you survive, you could bring some food back with you."

"Nice," he said. "If they kill me you can make do with octopus. In the meantime the bathroom's behind you."

She glanced over her shoulder. "I suppose he

has one of those space-age toilets that do everything but cook dinner."

"It doesn't work from across the room, Ji-chan. You have to go in and sit."

She glared at him. "And when I come out, you'll be gone. What if you don't come back?"

"I'll come back."

"What if they kill you?"

"I'm hard to kill. Go and use the toilet, Ji-chan. You're making me uncomfortable standing there with your knees together."

"You really are crass, aren't you?"

"And you're a puritanical American. People need to use toilets, even if you want to pretend they don't."

She was so tempted to stomp over to the sofa and sit, waiting for him to leave just to prove a point, but her body wasn't giving her that option.

"You know I hate you, right?" she said, turning her back on him.

"I hope so. That's what I've been trying to do for the past three days."

She ignored him, sliding the door shut behind her. Just once she wished she had a door to slam, loud. There'd been no time for her to even catch her breath since she'd arrived in Japan, no time to even think about whether she loved it here or hated it, but one thing was definite—she missed slamming doors.

Not that she made a habit of it in her normal life, but recently things had been far from normal. And she'd never been around someone as deliberately infuriating as Reno.

But why? Why was he trying to infuriate her? It made no sense.

The uber-toilet, however, made perfect sense, and for the time being she had more urgent matters to contend with. Maybe later she'd find out why he was trying to make her angry. And why she was jumping for the bait so readily.

Jilly was pissed off, just the way he needed her to be. As long as she was angry she wouldn't be frightened, and as long as she wasn't frightened he could handle things.

He should have known she wouldn't scare easily. Wouldn't run, as he'd told her to. For a supposed genius she was damned stupid when it came to her own safety. And when it came to him.

He'd seen her looking at him. And he'd known she wasn't going to just walk away. Any more than he would, even if he'd had the chance. But he also wasn't going to get any closer.

So pissing her off was the answer.

Except that she still looked at him. He must be some sort of adolescent rebellion on her part. And then, danger tended to heighten some people's emotions, sexuality. Maybe that was why he couldn't keep his hands off her.

It didn't matter. He'd scared her enough that she'd stay put while he went in search of food and clothing for her. And answers. Those answers were the most important on his mind right now.

Not thinking about taking off her clothes. Not seeing if she tasted as good as she felt…or if he could make her come again, this time with him inside her.

Holy motherfucker, he was doing it again. He needed to get out of there, fast. Before he decided that he didn't need to get out of there at all.

It was her second shower of the day, and no less wonderful. She stayed there until the water turned cold, then stayed longer, stepping out when it finally became icy. Hiromasa Shinoda's spotless apartment came equipped with new toothbrushes still in their packages and what Jilly devoutly hoped was toothpaste and not minty hemorrhoid cream. She even stole Hiromasa's comb to run through her wet hair, and his enveloping blue-and-white *yukata* to wrap around her body before emerging out into the studio apartment.

Reno was gone, as she'd expected him to be. There was food on the tiny counter in the kitchen, all unidentifiable, but something looked vaguely chiplike and crunchy, so she tore open the bag and ate it, accompanied by a bottle of what was euphemistically called Pocari Sweat. She was past the point of being picky—once she finished with them, she started hunting through the cupboards, coming up with tiny cans of coffee with names like Fire and Boss, strange-colored candies with gummy textures. It didn't matter. She was so hungry she would have eaten the furniture.

Taking a bag of purple candy with her, she headed over to the computer, drawn like a magnet. She couldn't read most of the diplomas on the wall, but the one from the Sorbonne was in Latin. Hiromasa Shinoda was a student with highest honors—Reno was probably the equivalent of a Japanese slacker. It made for an unlikely friendship. The paintings on the wall were Hiroshige wood-block prints of Mount Fuji—not a movie poster or video game in sight. There was a small photo in one of the bookcases—she went closer, finally getting a look at the mysterious Hiromasa. He was tall, like Reno, if you could judge by the people standing next to him in the graduation photo. Short black hair, high cheekbones, narrow, clever face. The same full, luscious mouth that Reno had, the same nose. Was he some kind of cousin? He looked like an ordinary version of the exotic Reno....

She picked up the photo, staring at it. The stress of the past few days must have been even worse than she realized, to have it take so long to make the connection. The conservative-looking, soberly dressed young gentleman, the brilliant graduate of several universities, Hiromasa Shinoda, didn't just look like Reno. He was Reno.

She hadn't heard the door open. Suddenly he was there, plucking the photo out of her hand and putting it facedown on the low table. "He's not your type," Reno said.

She stared at him. The red tattooed tears, like drops of blood, on his high cheekbones, the cat's-eye contacts that gave him a feral look, the three earrings in one ear and the long, flame-colored braid. "So you've been telling me for the past three days," she said with utter calm.

She made him blink. It was the strongest response she'd been able to elicit from him in days, and she took her small triumphs where she could. "Did you bring me back some food?"

He glanced over at the tiny kitchen area. "It looks as if you've already devoured everything here. Including the dried octopus. I thought you didn't do tentacles."

"I couldn't afford to be picky. And I'm still hungry."

He just looked at her. Her blush was instinctive, uncontrollable. Okay, so he won that round. "I brought back food, since you seem to be obsessed with it."

He was standing too close to her. She pulled the blue-and-white *yukata* more closely around her, and the slow smile on his face was just a little too close to a smirk, as if he could read her mind, her skittishness, and found them funny.

She was going to wipe that look off his face. "So, Hiromasa-san," she said, her voice cool, "why do you keep this apartment?"

The smirk vanished, and his eyes narrowed. "You can call me Reno."

"Is that what your grandfather calls you?"

"My grandfather calls me a disgrace to his name since I turned my back on the family business. And I don't blame him—if I hadn't left, he wouldn't be in this mess now."

"What mess? Exactly what's going on with your grandfather besides a little gang warfare?"

"You have no idea," he said, his voice like ice.

"You could tell me."

For a moment she thought he'd say nothing. "My grandfather is old school. Very old school. And his family follows his code. He won't touch drug dealing, the sex trade, arms trading. He's part of the old Robin Hood ethic. And Hitomi and the men who are listening to him are part of the new wave."

"If they don't deal drugs or prostitution or weapons, what is it they do? They sound pretty harmless to me."

"They're *bakuto*. They mostly deal with gambling, protection, counterfeit luxury goods. Mostly soft crimes that are committed without force. Unfortunately, they don't bring in the kind of money and power that the *gurentai* could give them."

"*Gurentai?*"

"More like your American mafia."

"And Hitomi is part of that?"

"It seems like it. And I don't know how far it goes. I never would have thought Kobayashi would turn his back on the old man." He moved over to the window, looking out into the darkness. "Until I find out, there's nothing I can do but keep you here. No matter how much I want to get rid of you, I can't risk it," he said, his voice flat. "I've put up with you for too long to fail now."

"What about my parents? My sister? They don't think I'm dead, do they? I don't want to put them through that kind of grief. And yes, as hard as it is for you to believe, my death will upset my family. Not everyone finds me a royal pain in the ass." She paused, thinking about it. "As a matter of fact, I don't know anyone who considers me a royal pain in the ass except you. Why?"

"They haven't been trapped with you for three days," he said, turning his back on her and heading into the kitchen area. "Maybe everyone else has only seen your best side. If you've lived your life without annoying anyone, then you must be very boring."

"You don't find me boring," she said, watching him.

He didn't turn back, concentrating on opening the carton. "Life would be easier if I did," he muttered.

Okay, that was interesting. Had she somehow managed to get past his cool, heartless soul? Now he was reminding her of something out of Kingdom Hearts, her favorite video game, though she couldn't remember who.

But he was no Disney-anime cross, and she

needed to remember that. He was a man—granted, a hot one—but more trouble than he was worth. Besides, Summer would kill her.

"So you brought me food?" Anything was better than thinking about something she could never, should never, have.

"You're obsessed. The sashimi is for me—I wouldn't want to waste it on an inexperienced *gaijin*. I brought you *oyakudon* and miso soup. The Japanese version of macaroni and cheese and chicken soup."

"You think I need comfort food?"

He turned his head to look at her. "I'm just trying to keep you quiet and docile while I figure out what to do next."

"I hate to tell you this, but the price of inner peace comes a little higher than macaroni and cheese."

"I don't give a shit about your inner peace—it's your silence I'm looking forward to." He turned back, then jumped a bit, as if he hadn't realized how close she was. He was skittish, and she wasn't sure if that was a good sign or bad. It depended what was making him nervy. The danger? Or her?

She got out of his way, not wanting to risk brushing up against him, not after last night, and he headed to the computer. "Help yourself," he said. "I need to check a few things."

"Are you sure that's safe? Someone can hack into your IP address and find where we are if they're good enough."

"No, they can't. I know my way around computers." It was a simple statement, one she believed, so she busied herself with the food he'd brought. Enough for both of them. Did he expect her to serve him like a good Japanese hausfrau, or whatever you'd call it in Japan? If so, he was going to wait a long time.

He was right, though. The hot miso soup was like a mother's calming touch, not that Lianne had been much for nurturing, but the warmth spread through Jilly's body like a shot of whiskey.

The other dish was made of chicken, rice and egg, bland and lovely. She glanced over at him while she shoveled the food into her mouth, but he seemed intent on the screen, totally oblivious to her.

For the first time she could watch him, really watch him. With the studied swagger, the mocking grin vanishing, the glittering eyes focused on something else, she could see glimpses of the somber young man in the photo. The red teardrops still danced across his high cheekbones, and his eyelashes were still absurdly long, but without the protective, outrageous persona he suddenly looked just a little bit like Hiromasa Shinoda.

It should have wiped out any last lingering trace of fantasy. There was no Reno, there was simply a bright young man with a bizarre and compelling protective shell wrapped around him. And she wondered what he would do if she untied the cotton robe.

He swiveled his head to look at her then, and his eyes narrowed. "Seen enough?" he drawled.

She didn't even blink. "Why? Are you planning on showing me more?"

"I'm trying to save your life here. You might at least stop trying to distract me," he growled, turning back to the computer screen and typing.

"Am I distracting you?" she said sweetly. "Tough shit. I don't suppose you have any clean clothes that might fit me."

"I'm making arrangements."

"You mean, there's someone we can trust who's not out to kill us?"

"Someone I can trust. I don't think I'd risk leaving you alone with him. Kyo makes me seem like a pussycat."

"Kyo?"

"Five feet two inches of pure nastiness. Unfortunately he's the only person who's good enough to keep out of the way of Hitomi's spies. I can't guarantee you'll like what he comes up with, but at least you'll be decently covered."

"Lovely," she said, sarcastic. "And in the meantime?"

"In the meantime, try to get some sleep. We're not going anywhere for a while."

"Sleep where?"

He glanced up at her. The cut on his cheekbone looked nasty, and she wondered if it would leave a scar. It would only make him even hotter, damn it. "You can open the futon. Don't worry, I don't intend to sleep. I'm not going to touch you again."

The memory of the previous night came flooding back, his hands between her legs, her body arching in spasms of hot, breathless release. "Not if you want to keep your hands," she said, calm.

He turned away, and she had no idea whether he believed her. In the end it didn't matter. Whether she wanted him to or not, he wasn't going to touch her again. And she was grateful. She didn't want him touching her, didn't want him kissing her, didn't want anything at all from him except to get away.

And the sooner she believed that, the better off she'd be.

# *11*

Reno pushed away from the computer, beyond frustrated. He had a headache—he'd taken out his contact lenses hours ago, but even that didn't help. Hours on the computer with little or no sleep wasn't doing him any good, and it wasn't bringing him any closer to the answers he was seeking. Who the hell was Hitomi-san? Was he from another gang, like the all-powerful Yamaguchi-gumi family, or was he working on his own, trying to take control of an already established family? There was no record of him to be found, even through the various side alleyways of the Internet that he knew so well.

He looked over at the futon. She was asleep, her short streaky hair tumbled around her face, and he leaned back in the chair, watching her while she slept.

She wasn't his type—apart from the fact that

every female under the age of fifty was his type. She was *gaijin,* she was American, she was as tall as he was and she was trouble. He had very few rules in his life, but one was never to sleep with anyone who came with strings attached. Ji-chan was so tied up in his family she was practically an exercise in bondage.

And that was not what he wanted to be thinking of right now, when he was trying to keep his mind off his dick. She looked almost innocent as she slept, not the sharp-tongued pain in the ass he knew her to be. But then, he wouldn't be as drawn to someone so vulnerable. He kept away from the innocent and the needy at all times. It only led to trouble.

And that was exactly what Ji-chan was. Nothing but trouble of the most basic sort. He'd done his best to make sure he'd rid her of any lingering, childish fantasies about him. It was a lot better, safer, that way.

But now that she was over him he had to work on getting over her. Which might be even harder to do.

He was tired, so bone-tired he could fall asleep in the chair. Which is just what he needed to do. It didn't matter that she looked like she belonged on his futon. It didn't matter that there was plenty of room for him, too, if he slept close to her. She'd used his almond-scented soap, and the smell of it on her skin was making him crazy. If it weren't dead winter, he'd open a window.

A cold shower might help. Then he could stretch out on the kitchen floor, far enough away from her to be safe. He'd slept in worse places, and being uncomfortable would be good for him. He could look at her, a few feet away, and resent her.

The problem was, he realized half an hour later as he tried to get comfortable on the *tatami* mat, that now he smelled like almond soap, as well. And just to make his torture complete, this was the night she decided to toss about in her sleep, her long, bare legs kicking out from his plain cotton robe, the neckline pulling away, showing too much of the soft curve of her breast. And when she turned her back it was even worse. The nape of her neck had to be the hottest thing he'd ever seen, vulnerable, the spiky blond hair curling slightly above it. There was a reason geisha wore their kimono pulled down slightly in the back. The delicate nape of a neck could be a more powerful turn-on than a spread shot in *Penthouse,* or so his grandfather had always told him. And damn if the old man wasn't right.

He rolled over on his side, turning away from

her, but the scent of almonds on his own skin was almost enough to get him to go shower again, this time with dish soap. But he didn't need to. The day that he couldn't control his need for sex was the day he was in big trouble. He could lie a few feet from Ji-chan and forget all about her. Or die trying.

She was never going to get used to sleeping on a futon, Jilly decided as she slowly opened her eyes to the shadowy apartment. Her entire body hurt, though part of that might be from the endless sprint away from the *yakuza* compound. She pushed up from the mattress, then realized her robe had come apart, revealing far too much of her breasts. She yanked it together quickly, peering around the darkened apartment for signs of life. Had Reno left her once more?

And then she saw the shape lying on the tiny patch of floor in the kitchen area. His back was to her, but there was no mistaking the bright hair, and the thin blanket draped over his long, lean body. He was lying on the floor, which had to be even worse than a futon. He'd probably rather lie on a bed of nails than have to be close to her, she thought glumly. She should be grateful, not miffed.

"Go back to sleep." His deep, sleepy voice came from the kitchen, even though he hadn't moved.

"I can't."

He turned, lifting his head. "I don't think you want me to come over there and help you out again, do you?"

The apartment was cold, but heat ran through her body. She didn't want to think whether it was from embarrassment or something else. She lay back down on the futon, shifting uncomfortably, the robe held tight around her, and closed her eyes, trying to regulate her breathing.

Clearly Reno, or Hiromasa Shinoda, didn't believe in central heating, either. She could see her breath in the darkened room, and the thin cotton wasn't much help. She could always put on her clothes again, and she would if she had to, but she'd run from the compound in nothing but a thin T-shirt that had been soaked with sweat by the time they'd gotten into the taxi. She'd been wearing the same pair of jeans since she left L.A., and her clean underwear was somewhere back at the compound with her backpack. She wanted clean clothes, she wanted a soft bed, she wanted Summer. And she wasn't going to get any of those things, so she might as well get over it and—

"Enough," Reno said, sitting up and throwing

off the thin blanket. It pooled at his waist, and he was naked from the waist up. Jilly knew she was in even deeper shit than she'd thought.

He was freaking gorgeous. His chest was smooth, lean and muscled, his stomach flat, and if she had even half her mother's gifts, she'd crawl over there and lick him.

Another flash of heat. Maybe if she just kept thinking random, embarrassing thoughts she'd keep from freezing to death.

"Stop it!"

"Stop what?" she protested. "I can't help it if I can't sleep."

"Don't look at me like that."

She could have been foolish enough to ask him what he meant, but she didn't. Looking at him as if he were a rare steak and she was starving. Looking at him as if he were a box of Godiva and she was a chocoholic. As if she were a drunk confronting a bottle of ancient Scotch. Like a stupid, semivirgin in love with the worst choice she could have made.

It wasn't as if she'd had any choice in the matter. If she had, she wouldn't think twice about him. But some things weren't up to her. She'd taken one look at him, years ago in Genevieve Madsen's garden in Wiltshire, and she'd been a goner. Familiarity, while it was breeding contempt, wasn't helping much with the lust part.

Which was actually rather reassuring. She'd been so disinterested in most of the men and boys she'd seen that she'd wondered if she were frigid or simply asexual. The moment she saw Reno again she knew that wasn't her particular problem.

Her problem was Reno, pure and simple. Though there was nothing pure and simple about him.

He shoved the blanket away and stood up, and Jilly let out a shriek. He was practically naked, all long, lean, gorgeous six feet of him, except for a strip of cloth wrapped strategically around his hips. It was the sort of thing she'd seen on sumo wrestlers. It looked a hell of a lot better on him.

"Close your eyes if you're embarrassed," he said, picking up the discarded blanket and tossing it to her. She resisted the temptation to pull it over her head. Except that she couldn't look away.

He looked alien, golden and savage, and the tattooed dragon snaking down one arm simply added to the effect, running from his shoulder down to his wrist, in vivid colors of red and gold. He strode past her, magnificent, and while she shouldn't have done it, she couldn't help but look as he walked past. He had to have the most gorgeous butt in the world.

She let out a quiet moan and buried her face in the blanket he'd tossed at her. And then quickly lifted her head. It smelled like the almond soap she'd used in his bathroom. And it smelled like his skin, something indefinable and unquestionably erotic. And at this point she'd be better off walking straight into a trap of *yakuza* thugs than spend another minute fantasizing about her unwilling protector.

When he came out of the bathroom, he was dressed again, in black pants and a loose white shirt and black jacket. She couldn't stop from wondering if he was still wearing that strip of cloth under the clothes or whether he'd gone to more traditional boxers. He didn't strike her as the tighty-whitie kind of man. Or maybe he wasn't wearing anything at all.

"It's called a *fundoshi*," he said as he headed back into the tiny kitchen alcove.

"What is?"

"The piece of cloth you couldn't keep your eyes off. I'll tell you what—we get out of this alive and I'll let you take it off me. With your teeth."

Her temperature went up another five degrees. "You are such a jerk," she said. "Use your own teeth." It came out sounding ridiculous, of course.

He just laughed. "Behave yourself and I'll make coffee."

Okay, all was forgiven. She'd rip the freaking *fundoshi* off him with her teeth in return for a strong hit of caffeine. "I don't suppose you did anything about getting me some clothes."

He looked at her over his shoulder, and there was a surprisingly wicked light in his eyes. "I wouldn't mind showing you how to wrap a *fundoshi*," he offered.

"Dream on." She rose, clutching the *yukata* around her in a vain attempt at dignity. "I'm going to take another shower."

"You're going to get waterlogged at this rate, Ji-chan."

"Why are you calling me 'Ji-chan'? I know enough Japanese to know that's a term of affection."

His cool laugh wasn't reassuring. "Your name has too many fucking *L*'s in it. Trust me, it's nothing personal. And you won't be able to wash it away."

"What?"

"Me."

If she had something to throw she would have. But in the spare, Zen-like apartment there was nothing to toss at him. "I like my coffee with cream and sugar," she announced, heading for the bathroom. She was expecting him to come out with another smutty comment, but for once he was blissfully silent.

She considered not using the almond soap—he was right, she'd washed enough in the past twenty-four hours, but at the last minute she steeled herself and used it. She refused to think of Reno using it, rubbing it on his body, over his chest, between his…

"What's wrong?" Reno's voice came from just outside the bathroom door.

"Nothing," she said. "I just banged my elbow." Shit, shit, shit. She was going stark, staring mad. She turned on the cold water full blast to cool herself off, letting out another shriek, and forced herself to stand under it, no matter how cold the apartment was, just letting the icy pellets of water sting her skin into submission. When she couldn't stand it anymore, she climbed out, wrapping a towel around her. She reached for the *yukata*, then stopped as she heard the sound of voices in the room beyond. Two men, one of them Reno.

She put the seat down on the toilet and sat down, waiting. Parading in front of Reno was bad enough—she didn't want any more of an audience.

She waited until she heard the outer door shut, and then silence. With any luck Reno would be gone, too, and she could have her coffee in peace. She pushed open the door to the bathroom, but Reno was back at the computer. And there was a gun on the table beside him.

"Was someone here?"

He didn't bother to turn around. "A friend of mine. I figured a gun would be a good idea."

"You didn't have one?" She looked at the cold, black, deadly piece of metal and shivered. All she could see was the man on the floor of the compound, the bullet between his eyes, the blood....

"I prefer not to use them if I can help it. There are other ways to face danger, quieter ways. Don't worry about it, Ji-chan. I promise not to shoot you unless you really annoy me."

She just looked at him. "People are dead. You've killed people. How can you joke about it?"

"Who says I'm joking?" he said in a cool voice. "When it comes down to a choice between me and them, I don't have any problem doing what needs to be done. And if I have to shoot someone to keep you alive, I'll do it, and I won't waste time making a fuss about it. Don't worry— you're not going to have to touch it. And Kyo brought you some clothes, as well as bringing me the gun. You aren't going to like them."

She looked away from the gun, simply because she had to. "Why am I not surprised?"

"Finding clothes in Japan for someone your size isn't easy. If I could find jeans that were long enough, they'd never fit around your hips."

"There's nothing wrong with my hips."

"By Japanese standards you're a walking sex bomb. This was the best he could do."

She looked over by the door to the mound of black-and-white fabric, and a sudden feeling of horror swept over her. "Oh, no," she said. "You're not dressing me up like one of those baby dolls."

"Gothic Lolita," he corrected.

"You couldn't find a simple T-shirt and some baggy pants?" She kept the plaintive note out of her voice.

"The T-shirts in your size are for tourists and they're very thin cotton. And while you're almost as flat-chested as most Japanese women, the bras would still never fit you and your breasts would cause far too much attention."

She resisted the urge to cross her arms over her chest. "Would you stop comparing me to Japanese women? I've spent my life towering over most people my age—I don't need to be reminded what an oversize freak I am."

He turned away from the screen for a moment, and his eyes narrowed. Reno was back. "Get over it."

"You know, sometimes I think your mastery of American idioms is a little too good," she said, scooping up the mounds of lace and fabric and heading for the bathroom.

But he was already staring at the computer screen again, dismissing her as easily as if she'd been a one-night stand.

Of which he probably had many, she thought. And she wasn't going to be one of them. She wasn't into masochism, and a night in bed with Reno wouldn't be something she could just shrug off. Not to mention the family repercussions.

He was a snake. And she wasn't getting anywhere near him again if she could help it. He could save her life, though why he felt it was his responsibility was beyond her, and then she wouldn't have to see him again. Or at least, not until Summer and Taka had babies, and even then she could probably avoid him, given his dislike of American women.

The outfit was even worse than she'd imagined. First, a black lace thong that she was tempted to ignore. White, lace-trimmed bloomers. Fishnet stockings with a black lace garter belt. Billowing black skirts trimmed with lace, a corset and fingerless black lace gloves, charmingly accented with a little apron and a bonnet. She looked like a deranged French maid crossed with Morticia Addams. The shoes were the final touch.

"I'm not wearing them," she said, storming out of the bathroom in her new rig, still in bare feet.

He didn't bother to turn around. "They're the only clothes Kyo could come up with. Don't tell me they don't fit."

"The clothes fit. So do the shoes, but I'm not wearing them. They're four-inch platform heels—if I don't fall over and kill myself, I'll still look like a basketball player."

He turned then, his eyes drifting down over her absurd body. There was way too much leg showing, with the garters and the fishnet and the bloomers peeking out from beneath the ruffles, and the corset made her boobs look distressingly prominent. She stuck out her chin, just daring him to laugh.

He was wise enough not to. The corner of his mouth jerked for a second, in the faintest beginning of a smile, but he managed to look somber. "Maybe I can find some sandals," he said. "Won't go with the outfit, though."

"I'm not that interested in accessorizing right

now. I just need something I can walk in. And how the hell did your friend find shoes like that in my size? I have big feet."

"Where I found the clothes. In a shop made for *josohumisha*."

"What?" she echoed.

"Cross-dressers," he said. "I thought if we put enough makeup on you you could pass for a man."

She threw the shoes at him. He caught one before it hit his head, the other knocked his picture off the shelf. He rose, slowly, moving toward her with sinuous menace, and if Jilly had been any kind of coward, she would have backed up.

"I told you not to hit me again," he said in a low, dangerous voice.

She wasn't going to react. "I didn't hit you. You caught it."

"The intent was there."

Okay, so she took a step back. A couple, as a matter of fact. But he just kept on coming, and the studio apartment was very small, and he was very big and there was nowhere to run.

She ended up against the wall, trapped, and he put his hands on either side of her, keeping her there. "Don't tempt me," he said in a low growl.

But she was tired of being bullied. "Go ahead and strangle me if you want to so damned badly."

There was an odd light in his eyes as they looked into hers, and she realized he'd taken out his contacts. She was looking into dark brown eyes, with no artifice between them. "That's not what you're tempting me to do, Ji-chan," he said.

He brought his body up against hers, hip to hip, belly to belly, his hard chest against her corseted torso, and it was like a strange, hot embrace, with his hands still against the wall, trapping her there. She looked into his eyes, hoping he thought she was fearless, but she could feel her mouth tremble slightly, and she couldn't keep it still.

Her heart was pounding, as well, hard and fast. And she could feel his heart, hard and fast, too, and she wondered what the hell was going on.

And then he kissed her.

# 12

It wasn't the kind of kiss she'd expected. For two years she'd thought about what it would be like to kiss Reno, for two years she'd imagined something out of a romance novel.

The reality was a shock. His open mouth covered hers, and he slowly, deliberately, ground his pelvis against her.

They were the same height. She could feel the explicit bulge of him through his pants, through the layers of her petticoats, and his mouth was hard, almost brutal. He was kissing her as if he hated her, and she put up her hands and shoved, hard.

He was immovable. He lifted his head, though, and her mouth felt bruised, swollen.

"Why are you kissing me?" Her voice was husky, and she could feel inexplicable tears form in her eyes. She blinked them away, angry.

"I don't know." He hadn't moved—his hips

were still pinning hers to the wall. "Do you want to fuck?"

She tried to kick him then, but he must have sensed her movement, and he wrapped one leg around hers, further imprisoning her. "No," she said, furious.

"Don't pretend, Ji-chan. You've got a crush on me. I'm about to fulfill your dreams." His voice was breathless, mocking.

"You're about to get kneed in the balls, and then you won't be fulfilling anyone's dreams, not even your own," she snapped.

"You know I'm not going to let you do that. You know you can't do anything unless I let you. I'll ask you again—do you want to fuck?"

"I don't know why you're asking me," she said bitterly. "We've already established the fact that you're not interested, and—"

"Does this feel like I'm not interested?" he said, pushing against her.

"So you're perverted enough to get turned on by women dressing in little girls' clothes. It has nothing to do with me."

"So take them off and we'll see if I'm still turned on," he suggested reasonably.

She looked into his eyes, at the tattooed tears beneath them. "Reno," she said in a calm voice, "if you're so bored, then go out and get laid. I'm sure you'll find someone who's interested."

"You're interested," he said. And then he released her just as suddenly as he had caught her, and he grinned. "No, you're right. You're not my type. Besides, I have a healthy respect for Taka, and he'd kill me if I fucked you."

"Would you stop with all the 'fuck' talk!" she said, exasperated. "It's called making love."

"Jilly, I don't make love. I fuck."

"Not me."

He tilted his head to one side, watching her. "Want to bet?" And pulling her back into his arms, he put his mouth on hers once more.

It wasn't as if she hadn't been kissed before. When she was seventeen, she'd decided, in the spirit of scientific discovery, to explore making out, and she'd found her Advanced Physics tutor to be up to the task. She'd learned to use her tongue, her teeth, how to tease, how to demand, how to suck gently, and while the whole experiment had been rather wet and sloppy, it left her with a better understanding of what people were doing when they were grinding their faces together.

Wrong. Reno didn't kiss the way Jeffrey did, or anything like the rudimentary kisses Duke had given her during their miserable, botched coupling. He kissed her like an angel, sweet and sad and so wonderful that her body seemed to lift into his, trying to get closer. He kissed her like the devil, hot and hard and deep, and she closed her eyes and wanted to sink, skin to skin, into some dark whirling place where there was nothing but heat and sex. He kissed her mouth, using his tongue, he kissed her eyelids, which had fluttered shut, he kissed her jaw and her temple and then her mouth once again, and she simply leaned against the wall, stunned, unable to move, unable to do anything but let him kiss her.

He moved his mouth down the side of her neck, nipping slightly, and his breath was warm on her skin, his hands were moving up her thighs, slowly, his fingers threading through the long lace garters, and she moaned quietly, a soft, impossible sound of surrender.

"Shit." The word muttered against the delicate skin of her neck was enough to throw her right out of the moment. Her eyes flashed open, and she looked into his, momentarily dazed.

She opened her mouth to say something, but he shook his head, silencing her, and the hot, stolen moments might never have happened. He was still pressed up against her, pinning her to the wall, but there was no sex in the air. There was violence.

"They're here," he mouthed.

"Shit," she said, just a breath of sound.

His eyes met hers, for a long, silent moment, and she had the sudden, terrible feeling that he was saying goodbye. And then he grabbed her shoulders and shoved her, hard, practically throwing her across the room, so that she slammed against the computer chair, knocking over the small table and landing hard on the floor.

She scrambled as far back as she could into the corner, trying to stay out of the way of the melee. It seemed as if an army had invaded, and it took her a moment to realize there were only three of them, in their fancy suits and their pomaded hair, closing in on Reno.

He wasn't going down without a fight. He was a blur of motion, leaping in the air and kicking one man in the throat, and the man went down, choking, as Reno spun around. He slammed his fist into the second man's belly, then brought them down on his neck, knocking the man flat.

But the third man was on him, bigger, catching him around the neck and pulling his head back. Reno kicked out, struggling, but the man was too strong, and he was being pulled backward as he struggled, clawing at his captor's hands.

He was going to die. The man would either

choke him to death or break his neck, and then he'd turn to her. And she didn't have any choice.

The gun had fallen on the floor when she'd knocked over the table, and she picked it up, cold, deadly metal, as Reno and his opponent flailed around the apartment. Reno was strong, knocking the man holding him back against the wall, but the man didn't break his grip. She could hear Reno choking, and his struggles were getting frantic.

She should have said something. A warning, anything. She didn't. The man smashed Reno down on the floor, and for a moment Reno lay still, dazed, staring up at him as the larger man loomed over him, and Jilly could see the gun in his hand, and there wasn't any time.

She wouldn't have thought it would be so easy. She pointed the gun and pulled the trigger, and the kickback knocked her hand up, the sound deafening in the tiny apartment. She squeezed her eyes shut, horrified.

She heard the thud of a body falling, but then nothing but someone's labored breathing. Her own?

She knew someone was moving toward her, and she didn't care who it was. She must be in shock, she thought dazedly. Any of those men could have gotten up and come after her, and it wouldn't matter. If Reno was dead, then nothing mattered.

Someone squatted down in front of her, and she felt a hand touch her face. She flinched, but the hand was gentle, brushing the hair out of her face, and she recognized his touch, the scent of almond soap on his skin, and she knew she should open her eyes, just to make certain he was still alive, but she couldn't do it. She couldn't move.

And then he leaned over and kissed her, the soft, light brushing of his lips against her closed eyelids. He took the gun from her limp hand. "We need to get out of here," he said, his voice oddly gentle. "Someone will have heard the gunshot. We need to leave before the police get here."

She opened her eyes. He was all she could see; he was blocking her view of the trashed apartment.

"You need to come with me." He was still being oddly gentle with her, and she wondered why. "Give me your hand."

She put her hand in his, the hand that had pulled the trigger, that still tingled from the feel of the gun, and let him draw her to her feet. "Don't look," he said.

But she did. The man she shot lay facedown on the floor in a pool of blood. Half of his head was blown away.

She started to gag, but Reno caught her, holding her. "Take deep breaths," he whispered.

"Don't think about it, don't look. Just look straight ahead and come with me."

She had no choice. She stumbled forward, and then realized she was still wearing only fishnet stockings on her feet. She started to turn back to look for the platform shoes, but he wouldn't let her, pulling her away from the horrifying scene. He put her into the hallway, and she leaned back against the wall, trying to breathe, while he disappeared into the apartment for a moment. Then he was back, with her sneakers and his boots. And the gun, the gun that she'd used, was tucked in the waist of his dark pants, almost hidden by his black jacket.

She stood patiently while he put the sneakers on her feet, and then she followed him, down the three flights of stairs, out into the bright winter daylight of a Tokyo morning.

Reno wasn't used to feeling powerless. He didn't believe in coddling himself or others; he did what he needed to do without hesitation, and expected others to do the same.

But he hadn't expected Jilly Lovitz to blow someone's head off to save his life. And he wasn't sure how to make it better.

She was in shock, which he supposed was a

good thing. She hadn't said a word since she'd fired the gun, and she'd done everything he'd told her to do, an obedient robot, silent and lost. Things would have been easier if she'd been this way from the start—he wouldn't have had to explain, to fight her, to fight himself. If she'd been like this he would have taken care of her, put her someplace safe and forgotten all about her. This ghost woman made him think of the grave, not a bed.

He needed her to wake up, but he wasn't sure how to do it. And maybe it was better this way, letting her retreat into a safe place of shock and denial. He didn't make the mistake of thinking killing was easy. It never was, no matter how well trained you were, no matter how many times you had to do it. For Jilly it would be devastating.

The people of Tokyo were too polite to stare as he led her through the subway system, still holding her hand. When they emerged at Harajuku she didn't even look up at the brightly dressed cosplayers parading around in the chilly air. She was lost.

And he was taking her to the only place he could think of that would be quiet and soothing. The Meiji Shrine was a huge park in the middle of the Harajuku district, but a world and a century removed from the shopping and dress-up. He drew her through the huge cypress *torii* entrance, down the winding path. There was no one else in the gardens that early in the day—the place was deserted, away from prying eyes, away from men with guns. Even the notorious Yamaguchi-gumi, the worst *gurentai* gang in history, wouldn't defile a sacred place with gunfire. They would be safe in the gardens, at least until they chose to leave.

She looked cold in the tight-fitting corset and the short, frilly skirt, but he couldn't give her his coat. There was blood on his shirt, and he needed to keep it hidden from her until she managed to pull herself out of this wounded daze.

He pulled her arm through his, still holding her hand, and he knew they looked like two cosplaying lovers who'd wandered in from the street. But no one would mind—the Meiji Shrine was a calming, welcoming place for whoever chose to come there. He drew her closer to him, trying to share some of his body heat, and she let him, not putting up any kind of fight. She was even colder than she should be, and she felt light, almost weightless.

"I'll find you some food," he said, trying to sound casual. "They've got a cafeteria here. More miso soup will do the trick."

She said nothing. Her face was expressionless,

eerily so, as she let him guide her along the pebbled path. Why the fuck did he ever think he wanted her to be docile? She was annoying as hell when she was talking back to him, but anything was better than this passive, lifeless doll.

He circled the shrine itself—there were people there, and he'd failed to bring anything to cover his telltale hair. He was an idiot to keep it. The first thing he was going to do when they got someplace safe was cut it off and dye it black. He was like a walking neon sign—in the past his notoriety and that of his grandfather's had kept him safe. Now it was drawing the enemy closer to him like a beacon of light.

He bought her a can of coffee from one of the vending machines, and he made her sit while she drank it. She swallowed miso soup and picked at the bento box from the cafeteria—another sign of hope. As long as she could eat, she'd be all right. He'd never known anyone so intent on food, which would have been annoying if it didn't turn him on.

Right now, on this rare occasion, sex was the last thing on his mind. He had to keep her safe and hidden until she snapped out of this, and wandering down the hidden pathways of the park could only take so long. Besides, she looked as if she was freezing in her skimpy, undeniably erotic get-up.

Okay, he wasn't going to think about sex. He'd keep his eyes straight ahead, remember she was in shock, and forget about the glimpse of black lace garter he could see if he stepped back. Besides, she needed him beside her, not lusting after her.

It was late afternoon by the time they left the massive gardens and she still hadn't said a word. Businesses were spilling out onto the brightly lit streets, and in Harajuku it was easy enough to blend in, even with a giant female *gaijin.* He managed to cram her onto one of the trains, shielding her with his body from curious looks or the roaming hands of salarymen. He switched them over to the Marounouchi Line, which circled around the center of the city, put her into a seat and guarded her. They could ride for hours while he figured out what the hell he was going to do with her.

She was in shock, and he knew people could die from shock. But the last thing he was going to do was take her to a hospital; there'd be too many questions, not enough answers. And if they decided to keep her there, he wouldn't be able to protect her.

But he had to do something. The blank-faced, eerie silence was making him crazy. He wasn't stupid enough to feel guilty that he hadn't been able to protect her—he'd done his best, and if she hadn't capped the man, they'd both be dead. She'd get over it. As soon as he found her a safe place to crash.

Jilly supposed she was cold. Her hands felt numb, her legs and knees were icy, but it didn't seem to matter. She didn't know where she was, but that didn't matter, either. As long as she kept hold of Reno, she didn't have to think. She could stay in the safe place she'd found, where nothing could touch her, nothing could intrude on the peaceful cloud she'd enveloped herself in.

The cold was nagging at her, pulling at her short skirt, trying to drag her back into the present, and that was the one place she refused to go.

He put his arm around her, only it wasn't the iron grip he usually used. He must have known she'd given up. She wasn't going to argue anymore. She was going to do exactly what he wanted her to do. As long as he didn't try to talk to her, she was fine, perfectly fine. Because if she opened her mouth, she'd start screaming, and she didn't think she'd be able to stop.

But everything was safe around her, a bubble of tranquillity that nothing could break. And she tucked her arm in Reno's, leaned against him and followed him wherever he led her.

In the end the hotel was probably a stupid idea, but he couldn't think of anywhere else to take her. He considered a love hotel, just to see if that would jar her out of her blank-faced stare, but most of them were run by the various *yakuza* families, and it was too great a risk for them to take.

A hotel built for rich Western businessmen was a compromise, and even if word got out that they'd been seen, the security at those hotels was usually excellent. He could be reasonably sure they'd be safe for at least a few hours, probably for a night or more. If anyone tracked them, they'd simply wait for them to emerge from the hotel.

He managed to pick up a baseball cap from one of the street vendors. He put it on backward, the bill hiding the bright red hair as it trailed down inside his jacket. It wasn't much of a disguise, but it would have to do. And they wouldn't be looking for a *gaijin* Gothic Lolita who was taller than most Japanese men, either. If luck, which had been piss-poor so far, decided to improve they might just be able to buy a little time. Enough time to get in touch with Ojiisan and warn him about Hitomi and Kobayashi.

At least he'd been smart enough to bring the extra passports and credit cards the Committee always provided. Jilly's documentation wasn't as flawless, but he'd had to take what he could get on such short notice from his friend Kyo. He checked in as a Korean American and his girlfriend, and the exquisitely polite staff of the Trans-Pacific Grand Hotel didn't give them a second look. If they did, they probably thought Jilly was so stoned she couldn't walk on her own, but they wisely said nothing, ushering them to a corner room on the thirty-second floor.

Once alone he gently pushed Jilly into a chair and headed for the door, planning on checking out the emergency exits and stairwells in case someone caught up with them. But before his hand was even on the door she was behind him, the same dazed look on her face.

He put his hands on her arms, moving her back to the chair once more. "You need to stay here," he said patiently, kneeling down and taking off her sneakers. "I have to make sure we have another way out." He started to move away and she rose again, ready to follow him.

He began to curse. "You know, you're really

beginning to annoy me," he said. "I get it—you're traumatized. But unless you want to get over it you're going to get us both killed. Sit the fuck down and wait for me."

She sat. When he slipped back inside the hotel room, she was still there, unmoving, her hands clasped lightly in her lap.

He double-locked the door, then pulled the curtains on the winter-dark night. He went straight to the minibar, removed a tiny bottle of Scotch, opened it and poured it down his throat. Then he took another, twisting off the cap and advancing toward her.

"Drink this."

She ignored him, averting her gaze. He grabbed her chin, rough, and forced her mouth open, pouring the Scotch down her throat.

She started to choke, and for the first time she moved, hitting at him, and the tiny bottle went flying across the room.

"Say something!" he said in a fierce voice. "Holy motherfucker, just say one goddamned thing."

She closed her eyes, shutting him out. That was the final straw. He caught her arms and hauled her up against him. "You killed a man," he said. "You didn't have a choice. If you hadn't, he would have killed me and then you and then he would've gone out and killed more people. He was a bad man and he deserved to die and you did the world a service by blowing his fucking head off."

She blinked at that, her first sign of life, and he shook her, hard. "Would you rather be dead? Maybe you would, if you'd known just how empty you'd feel once you'd done it. And it doesn't get easier. Each death takes a little piece of you, a piece you can never get back. You'll never be the same, Ji-chan, and it won't do you any good to fight it."

Another blink. He slid his hands up her neck, forcing her to look at him, and frustration and pain boiled over. "Well, if you're not going to talk to me, I may as well take advantage of it," he said in a savage voice.

He scooped her up, all six feet of her, and carried her into the bedroom, throwing her down on the king-size bed as he stood over her.

"It's up to you, Ji-chan. I'm not going to stop until you tell me no." And he pulled off his jacket, tossing it on a chair, only to meet her horrified gaze. Staring at the blood that had stained his shirt, blood from the man she'd killed.

And she opened her mouth to scream.

# 13

No sound came out. She was frozen, staring at his bloodstained shirt. With a muttered curse he ripped it off, buttons flying across the room. Then he reached for the gun tucked at his waist, and she suddenly moved, trying to scramble away from him, across the wide king-size bed, but he caught her leg and hauled her back.

"It's a gun, Ji-chan," he said. "You used it to save our lives. It's just a tool."

She was fighting now, kicking at him, beginning to come alive beneath his hard hands. He took her hand in his, placing the gun there, forcing her to hold it. She let out an agonized whimper, the first sound he'd heard from her in hours, as she tried to shove it away.

"You have to accept it. You have to accept what you've done, that you had no choice." Was he talking to her, or was he talking to himself? He was no longer sure. For some reason he had to make her come to terms with what she'd done, because if she couldn't, what hope was there for him?

He wrapped her long fingers around the handle, and suddenly she moved, away from him, clutching the gun. She was pointing it at him, her hands shaking, pointing it at his head.

And she was just freaked enough to kill him, he realized. Her hands were trembling so badly she only had a fifty-fifty chance of hitting him, but he didn't like those odds. If he moved any closer, she'd shoot him.

"Do you want to kill me, Ji-chan?" His voice was low, calm. "I'm your best chance at staying alive, but maybe you don't want to stay alive. Maybe you want to take the coward's way out."

The gun was still shakily trained on his chest, and he knew it could go off at any minute. She'd managed to get the safety off the first time, in the heat of the moment, she could easily do it again. "Put the gun down," he said. "Or use it. One or the other."

She froze. And he moved, onto the bed, crawling toward her, and took the gun out of her hand. He set it on the nightstand, safely within reach. He sat back on his heels, looking at her. Watching her as she tried to retreat back behind the wall of blankness.

"Then we'll have to try it this way," he said. "Turn around."

At first he thought she'd ignore him, but a moment later she turned her back on him, her shoulders hunched over, shutting him out. Giving him a view of her narrow, elegant back, the ridiculously erotic nape of her neck, the zipper that ran the length of the black corset Kyo had brought for her.

She jumped when he put his hands on her, but she didn't move away, and he placed one hand on her shoulder as he began to unzip the corset. He could feel her tremble beneath his touch, but she didn't protest, didn't move.

Another man might have had trouble with the complicated corset, but it came apart easily in his hands, and he tossed it to one side, so that she was sitting with her back to him, in a mound of fluffy skirts and fishnet stockings and nothing on top. And he couldn't help himself—he leaned forward and put his mouth against the nape of her neck.

She shivered. A tiny shimmer of reaction, dancing across her skin. He unhooked the skirt, the two layers of crinoline. She'd been obedient all day—how long would it last? "Take off your skirts, Ji-chan," he whispered.

For an endless moment he couldn't breathe, waiting for her. And then she rose on her knees, her back still toward him, and pulled the layers of skirts over her head, leaving her in a pair of frilly bloomers and a black lace garter belt holding up her fishnet stockings.

It was his turn to groan. She was supposed to panic, come back to life, fight him. She wasn't supposed to do what he told her, strip off her clothes and wait patiently for him to touch her.

He couldn't do it. He knelt there, looking at her vulnerable back, hard enough to get off just watching her, and he couldn't do it. It wasn't fear of Taka, it wasn't even fear of her thinking it meant more than a fuck, a simple release of tension.

He just couldn't do it to her.

He climbed off the bed and went to the closet, pulling out one of the *yukata* that came with the room. When he turned back she hadn't moved, and he put the robe over her shoulders, helping her put it on, resisting the impulse to even look at her breasts, because he was hard enough as it was.

She let him tie the belt. "You need to sleep, Ji-chan," he said, pushing her back gently onto the bed. "Get under the covers."

She was obedient again, sliding beneath the

covers. Despite her height she looked very small in the king-size bed.

Her hair was in her face, and he pushed it out of her eyes, gently. She blinked. And then she closed her eyes, shutting him out.

He picked a hell of a time to grow a conscience, he thought as he moved back into the sitting area of the suite. He couldn't remember a time when he needed the release of sex so badly, and whether he liked it or not, he wanted Summer's sister. Had wanted her from the moment he grabbed her in Taka's house. Hell, wanted her since he saw her in Peter Madsen's garden two years ago. And he could have her, right now.

He stripped off the rest of his clothes and stretched out on the sofa. It was too short for his body, but it would have to do. If someone wanted to get to Jilly, they'd have to go through him, and for now he could let himself sleep.

She must have made some kind of sound, because he was just coming awake when she screamed. He moved quickly, on top of her before the second scream could erupt from her throat, covering her mouth with his hand. "Hush, Ji-chan. It will be all right. I promise you."

She was fighting him, struggling, and he caught her flailing arms and imprisoned them between them. "Calm down. If you scream again, it will bring too much attention."

She shoved him, pushing him off her, and he let her go, watching her out of hooded eyes as she scrambled off the bed, backing against the wall like a cornered animal, panting with fear.

"Make it stop," she whispered. "Make it go away."

He shook his head. "Ji-chan, I don't know how to do that."

"Yes, you do." She looked at him through the darkness, and her eyes were glittering with unshed tears. "Make it go away."

He came off the bed, moving toward her, giving her time to change her mind, to panic, to retreat. But she didn't move, waiting for him.

He hauled her up, pushing her against the wall, and brought his body up against hers, so she'd know exactly what she was asking. "Are you sure?"

She was frantic, her fingers digging into his shoulders, trying to bring him closer. "Make it stop, make it stop, make it—"

He lifted her up, pressing her against the wall, and tore open the *yukata*. She was still wearing the garters and the bloomers, and he slid his hands up her thighs, flicking the garters open with his thumbs. The stockings stayed up anyway. He slid his hands up and tugged at the white cotton bloomers, drawing them down her long legs, only to realize she was wearing a tiny black lace thong.

He was going to kill Kyo. He was going to buy him a case of sake. He sank to his knees in front of her and pressed his mouth against the tiny scrap of fabric as he pulled the bloomers over her feet and tossed them aside. As if she wasn't torment enough, she was a walking sex dream, and his last shred of conscience disappeared.

She made a muffled sound, of need, of protest, as he started to pull the thong down, and he simply broke the thin lace straps so that he could use his mouth on her.

Her hands were on his shoulders, her fingers digging in, and he wasn't sure whether she was trying to push him away or pull him closer. It didn't matter. He loved going down on women—it was his second favorite thing in the world to do, and with each touch, each lick, each tiny bite she quivered in shocked arousal. She was saying something, but he decided not to listen. It wouldn't make sense, anyway, and he slid his hands up her body, pushing the *yukata* off as he felt her first tiny climax.

He wanted more. He slid his fingers inside her, and she moaned. He couldn't believe how tight she was, tight and wet, and then he stopped thinking as he felt her shatter, her breath coming in deep, gasping gulps as her body arched.

He rose, lifting her, pressing her against the wall, pulling her legs around his hips, so damned ready for her, and he wanted to slam into her, hard, but he held back, controlling himself. He started to pushed inside her, just a little bit, into the tight wet heat of her, slowly, then pulled out again, so that she made a little mewling cry of need, and then he went deeper, a shallow, taunting rhythm just to drive every thought, every memory, out of her mind, just to drive himself crazy.

He went deeper with each thrust, getting her used to him, and she dropped her head against his shoulder. He could feel the wetness of her tears, the trembling of her body, and it wasn't enough. He had to bring her all the way there, with nothing held back, and he thrust into her, completely, and she let out a small cry that sounded like pain.

He froze, ready to pull out, but she clutched him even tighter. "Don't stop," she whispered. "Don't stop."

And then there was no way he could have. His body took over, slamming into her. With each thrust she tightened around him, and when the climax hit her it brought him along with it, and he pulled out, quickly, still holding her against the wall as the orgasm ripped through her body. It should have been enough, but he was greedy, and he put his hand between her legs, touching her, and she slammed her face against his shoulder, muffling her scream.

He made it last. Long enough that all conscious thought had left her, and she was animal, elemental and his. He turned her from the wall and pushed her down on the bed, following her, and he was still hard, or maybe he was hard again; he'd been too busy paying attention to her to even notice whether his erection had ever faded. It only mattered that he was hard and he still wanted her, and when he pushed her back and moved between her legs she arched her hips, her hands reaching out for him, to pull him into her, deep and tight, and she climaxed again when he filled her.

This time he could keep it up forever—she needed oblivion and she was right, he knew how to give it. He could last all night long if she needed it, and even if his cock gave out he could still make her come from a dozen other ways. He didn't want her thinking, feeling, anything but him, inside her.

By the time she fell asleep there wasn't a space on her body that he hadn't touched. She lay sprawled on the bed, in a deep, dreamless sleep, and he lay beside her, watching her, as the sun rose over the Tokyo skyscrapers. Watched her as he felt something inside him knot. Dread, and longing, and something he refused to even think about.

There was a smear of blood on the bed, and he stared at it. There was no such thing as a twenty-year-old virgin—maybe she was just coming off her period. He wasn't squeamish about such things, but that wouldn't explain her initial pain, or her unexpected tightness.

Shit. It was impossible. When he'd kissed her, back at his apartment, she hadn't responded, but he'd thought that was because he'd been goading her. Maybe she really didn't know how.

He pushed off the bed. She'd sleep for hours now, the nightmares chased away for the time being. And maybe his nightmare was just beginning.

The sun was beating against her eyelids, determined to wake her, and she didn't want to move. Her entire body hurt, and yet for once she was lying on a real mattress, not on a thin futon or in a plastic capsule. She stretched, and every muscle, every joint, felt achy in a deliciously decadent way she'd never felt before.

And then memory came flooding back with a horrifying swiftness. Reno's apartment. The gun. The dead man.

After that she couldn't remember anything until she woke up in bed in the middle of the night and Reno came in....

The whimper came from her own throat as she sat up. There was no sign of him. Her clothes were scattered all over the bedroom, but there was no way in hell she was going to touch them. She dove for the *yukata* that lay in a pile in a corner, and she remembered what he'd been doing when he stripped it off her. *Oh, God.*

The bathroom door was open, but it was empty. She could smell shampoo and water—he must have just left. She rose on unsteady feet, moving toward the window to look at the view of Tokyo. There were snow flurries dancing around the window, and far below the thick pack of pedestrians were bundled against the cold. She leaned her forehead against the window and closed her eyes.

She was a heartless, shallow, miserable excuse for a human being. Not because she'd killed a man. But because right now she was much more horrified about what she'd done with Reno in that huge bed.

When she finally moved, the snow was coming

down more heavily. There was a clock beside the bed—the tumbled, messed-up bed. It was early afternoon, and Reno had disappeared. Which at this point was a good thing.

There was a pile of clothes on the sofa. He'd clearly thought better of the Gothic-Lolita look, and he'd somehow managed to find loose silk pants and a silk shirt and camisole. And a goddamn thong. She moaned again at the memory.

No bra, but she'd have to make do—she'd left hers in Reno's apartment, and either he hadn't been able to find one in her size or he'd chosen not to. She opened the *yukata* to look at her breasts. There was a bite mark on one, and chafe marks from his skin. Against hers. In that bed.

She grabbed the clothes and practically ran for the bathroom, cursing herself up and down. Had she gone out of her mind? Why couldn't she be like a normal female, with a reasonable amount of experience? She'd tried, with Duke, but she could see by the stain on the sheet that he hadn't quite succeeded. Reno had.

She took as long in the shower as she could, scrubbing every inch of her body. Trying to ignore the fact that he'd used the soap on his body. On the parts of his body that had been inside her body. Again and again. And again.

She hurt. She didn't remember making any protest, but a hot, soaking bath would have made her more comfortable. By the time she turned off the shower her skin was pink from scrubbing. At least the silk pants were loose-fitting—tight jeans would have been an agony she didn't want to think about.

She was just getting ready to leave the bathroom when she smelled the coffee, and for the first time in her life the smell of coffee made her sick. In this hermetically sealed modern building the only way the smell of coffee would reach her would be if someone had brought it into the suite.

She had to face him sooner or later. She looked at her reflection in the mirror. Her short hair was damp and curling slightly around her face. She looked at her mouth, and an even more awful memory came back to her. With all the things he did to her, all the things she'd willingly participated in, he'd never kissed her. Not once.

It was enough of a shock to give her the courage to face him. She walked out of the bathroom, to see him lounging on the sofa, a paper cup of Starbucks in his hand, a second one on the table.

He lifted his head, looking at her, and there was something about his cool, lazy expression that warned her things were about to get a lot worse.

He didn't say a word when she came forward and picked up the coffee, and the silence was making her want to scream. "This is for me?"

"Yes."

More silence. "I found the clothes you got me," she said, then could have kicked herself for such an inane statement.

He tilted his head to one side. Mocking Reno was back, and he'd even found another pair of sunglasses that were now perched on top of his flaming hair. "Obviously," he said. "I take it you've gotten over your traumatic experience."

"Which one?" The words came out unbidden, and his smile was cool and unpleasant.

"Take your pick, Jilly. I don't know which was worse for you—blowing a man's head off or blowing—"

"Don't!"

"Though actually you didn't blow me, did you? You just lay back and enjoyed yourself. Except you're not thinking it was that enjoyable after all, am I right?"

"I don't know what I'm thinking."

He put his feet on the floor, and she backed up nervously. He laughed. "Don't worry. I'm not going to touch you again. I make it a practice to keep away from virgins."

"I wasn't… I mean, not really."

"There's no such thing as a semivirgin."

"Actually, there is, but I'm not about to explain it to you. You're acting as if I did something terrible to you."

"Instead of the other way around? You're forgetting one thing. I didn't offer. You asked."

"What?"

"'Make it stop,'" he said, echoing her words. "So I did what you asked. I made it stop. A very big mistake."

She just stared at him. The coffee was warm in her hand, the smell teasing her. But she couldn't move.

"What do you mean?"

He gave her his lazy smile. "I mean, that when I'm looking for sex, I prefer a woman who knows what she's doing."

She could feel her face whiten. He leaned back again, nonchalant. "You know why I hate American women?"

"No." She could still talk. Amazing.

"Because my mother was American. She thought it would be fun to play *yakuza* royalty for a while, but then she tired of it, and she left me with my grandfather and never came back. Poor, poor little Hiromasa with his abandonment issues and his mommy fixation." He took another sip of his coffee and smiled at her, that cruel, ugly smirk that she'd hoped was gone. "So every now and then I like to fuck American women so I can fuck my mother. And then tell them to fuck off."

She threw the coffee at him. The top came off and the hot liquid went flying, soaking his new white shirt.

"I told you not to do that," he said in an even voice. "I don't like being hit or having things thrown at me. I tend to react badly."

"As opposed to what?" She'd managed to find her voice and her fury.

He rose and headed for the bathroom at a lazy stroll, pulling off his jacket and the coffee-stained white shirt as he went. Exposing his chest and his back. And the scratch marks. "I'll give you this one," he said as he headed into the bathroom. "But next time I'll hit you back."

He closed the door, and she heard the water running.

Her shoes were by the door. It took her less than a moment to slip them on. And then she was out the door, closing it quietly behind her, and she never looked back.

# 14

Reno looked at his reflection in the mirror as he wiped the coffee off. He'd set things straight; she knew exactly where she stood. Last night was only an aberration, a one-night stand, the sort of thing he excelled at. It meant absolutely nothing.

And the added side benefit—unless she was a masochist, she'd be completely over him, which is just the way he wanted it. He never wanted another night like last night. When he couldn't get enough of her, no matter how he pushed it, no matter what he lured her into doing. It wasn't enough. It would never be enough, and that scared the hell out of him.

Attacking a woman's sexuality was always an effective way to get rid of an unwanted leftover. There's no way she'd ever let down her defenses with him again—he'd scarred her too deeply. He had no doubt she hated him more than she thought she had the capacity to hate. He could have told her otherwise. Humans, even the least experienced, had an infinite capacity for hate.

Hating him was the best thing he could do for her. She'd be able to turn her back on everything that had happened in Japan. And he could turn his back on her.

He shoved a hand through the spiky red hair. Yeah, he was a real hard-ass, he thought, putting his sunglasses back on his nose. She didn't need to see that his eyes were a dead giveaway if she had the chance to look closely enough. He didn't need or want anyone, ever. And this momentary insanity would be over as soon as he managed to dump her.

Hitomi's men would be on the lookout for him, but there were at least three secret entrances to the compound, made for a last-minute escape, and he doubted Hitomi had found them. Even Ojiisan's bodyguard, Kobayashi, didn't know of their existence.

She'd do what he told her now—he'd managed to strip away any remaining defenses when he'd stripped away her clothes. She'd stay put while he went out to reconnoiter, and if he had any doubts, he'd cut the electric cord off a lamp and tie her up.

But frankly, he'd rather not do that. For a

number of reasons, not the least of which was that it would turn him on. And he wasn't going near her, ever again. She was far too dangerous to his peace of mind.

His new white shirt was ruined, but he'd bought several, and he headed out into the living area, shirtless, ready to set things straight.

The room was deserted. Once more he'd underestimated her. She'd taken off, rather than spend another minute with him. And if he didn't catch up with her, and fast, she might have no more minutes left in her life.

Holy motherfucker, what an idiot he'd been. You never went in with more firepower than you needed, and he could have scared her off without bringing out the big guns. But for the first time in his life he'd been frightened, of her, of what he was feeling for her, and he'd miscalculated.

He was shoving his feet into his cowboy boots, pulling on a clean shirt as he stumbled out the door of the hotel room. He was going to kill her when he found her.

The snow was falling more heavily when he left the hotel. He'd checked with the front desk— no one had seen the tall *gaijin* leave, and she tended to stand out in a crowd. If she'd gone outside, she'd be easy enough to find. He ran out onto the sidewalk, searching through the throngs of people getting out of work. No tall, blond *gaijins* anywhere, and he had no idea which way she could have headed. She had no money, no identification, not even a coat, and the silk clothes he'd bought her had been an impulse on his part, a stupid one. She'd be freezing.

He pulled out his cell and began texting—he was going to need help if he stood any chance of finding her, and Kyo was his first choice.

A meaty fist appeared in front of him, picking the cell phone out of his hand and dropping it on the sidewalk. Kobayashi, always light on his feet, loomed over him. "You need to come to the compound."

He was faster than Kobayashi, and he didn't see anyone else around who could stop him. "I don't think so. I'm not walking into a trap."

"Yes, you are, young master. You would never stand by and see someone you loved be tortured and killed."

"My grandfather can withstand torture."

"I'm talking about your *gaijin.* Hitomi-san has her and there's nothing your grandfather can't do about it. If I don't bring you back with me, he's going to start cutting pieces off."

Odd, he could see his breath, but he wasn't

cold. He looked at Kobayashi, murder in his eyes. "You touch her…"

"No one will touch her, Hiromasa-san. Not if you come back. She has no value on her own; her only worth is to get you and Taka to come. If you don't care enough, Hitomi-san will get rid of her." He gave Reno a sorrowful look. "You should know I would never betray your grandfather. He has always known that something was going on, and he has had me go along with them. Your warning only gave him more proof. Your grandfather is smarter and stronger than five Hitomi-sans. You should know that."

"Then why did you let them take her?"

Kobayashi shook his head. "She is of little worth to your grandfather and none to me. If I do not bring you back, they will kill her, and they will know I failed. They will no longer trust me. You need to come back with me, young master. Or Hitomi will win me and your grandfather will fall."

There'd never been any real question. "What do they want with me?"

"Hitomi-san has said he will trade the girl's life for yours. He thinks you are sentimental enough to make such a bargain. I told him he was wrong, but he took her anyway, and he's awaiting word from me. If you refuse, he will kill the girl and then he will go for your grandfather, and I will not be there to stop him." There were tears in Kobayashi's eyes. "Please, Hiromasa-san. You're the only one who has any chance of stopping him."

Reno looked at him for a long, silent moment. And then he bowed. "Tell Hitomi-san I'm coming," he said. "And if he even touches her little finger, I'll rip his heart out."

For a moment Kobayashi looked disapproving. "Your grandfather will never approve. Look at the shame and trouble your worthless mother brought to the family. If you choose to marry a *gaijin* like your father—"

"I'm not marrying anyone!" he protested, truly horrified.

Kobayashi did not look appeased. "Your grandfather will be very unhappy. His days are not long, and you are his favorite grandson."

"I'm his only grandson," Reno said. "And I'm not going to let anything happen to the old man. Or to Jilly Lovitz. Is that understood?"

Kobayashi bowed in agreement, lower than Reno would have expected. Maybe it was true that the old man would eventually die, but that wasn't going to happen for many years, no matter how frail he'd suddenly become. He'd outlive

Hitomi-san and his fellow traitors—hell, he'd outlive them all.

"Tell them I'm coming," Reno said wearily.

"They already know, young master." He jerked his head toward the black sedan waiting by the curb, one of many at the upscale hotel.

No time to get in touch with Kyo, no time for backup of any sort. If he was going to keep Jilly alive, he was going to have to walk into the lion's den, just like that stupid story he'd learned in the Bible class he'd been forced to go to to learn some of his mother's culture. A waste of time, even if there were occasionally good stories.

He nodded. "Let's go, then." He yanked his long red braid from underneath his jacket, letting it hang loose down his back, put his sunglasses back on his nose and composed his face into a faint sneer. And then he strolled toward the sedan at a leisurely pace. Ready to do battle.

Why didn't she ever learn not to run away when things were difficult? Jilly thought. Not that there was anything else to do but think—she was tied up and dumped in some kind of a storeroom, filled with boxes and one narrow cot. Just to make sure she couldn't investigate, they'd tied her to the cot, and while she could probably hop across the room, dragging the metal bed with her, it didn't seem to be worth the effort.

How stupid could she have been? Almost three years ago she'd done the same damned thing in California. She'd run away from people sent to protect her, straight into the arms of a madman, and if it weren't for Isobel Lambert and the Committee she would have been brainwashed or dead or both.

And now she'd done it again. No matter how hurt, how angry she was, she still should have stayed with Reno. He was the only one who had managed to keep her relatively safe, from everyone else, if not from him. She could have given him the cold, silent treatment. Reno was unbelievably tough, but even the strongest man eventually cracked under the silent treatment. Even her ruthless father quailed.

But no, she had to run out of the room, straight into the arms of what could only be Hitomi's men. She was learning to tell *yakuza* from a distance—they wore garish suits and had carefully arranged hair, the polar opposite of Reno's red-dyed mane and black leather. But there was no mistaking the coldness in their eyes, the way they carried themselves.

She hadn't even gotten to the elevator. In fact, she couldn't remember exactly what had happened. Someone had put a cloth over her face, and everything went dark. They must have used chloroform or something equally nasty, because the next thing she remembered she was alone in this cold, dark room, bound and gagged. Presumably back in the huge cement warehouse that provided the front for Ojiisan's headquarters.

Were they going to kill her? If so, why were they waiting?

At least Reno would be relieved—she was no longer his problem. If she had any sense at all, she'd be much more upset about the fact that she'd been kidnapped and would most likely be killed. Not still obsessing over the night she spent with Reno in her bed.

Then again, she'd learned one thing in the past few days. Being a child brainiac with an astronomical IQ didn't do a spit of good if she had absolutely no common sense. And where Reno was concerned, she was brain-dead.

Whoever had tied the ropes was far too good at it—it probably came from practice. They weren't tight enough to cut off the circulation, and she could move her muscles enough to keep from cramping up. But there was absolutely no way in hell she could even begin to untie them.

She looked at her bound wrists. Maybe she could try her teeth....

Unbidden came the memory of Reno suggesting she undo his *fundoshi* with her teeth. She dropped her head down on her knees with a groan. It was bad enough being kidnapped and, probably, eventually murdered. Did she have to be haunted by the biggest mistake in the history of the world?

Though, maybe it wasn't that big a mistake. She'd never expected anything from him, and the fact that they'd had mind-shattering sex could be construed as a good thing. At least she wasn't going to die a semivirgin, even if she'd been as bad at sex as he'd told her.

But if she'd been that bad, that uninspiring, then why had he come back to her, over and over again? Why hadn't he walked away?

She lifted her head from her knees, leaning back against the wall with a groan. There was no way she was going to make sense of it, make peace with it. She wasn't going to be seeing him again—that was at least one small blessing of being kidnapped by a Japanese gangster. She could live out whatever days or hours she had left knowing she'd never have to look at his far-too-pretty face.

The door to the storeroom opened, and one of the blank-faced men appeared. Except that he was young, probably younger than Reno. He had a nasty-looking knife in one hand, and she wondered if it was going to be over that quickly. Why had they even bothered bringing her here if they were going to kill her so quickly?

If they thought she was going to go down without a fight, they were wrong. She waited until he got close enough, and then she kicked out with her bound legs, trying to knock him off balance.

He scrambled to his feet and backhanded her across the face, hard, and she saw nothing but a red haze for a moment before she shook her head to clear it. He was already slicing through the ropes, not through her. Okay, she could put up with being slugged if it meant she got to live for a while longer. She wasn't big on going gently into that dark night.

He hauled her to her feet, smart enough not to cut the ropes on her ankles while she could still kick him in the head. He only came up to her shoulder, and he had a sullen expression and a slick, black pompadour, but she didn't make the mistake of underestimating him. He was the one who held the knife.

He leaned down and sliced through her ankle

bonds, roughly, the blade nicking her skin as he jumped away, wisely not trusting her. She was considering making a run for it when he put the knife away, only to pull out a small, serviceable-looking gun instead. Maybe not; he was probably a decent shot and she didn't want to die with a bullet in her back, running away.

Without a word he pushed her out into the barren hallway, gesturing for her to precede him. For a moment she didn't move, wondering exactly what he'd do, but then she thought better of it. Her face still stung from his backhanded blow—*yakuza*-boy would not hesitate to hit her again to get her to do what he wanted. So she put her head down and began walking.

The hall was ill-lit and cold, and it looked like the corridor she and Reno had run down, stark and empty, the kind of corridor a trapped rat might race down. That eerie, trapped sense got worse as she turned the corner three times, at her captor's prodding, and each corridor looked exactly the same.

"*Dozo,*" he said, stopping her in front of a door, and her stomach knotted. It looked like the room where she'd seen the murder. But all these rooms looked alike, except for Ojiisan's throne room, and what were the chances of her being taken to the same room where she'd seen murder committed?

Very good, it turned out. She was pushed inside the large room, and the first thing she saw was the bloodstain on the floor, where she'd last seen a dead body.

There were half a dozen men in the room, talking in low voices, and they didn't look up when she came in. Her surly guide closed the door behind them, and she stood still, wondering if she could make a break for it.

Unlikely. "You know, if you brought me here to kill me like you did the other man, then you might as well get to it," she said in her most annoyed voice. "I'm really getting tired of all this drama."

One man lifted his head to look at her, and she had no doubt at all that this was the notorious Hitomi-san. His eyes were flat and cold, and he emanated an ugly kind of power. "You are very brave for a *gaijin*," he said in heavily accented English. "But we have no plans to kill you if Hiromasa-san does what he's ordered to do."

"Who?"

Hitomi's lips curled in contempt. "I believe he calls himself Reno. If he agrees to come here and trade his presence for yours, then you can go back home and never have to think about this place again. And that is what I would advise. Tokyo is not a very healthy place for you."

"I don't think I'll have the option. Reno isn't going to put his life on the line for me."

"He has been doing just that for the past four days. Why should that have changed?"

*Well, because we slept together and he found me wanting?* No, that was the last thing she was going to say. "You didn't give him the choice of him or me before," she said instead. "I don't think he's going to sacrifice himself for my sake."

"Then you do not understand Japanese honor."

"Do you?"

The silence in the room was absolute, and the man who'd brought her there, the one who'd hit her before, took a threatening step toward her.

Hitomi-san held up a hand to forestall him. A hand that was missing parts of several fingers, and he wore a gaudy diamond ring on one stump.

"For your sake, Miss Lovitz, I hope you are wrong. In the meantime you may sit over there and keep quiet. My men will never hurt you unless I give them the order, but it wouldn't be wise to test me."

Jilly had gone beyond fear, gone beyond hope, but she hadn't gone beyond common sense, so she swallowed her instinctive retort and let *yakuza*-boy push her into a chair in the corner. "I don't suppose the condemned woman could have a last meal?" she said.

Hitomi-san looked confused for a moment.

"I'm hungry," she said. "Can I have some food before you kill me?"

Hitomi's amusement wasn't the most reassuring thing she'd ever seen, but he sent *yakuza*-boy off with orders that were too muffled for her to understand. He'd probably bring back tentacles.

She sat, absently rubbing her wrists where the rope had chafed her. Her cheek was throbbing—she'd probably have a bruise, assuming she lived long enough for one to form. Life had taken on an air of absurdity—and she fully intended to treat it as such. If she was going to die in a warehouse in Tokyo, then she was going to do it with style. Lianne would be proud of her.

The door opened again, and she looked up, hoping it was *yakuza*-boy with tentacle-free sashimi, but instead the giant bodyguard filled the entrance. He bowed, and Hitomi-san gestured him to enter.

And then Jilly saw what was hidden behind his massive bulk. Reno.

She didn't move. Didn't blink. Just watched him as he strolled into the room as if he owned it, never glancing in her direction. There was a time when she thought that swagger was obnoxious. Right now it filled her with ridiculous hope. Maybe they weren't doomed.

Hitomi-san gave a short, sketchy bow, and Reno returned it with a flare that somehow reminded her of the Three Musketeers. "I believe you have something of mine, Hitomi-san," he said in Japanese.

"It was kind of you to join us, Hiromasa-san," he replied. "Though I felt sure you would come."

"Did you?"

"If not for the sake of the annoying *gaijin*, then for your esteemed grandfather."

At that point Reno shot a cool, ironic glance in her direction. "She is a pain, is she not? But hardly worth the trouble it would cause if she were to disappear. And you are a very smart man, Hitomi-san. You would never needlessly complicate matters over someone so trivial."

Hitomi-san's malicious smile didn't help matters. "Aah, but Hiromasa-san, you know I'm a man who pays attention to even the smallest detail. It is the reason behind my success. There's no way to trace her disappearance back to us. Enough people know that Russian mercenaries were in the country and she got in the way."

"With your help."

"Of course. Details, Hiromasa-san. Your grandfather is old, and his organization belongs to another age. You and I both know that. We can bring it into the future. As your grandfather's natural heirs, both you and your cousin are welcome to join us, of course."

"I don't think so," Reno said, his voice cool.

Hitomi's faint smile wasn't reassuring. "No, I didn't think so, either. And as long as you're around, there will still be a faction of the family who look to you for power. So I'm afraid you will need to be disposed of. You and your cousin and his wife."

"And how do you intend to get to O'Brien-san? He was warned."

"He was also told the sister of his wife has been killed. He won't stay hidden for long with that kind of information."

"Oh, shit," Jilly said.

Reno didn't turn to look at her. "You know she and her sister won't be any threat to you."

"Details, Hiromasa-san. If you had longer to live, you would learn to appreciate the necessity of paying attention to them. As it is, you'll have to wait for your next lifetime."

Jilly rose. "Look, haven't we had enough of

this evil-warlord shit? Why don't you just—?" She'd forgotten that *yakuza*-boy was still behind her. Forgotten that he had a gun in hand. She felt the blow to the side of her head, and everything turned dark as she sank down onto the cold, hard floor. A roar of rage echoed around her as she lost consciousness.

# 15

"You're an idiot."

Not the best words to wake up to, particularly when she didn't want to wake up. She felt fuzzy, disoriented, as if she'd been kicked by a horse, and she would really much rather keep her eyes closed and wait for the world to settle down.

"Don't pretend you're still unconscious—you don't fool me. He didn't hit you that hard."

Jilly didn't open her eyes. She was lying on something hard; it felt like the tiny cot in the storage room. She moved slightly, just to check, but she didn't seem to be tied up. That was another improvement, even if someone seemed to have ripped off the top of her head and poured lye inside. Or tentacles.

"Go away," she muttered into the mattress. She was facedown, and that was fine with her. It felt safer that way.

"I don't seem to have that option."

"Shit." She lifted her head, slowly, gingerly, and looked toward the voice. It was Reno, of course, sitting cross-legged on the floor. Even in the dim light she could see he was a total mess. His white shirt was filthy, blood and dirt ground into it. Dried blood darkened his flame-colored hair, the cut on his cheek had opened again and he looked totally thrashed.

"What happened to you?" she asked, starting to sit upright when her head exploded. She lay back down. "Did you finally annoy someone enough to have them beat the shit out of you?"

"Let's say someone annoyed me enough," he said, his voice dry. "How's your head?"

"It hurts. Why the hell do you care? And why are you here? Don't tell me you came to offer yourself in my place, because I won't believe you." She didn't bother disguising her grumpiness. It had been a very bad day.

"Of course you wouldn't. You're not stupid, and neither am I. I knew Hitomi-san had no intention of ever letting you go. He just wanted to get me in here, as well. As soon as Taka shows up, then nothing will stand in the way of his taking over my grandfather's organization."

A memory fought its way through her clouded brain. "He's not really going to kill my sister."

"He's going to try. However, she's well out of reach, and I don't think she's stupid enough to get her feelings hurt and go running out into the streets, straight into the arms of people who've been trying to kill her."

"Feelings hurt?" she echoed, sitting up, her rage more powerful than her pain. "That's what you call it? You miserable rat bastard, it was leave or kill you myself, and it's not like I haven't killed anyone before." Her voice only wavered slightly.

He leaned his head back against the wall, and she could see a dark bruise forming on his chest beneath the ripped shirt. "You're still an idiot. Why didn't you keep your mouth shut in there?"

"Would it have made a difference? Would they have let us leave?"

"No. But at least you wouldn't have a headache."

"Thanks for the concern," she said. "Give me a couple of aspirin and I'll be fine in the morning."

"You'll be dead in the morning."

"Aren't you a bundle of laughs?" she said.

He pushed himself off the floor, carefully, and moved over to the bed. She scrambled out of the way, but on such a small surface there wasn't far to go, and she wasn't about to go for the floor.

He sat down, leaning back against the wall and letting out a sound halfway between frustration and exhaustion. "Just be quiet for a moment, Ji-chan," he said. "I need to think."

"You don't need to think," she said. "You need to get out of here and find out if your grandfather is still alive. You need to warn him about Hitomi."

"He already knows about Hitomi-san. And he's still alive—I would know if he wasn't. My grandfather is not going down easily. But Kobayashi may not have had the chance to tell him that Hitomi's made his move."

"So?" she said. "Make some daring escape. Get us out of here, warn your grandfather and save the day."

"You've been out for a while. I've been trying. The door is locked and bolted from the outside, the windows are barred and I have nothing to use as a weapon."

"What about all those boxes? Maybe there's something in there...."

"The boxes are filled with fake Chanel handbags. I don't think we can beat someone senseless with a purse."

"In every box?" she said, looking at the huge pile. Each one was almost four feet square, which made for a hell of a lot of fake Chanel.

"I dumped a couple while you were still out. We can always try hiding, but I don't think that would buy us more than a few minutes. And it's not my style to hide."

"And it's mine?" she said, insulted.

"You're not going to have any say in the matter."

"Now, why does that sound familiar?" she said. They were back to scrapping—she could almost forget the dark, hot hours in the king-size bed. Almost forget the casual cruelty of his words just a few hours ago.

"They beat the shit out of you," she said after a moment, quieter.

"Yes. But Azuki's in the hospital."

"Who's Azuki?"

"The kid who hit you."

Silence. "Isn't that a little extreme?" she said.

"He's lucky I didn't kill him."

Another silence. "Why?"

He closed his eyes. "Why what?"

"Why did you want to kill him? Why did you come here when you knew you were walking into a trap? Why did you spend the night in bed with me and then tell me I was lousy at sex? What the hell is going on?"

He opened one eye to look at her. "I thought we agreed you weren't stupid, Ji-chan. Figure it out."

The problem was that the room was dark—the bare lightbulb barely penetrated the cavernous space. And darkness made everything more intimate.

She tried to retreat farther on the narrow cot, but there was nowhere else to go, and she'd inadvertently gotten his attention.

"Are you trying to melt into the wall, Ji-chan? I don't think that's a reasonable way out of here."

"So we just wait?"

He gave her a long, considering look. "If you're bored, I can offer a suggestion."

"No!" she said, her voice a nervous little squeak.

He laughed then. *Rat bastard, indeed.* "You can only be a virgin once, you know. It would pass the time."

"Go fuck yourself."

"That wasn't what I was thinking of." He had a lazy half smile, and he stretched, wincing slightly as something pained him.

"You must practice that look in the mirror," she said, going for caustic.

"What look?"

"That 'I'm such a hot bad boy that you can't resist me' look," she said.

He laughed at that. "I didn't know it worked."

"Why the hell are you so cheerful?" she demanded, incensed. "We've been imprisoned by murderous *yakuza,* we can't find a way out and we'll probably be dead by tomorrow."

He shrugged. "At this point we don't have anything to lose, and it's going to be a long night."

"For you, maybe. I intend to sleep."

"The bed is very small."

"You can take the floor."

"I can take you."

She froze. "The hell you can. I'm never having sex again in my entire life."

"That's not much of a vow if you're only going to live one more day," he pointed out.

"You said I was lousy in bed."

"I said I prefer experienced women. So I'm offering you a chance to practice and distract me at the same time. Besides, I don't have any other choice."

"Use your hand," she snarled.

She was in the wrong place, backed into a corner of the room on the tiny cot. When he moved toward her there was no place for her to go. She could dive onto the cement floor, but that wouldn't slow him down, and he had a dangerous look in his eyes. "I don't think so," he said softly.

"If you touch me, I'll kill you."

"I don't think so," he said again. "You want me."

She let out a hoot of laughter that sounded very convincing. She almost believed it herself. "Dream on."

He was close now, very close, moving like a panther across the tiny space, and his mouth was dangerously near hers. She could feel her heart pounding, her palms were getting sweaty and she'd forgotten all about her headache.

"Say no, Ji-chan. Tell me you don't want it." She opened her mouth to say it, but he stopped her. "But only if you mean it. Tell me you don't want me to put my hands on you." He let his fingers trail down her neck, so soft, so sexual. "Tell me you don't want me kissing you." He brushed her mouth with his, barely a glancing touch. "Tell me you don't want to come with me inside you."

Any self-respecting female would tell him to fuck off. She'd tried that, but it hadn't seemed to sink in. She could tell him no, right now, and he'd move back, away from her. Like a predator who thought better of the tasty snack he'd come across.

But she might die tomorrow. And if that was going to happen, she didn't want to be alone tonight.

He was on his knees on the cot now, and his hands had slipped down to the front of her blouse, and he was slowly unbuttoning it, pushing it off her shoulders so that it puddled around her, and she only had the silk camisole to cover her. "Say no, Jilly," he whispered in her ear. "Tell me to leave you alone. Tell me you don't want me. Go ahead and lie." His mouth was at her ear, and she could hear soft, seductive whisperings, and then he bit her earlobe, a tiny sting of pain and pleasure.

She gathered her self-respect for one last time. "I don't want to spend the last night of my life having sex with someone who doesn't care about me," she said, waiting for him to retreat, waiting for a mocking comment, waiting for the end.

He sat back on his heels, looking at her, and for once his beautiful face was still and thoughtful. "I'm here, aren't I?"

For a declaration of emotion it was piss-poor, but it was enough. She sat very still as he pulled the camisole over her head and tossed it on the floor, and then his hands started up her sides, slowly.

"Did I tell you that you have beautiful breasts?" he whispered as his hands closed over them. "Just perfect. Not too big, not too small. And they taste delicious." He leaned forward and put his mouth on one, and she jumped as she felt a powerful current move through her body, ending between her legs. He moved his mouth to her other breast, sucking it, and she heard a quiet little moan that could only have come from her.

"I don't know which one I like better," he whispered, using his tongue to tease her nipple into a hard knot. "This one—" he moved to her other breast, using his teeth this time, just letting them scrape lightly over it "—or this one."

"Oh, God," she whispered, losing it.

"I take it that's a yes?" he said, kissing the underside of her chin, nuzzling her lightly.

She tried to gather one last shred of dignity, even though she wanted to throw it to the winds. "You used me last night," she said.

"If you say so."

"So I'll use you tonight." It seemed to make sense, at least to her.

"My pleasure," he said, and pulled her down onto the narrow cot so that he knelt between her legs.

She'd never felt more vulnerable in her life. She was half naked, he was fully clothed, and she'd just given him total power over her, for all that she thought she'd be using him. There was no way she could feel in control when his hands were touching her, his long fingers brushing against her skin. It was a lost cause. She didn't move when he slid his fingers beneath the drawstring waist of the silk pants and began sliding them off her legs.

Leaving her in a thong again. Exposed. Waiting.

He pulled off his torn jacket and tossed it on the floor. He yanked off his ripped and stained shirt, as well. There were bruises on his beautiful chest. Things were beginning to fall into place. He'd tried to kill *yakuza*-boy and had been beaten. He'd tried to kill the man who'd hurt her.

She rose on her elbows to look at him. He was bruised, bloody and beautiful. And he was hers, whether he knew it or not.

She put one hand flat across his belly. And then she began to undo the button on his pants, and then the zipper, and he watched her, making no move to help or encourage her.

She didn't need help or encouragement. Tonight she knew what she wanted, knew what she needed, and she wasn't going to let anything get in her way. Tonight she would show him just how good she could be.

He was already hard, as she expected he'd be. He was wearing silk underwear, not the *fundoshi* that she'd planned to tear off with her teeth. Maybe that would come later. If there was a later.

"Sit back," she said in a low voice.

He raised an eyebrow but did as she asked, leaning back against the wall as she sat up.

She started with his neck, the fragile spot at the base of his throat, kissing him, moving carefully across the bruises until she reached the flat male nipples. She licked and he groaned, reaching his hands up to touch her hair.

She pushed him back down on the cot. "This is for me," she said sternly.

He tasted of sweat and blood and almond soap. She sucked at his nipple, and it hardened in her mouth.

She moved down his stomach with her lips. She could feel the increasing beat of his heart, the tremor when her tongue touched a new sensitive spot. He was so delicious she wanted to bite him, and she did, lightly, just below his navel.

He muttered a word in Japanese, one she hadn't heard, but she had no doubt it was positive. She ran her tongue over the bite mark, and moved on.

"Lift up your hips," she whispered, and he did what she told him to, letting her slide his black pants down his long legs.

If she'd had any doubts as to whether she was being effective, it was wiped out. His cock was hard, bigger than she'd expected. No wonder it had hurt in the beginning.

"I thought Japanese men were supposed to be smaller than average," she said.

"Whoever did the measuring hadn't been around you. Shit!" The exclamation came out as she touched him, carefully wrapping her fingers around his silken length.

"No cursing," she chided him, her fingertips dancing on the smooth, beautiful skin of his cock. "You have to behave yourself."

"And when have I ever behaved myself?" he said, his voice strained.

"If you don't, I won't do this." And she let her tongue drift across the head, tasting the dampness that had already gathered.

"Shi—" He broke off the word and said something in Japanese. More words she hadn't heard.

She lifted her head to look at him. His eyes were half closed, and his hands were fisted on the thin blanket beneath him. "What are you saying?" she asked, suspicious.

A half smile tugged at his perfect mouth. "Just compliments, Ji-chan. Do it again. Please."

The odd thing was she wanted to. She wanted to take him into her mouth and make him groan again, she wanted to make him as out of control as she'd been the night before, and she wanted to do it with her mouth.

She'd read all sorts of terms in the romance novels she loved. Alabaster shaft. Rigid pole. Turgid, tumescent rod....

It was a cock, big and hard, and she slid her lips over it, bringing as much as she could into her mouth.

He muttered something incomprehensible, and for a moment his hand released the blanket he was gripping to hover over her head, and then he put it back again, tense, aroused, incredibly patient as she tasted him, explored this strange part of his body that was so mysterious and powerful.

She tried to remember the books, but her brain was going on autopilot, and she lifted her head to look up into his dreamy face. "I don't know what I'm doing," she said, suddenly worried.

"Do anything you want," he murmured, and this time he let his hand touch her face, a reassuring caress. "Just don't bite too hard."

She laughed, still a little uncertain, but she wanted him in her mouth too much to worry. She wanted him everywhere, over her, inside her, wherever he wanted to be. Her own body was trembling now, and she could feel her arousal so strongly that it distracted her. She wanted, she needed more, and she didn't know what to do.

His hands cupped her head, gently, guiding

her into a rhythm, and he took her hand and placed it around the base of his cock, the part that was too big to fit in her mouth, and his hands guided her, pressing, squeezing.

She gave up any pretense of control, lost in the sensations she was drawing from him. She was moving faster, sucking harder, and she wanted him to come in her mouth, she needed it….

But just as she felt him begin to peak, he pulled her away, lifting her with seemingly effortless ease and putting her astride him so that she was straddling his cock, with only the thin scrap of cloth between them.

"I don't know whether I love thongs or hate them," he said in a shaky voice. He broke the straps and tossed it to one side, and then he placed the head of his cock against her. She waited for him to push it in, to finish it, but he didn't move.

"It's up to you," he said. "Take what you need."

"I don't…I can't…"

"Of course you can," he said, his soft voice at odds with the tense control she could feel rippling through his body. "Just take what you want." And he put his hands on her hips, to reassure her, not to rule her.

She sank down, just a little, and she could feel him filling her, pushing into her, and a little spasm of release shook her. He held her steady while it lasted, and then, when she was breathing again, she took more of him, and another small climax hit her.

She looked down to where their bodies were joining and began to tremble. "Please," she whispered.

His fingers tightened on her hips for a moment, then relaxed again. "If you want it, Jilly, you have to take it."

Somehow her hands had gotten to his shoulders, clutching them. She pushed his head back and kissed him as she took him deep inside her with one, fluid move.

His hand was tangled in her hair, and he was kissing her, with a kind of desperation that was the finish for her. She started to climax again, in slow, powerful waves sweeping through her body, and she dropped her head on his shoulder, holding on as the convulsions shook her body.

She thought she'd finished when he turned her, pushing her back onto the narrow bed, still inside her, but the change just set off a new round of orgasms, and with each of his hard thrusts she went further, until he put his hands between them, touching her, and everything vanished in a flash of white heat, spiraling into darkness, and the only sound was his muffled cry of release.

He was still inside her when she floated back out of the roiling darkness, and her face was wet with tears she hadn't known she'd shed.

He wasn't that heavy; for all the strength and muscle, he didn't weigh that much, but he pulled out, moving onto his side, pulling her with him, so that they were facing each other on the tiny cot, their bodies pressed up against each other's.

His hair had come loose from its long braid. His face was wet, too, but she couldn't believe they were tears. He smiled at her then, a smile of such devastating sweetness that she was lost.

"Sleep now, Ji-chan," he whispered. "We've only got a few hours left before they come for us. Rest now."

She wanted more, but she was too drained to say a word. Any more would probably kill her, she thought, smiling to herself as she pressed her face against his sweat-slick shoulder.

"What's so funny?" he asked in an absent voice. His long hair was covering them both, and she felt him drape some of it over her shoulders, like some sort of powerful bond, tying them together.

"I'm happy," she said.

"You're probably going to die tomorrow and you're happy? I'm not that good."

"Yes, you are. And I'm not going to die. You're

going to rescue me, as you've done so many times already, and we're going to live happily ever after."

She almost thought she felt his body freeze, but she ignored it, drifting into a blissful, dreamless sleep, held tight in his arms.

Holy motherfucker. What the hell had he done? Just when he thought he'd driven her away forever, he'd managed to sabotage himself. It was going to take nothing short of a bomb to get away from her now. Happily ever after? There was no such thing.

He didn't want her. He didn't want to care about her, he didn't want to get so turned on by her amateur and earth-shattering efforts at sex. He wanted his life the way he had it, with no room for a clinging *gaijin*.

He could tell himself he had a good reason for making such a terrible mistake, fucking her again. They were facing death in the morning; it was a natural human response to try to deny it. But the problem was, he had no intention of dying. Or of letting her be killed, no matter how convenient that suddenly seemed. He'd just used it as an excuse to get inside her.

In the cold light of day she'd know there was no such thing as a happy ending.

And if she didn't, he'd have to show her just how cruel the world could be to innocents who still believed in fairy tales. Whether he liked it or not.

# 16

She'd looked so peaceful when he yanked her out of her deep sleep. She was curled up next to him like a cat in the sunshine with a stomach full of cream when he leapt off the cot, dragging her with him.

"Someone's coming," he said in a low voice. "Get in the box."

"The hell I will."

He was shoving her discarded clothes at her, what there were of them, at the same time pulling on his pants. "Don't make me hurt you," he said, his voice flat and cold.

"I don't hear anything."

"I do." He grabbed her arm and hauled her over to the pile of boxes on the right, tipping one up. It was big enough, and empty, and she yanked on her pants as he shoved her under it, buttoning up her shirt as he dropped it down over her.

"Don't make a sound," he said in something close to a growl.

For once she did as he told her to. He moved silently to the door, waiting behind it. All he had was the element of surprise, and he probably wouldn't have that. They'd be smart enough to guess that he'd try something. Most of the men who worked for his grandfather were smart, though following someone like Hitomi and betraying the old man was not only stupid but dishonorable.

Someone was outside the door, trying his best to be quiet. There was only the one dim lightbulb, creating enough shadows in the cavernous room to give him a fighting chance, and he moved back. He could hear the lock click open—whoever was outside was picking the lock, not using a key. Which meant they were acting outside of orders, which could be either a bad thing or a good one.

He flattened his body against the wall as the door opened, waiting, soundless, breathless, until the very last second before slamming it hard against whoever was sneaking in.

The door hit solid rock, slamming him back against the wall. A moment later he was looking into the furious eyes of his cousin, Takashi O'Brien, as he shut the door behind him.

"I thought it might be you locked in here," he

said, his voice cold and deadly. "What the fuck is going on? Why are you locked up, and why is Great-Uncle in seclusion?"

Reno relaxed his body, just marginally. "Nice to see you, too, cousin. Here to play rescuer? All hell has been breaking loose while you've been in hiding."

"Are you accusing me of cowardice, little cousin?"

He knew that tone of voice of Taka's, knew the kind of danger it signaled, but now was no time to get into a fight. "You had no choice," he said grudgingly. "The Russians who were after you were being paid for by Hitomi-san, Ojiisan's new second in command. His family have gotten greedy, and they don't like his rules, and neither of us was around to stop him."

"And?" Taka was practically vibrating with rage—not a good sign.

"And they're planning on getting rid of him and anyone who would inherit leadership. Which means you and me, and you just walked right in here, meaning we're screwed," Reno said bitterly.

"You're screwed," Taka said. "They don't know that I'm even here, and I'm not about to enlighten them. How many are there?"

"I don't know. I don't think the older generation would turn against Ojiisan, but I don't know who we can trust. You got any ideas?"

"Of course," Taka said, his voice clipped. "I'll get out of here the way I came in and get backup. In the meantime you can stay put so they don't get suspicious."

"And if they kill me?"

"Probably long overdue. But I have something even more important to ask you."

He knew that tone of voice from his older cousin, knew that flat, deadly expression, and he was wary. "What?"

The fist came first, and it was only Reno's lightning-fast reflexes that stopped it from landing in the middle of his face. He spun, and it landed on a rib that had already suffered a number of kicks from the night before, and he groaned.

"Christ, Taka, give me a break," he said, knowing exactly what the problem was. "She…"

He came at him again, but this time Reno was ready for him, ducking in under him, knowing that Taka tended to head for the right. Taka fell back, murder in his eyes. "I'm supposed to tell my wife that my family failed her? I'm not going back to her until I beat the shit out of you."

"Don't you think dealing with Ojiisan's problem might be a higher priority?" Reno shot back, panting.

This time Taka's fist landed on his chin, a glancing blow since he saw it coming, but as he whirled backward he came up against the wall, and he stayed there, out of breath, glaring at his cousin.

"If I beat you to a bloody pulp, they may leave you alone while I go for help. Consider this a gift," he said, slamming his fist into his stomach.

Reno doubled over in pain. Taka had learned a new fighting style in the past few years—he was no longer as predictable.

"You don't…" he said, choking.

"Stop it!" The voice was muffled, the cardboard box thrashing around as Jilly tried to fight her way out from under it. Taka froze, staring, as Jilly finally managed to unbox herself. "I'm okay, Taka. Reno saved my life. Many times. He wouldn't do anything to hurt me."

Taka didn't move as he took her in. And then he stooped down, picking up a scrap of cloth from the floor. It would take a monk not to recognize the ripped thong, and Taka was no monk.

Added to that, Jilly's shirt was misbuttoned, she had a very visible love bite on the side of her neck, and she simply had that well-fucked look that was impossible to mistake.

"I'm going to fucking kill you," Taka said in a quiet voice, leaping on him in a white-hot rage. They both went down, rolling around on the dusty cement floor, flailing at each other. Taka was a little taller, a little stronger, but Reno had more street smarts, and besides, Jilly was watching. Some other time Reno would take the punishment he endured like a man, but not right now.

He shoved his fist into Taka's gut, getting no more than a muffled grunt in response, and then Taka was pounding him, a lot harder than when they were kids.

Reno kicked up and Taka went flying, landing on his back with Reno following him, grabbing him by the shirt and preparing to slug him. There were more important things to worry about. Like Ojiisan and Hitomi's ruthless plan. Like Jilly bashing them both with a huge fake Chanel purse so loaded with chains and buckles it could cause permanent damage.

Reno rolled off, lying back on the floor and panting, and Taka just lay there, breathing heavily. Reno was tempted to kick him, but they'd work that out in private.

Taka pulled himself into a sitting position, looking pissed. One of Reno's fists had landed near his cheekbone, and he was going to have a hell of a black eye in a matter of hours, which at least was more noticeable than the cracked rib Taka had delivered. Reno sat up, as well, hiding his instinctive wince of pain.

"How many times did we warn you to keep your goddamned hands off of Jilly?" Taka demanded in a dangerous voice. "Summer told you she had a crush on you—you knew better than to take advantage."

He heard Jilly's swift intake of breath, and he didn't make the mistake of looking at her. "Things don't always work out the way you plan, Taka-san." He went with the honorific name— Taka might hit him again if he went with the more affectionate "chan." "It was an accident—it's certainly not going to happen again."

"How does sleeping with my sister-in-law, the girl you were told to keep away from, constitute an accident?" Taka demanded bitterly. "You tripped over her and your cock accidentally landed inside?"

This time Taka heard Jilly's involuntary sound of distress, and he turned to look at her, and Reno's eyes followed, as well. She was pale with shock and pain. "Sorry, Jilly," Taka said belatedly. "It's not your fault. Reno nails everyone he can. He knew you were vulnerable and he had orders to keep away from you."

"Someone had to save her life," Reno snapped. "You were out of reach and the Committee's in a mess."

"That someone didn't have to screw her senseless," Taka retorted. "Sorry, Jilly," he added again.

Reno rose to his feet, wincing slightly. "I think we can put off this argument until later. It's a moot point—I'd already decided I wasn't touching her again. We need to concentrate on getting Ojiisan the hell out of here. Along with us."

"I told you, I couldn't get anywhere near him. All the approaches are heavily guarded. Where the hell is Kobayashi? Is he in on this? He's always been devoted to the old man."

"He's playing spy for Ojiisan. I don't know how much Hitomi trusts him—everyone knows Kobayashi would die for Ojiisan." He reached for his discarded shirt.

Taka frowned. "And where does this Hitomi-san come from? Is he a long-term member of the family? I don't remember him." Taka scrambled to his feet, as well, touching the welt on his face carefully.

"He's from one of the *gurentai* families—I haven't been able to find out which one, though I'm guessing it's the Kuromaku gang. They've always been ultra-violent, but most of their membership has been killed off by the Yamaguchi-gumi. They need new *kobun,* and taking over Ojiisan's family is a smart move." Reno allowed himself a furtive glance at Jilly. She'd rebuttoned her shirt correctly, and she'd moved to one corner of the room, sitting cross-legged and remote. Totally emotionless, silent. He could only hope and pray that would last until Taka got her out of here.

"You need to take Jilly to safety," Reno said. "I'll stay here and find a way to get to Ojiisan." He half expected Jilly to argue, but she said nothing.

Taka shook his head. "We can't handle this on our own, particularly if the old man is being kept prisoner, and I don't have any place to take her where they can't find her. She needs to stay with you while I get help. Apparently you've saved her life more than once—I can count on you not to let anything happen to her. Just keep your goddamned hands off her."

"I'm not touching her again, I told you." His voice was clipped, emotionless. "You know me, I don't believe in commitments and relationships. I like novelty. I've already had her—I don't need to revisit old territory." He didn't know who he was trying to fool—Taka or Jilly. Or maybe himself.

Taka's eyes narrowed, and Reno braced, ready for him to rush him again, but in the end he just nodded. "I'll let Summer deal with you. In the meantime, you're probably safer if you stay put. I tried to pick up as much intel as I could, and they're not planning on doing anything with you two until they get their hands on me. So you should be safe. Otherwise I expect you to die trying to save her."

"She's too much of a pain in the ass to die," he said, glancing in her direction. She didn't react— she just sat there, silent, waiting.

Ignoring Reno, Taka turned and went over to her, kneeling down beside her, taking her hands in his. Which annoyed Reno—Taka had no business holding her hands. That was his business. It didn't matter that he didn't want anything more to do with her—he just didn't want anyone else touching her, even her brother-in-law. He'd work out the logic of that later. In the meantime, all he could do was seethe.

"Is this all right with you, Ji-chan? I hate leaving you with that miserable son of a bitch, but I don't have any choice. He'll keep you safe—I trust him that much." His voice was gentle, another annoyance. It wasn't Taka's place to be gentle with Jilly, it was his. If he felt like it, he reminded himself.

"Of course, Taka," she said in a voice so calm

Taka knew it was a lie. "Reno's very good at protecting people, and I know you'll do everything you can to help us. I wouldn't want to slow you down."

Taka looked unconvinced. *No shit, Sherlock,* Reno thought, fuming. That calm, reasonable voice was a sure sign that Jilly was about to erupt.

"Maybe I can get you to the American embassy before I—"

"There's no need," she said. "I've put up with him for at least four days by now. I'm not sure— I've kind of lost track of time. I can survive another day or more. Particularly since he's going to keep his hands off me." At that she did look in his direction, her usually warm brown eyes looking flat and dark. She turned back to Taka and smiled with a sweetness she'd never shown him. "We'll be fine."

Taka rose. "I promise you, Ji-chan, that Summer will make him wish he'd never been born."

She even laughed. A fake laugh, but Taka wouldn't know that. Taka didn't know her as well as he did, Reno thought sourly.

"I'm sure she will," she said. "I just wish I could be there to see it. But as soon as we get out of here I'd better head back to L.A. I have to get back to my classes. I'll wait till you two can get away for a visit with my sister."

This was the best news Reno had heard in days. She was removing herself voluntarily. She'd live half a world away and she would no longer be his problem. It wasn't like it was her first one-night stand.

Or maybe it was, given her virginal state. Though she'd never explained what semivirgin meant. Presumably nothing that involved penetration.

And he needed to stop thinking about words like that when he was looking at her.

"I'll be back as soon as I can. No longer than twenty-four hours," Taka promised her.

"And what if they catch you on your way out of here?" Reno said. "You can't be the hero and save the day if you're already strung up."

He didn't like the look Taka gave him. Instead of the hostility that had been bristling from him, he looked faintly amused. And then he answered, "I never get caught, Reno. You should know that. Only if I want to be, and right now I need to be free to roam around. Just keep her safe or I'll rip your throat out."

And he gave him a rough, cousinly embrace, leaving Reno astonished, and then he was gone.

"Holy motherfucker," Reno muttered. "He thinks we're going to die. Taka never hugs me unless something big is happening."

Jilly didn't say anything. She was still sitting on the floor, her knees pulled up to her chest, and she was staring off into nothingness. For a moment he panicked, wondering if she'd retreated back into that crippling state of shock that had possessed her after she blew the man's head off.

Though, maybe it wouldn't be so bad if he had to wake her up the same way he had last time.

No, she wasn't in shock—she'd been conversing normally with Taka. And being told he had no interest in her anymore was a lot milder than blowing someone away.

"Are you going to just sit there and ignore me?" he said, determined not to sound irritated. All his adult life women, annoyed with him, had tried to get to him with the silent treatment, and he was immune to it.

Nothing from her, not even a glance. "Well, that certainly makes things easier," he said, stretching out on the cot and trying not to think about what he'd been doing there a few short hours ago. "Taka may or may not be able to come up with some help. In the meantime, I don't intend to sit around waiting for an execution."

She didn't even blink.

"If Taka can get out of this place, so can I," he continued. "I'm even better at picking locks." Of course there was no doubt that the silent treatment was extremely annoying. He was just able to ignore it, not let it irritate him into showing any emotion. Emotion was what led him into this mess with her in the first place, whether he wanted to admit it or not.

"I'll give it a couple of hours. If Taka doesn't make it out, they'll come for us—no need to keep us hanging around if they've got what they wanted." He glanced up at the bare lightbulb overhead. "I'm going to sleep for a little while. If anything happens you can wake me."

To his astonishment he heard a noise coming from her direction. She didn't have the stubbornness he expected—he thought she'd hold out longer than that. It wasn't speech actually, just a derisive snort.

He lifted his head, but she still wouldn't look at him. "You know, it's your fault we're here. If you hadn't gone racing off like that, I wouldn't have had to follow. We'd both be safe back in that hotel room. Or at least you would—I would have been trying to figure out what was going on."

Silence. "It's nice being able to hear myself think for a change, without interruptions. The question I'm trying to figure out is what they've done with my grandfather, and whether or not he knows how far things have gone. Hell, whether or not he's still alive. But I know he is—he's been my only family, aside from Taka, for most of my life. I'd know if something had happened to him. I'd feel it inside." That sounded a little too sentimental, but it didn't matter since she was ignoring him.

"You know, if I have to choose between keeping you alive and saving my grandfather that I'll go for my grandfather. You'll be on your own. I expect if Hitomi decides to torture you, you can always talk him to death. Unless Azuki gets out of the hospital and decides to go for revenge. He knows he can't kill me, but he won't think twice about blowing your head off. Sorry, didn't mean to remind you."

That was exactly what he'd meant to do, but she still didn't react. She leaned forward to rest her face on her drawn-up knees and she looked very young. Very sexy.

*Snap out of it, Reno!* he told himself. *You've just managed to rid her of any romantic notions. Don't blow it by thinking with your dick again.*

The funny thing was, it wasn't his dick that was giving him trouble. Yeah, for some crazy reason he still wanted to screw her when he should be concentrating on other things. But even more, he wanted her lying on the narrow cot with him, her body crammed up against his, her arms around him, her face against his shoulder, her heart beating against his.

Hell, it was worth a try. "There's room on the cot if you want to be more comfortable."

He got another derisive snort out of her, a small triumph. As long as she was fighting back, he was doing fine. Now he just had to figure a way to get out of there and find his grandfather. Before Hitomi realized that getting rid of all of them would be the smartest and easiest thing to do.

He knew what was stopping Hitomi-san. There were enough members of the *kobun* who had, if not enough loyalty, at least respect and admiration for his grandfather, and they wouldn't let Hitomi dishonor him. But that would only slow Hitomi's hand for so long. And the respect shown Ojiisan wouldn't necessarily translate to his hotheaded grandson and a *gaijin* interloper.

He could wait for Taka to come back. Nothing had ever been able to stop Taka when he set his mind to it, and Reno had no doubt that he'd eventually show up and save the day. It would be the smartest thing he could do; making a move on his own would endanger Jilly and force him to interact with her. If he just stayed stretched out on the cot, forgetting what had happened on there just a short while ago, he'd end up as free as a bird.

He glanced over at her, wondering if she was crying. She wasn't. Her face had an almost eerie calm, an expression that was making him very uneasy. He wasn't foolish enough to think she was taking his instant repudiation well. He was just hoping the silent treatment was her only way of making him pay.

But he had the gloomy feeling that she had something far worse in mind.

# 17

The floor was surprisingly comfortable. In fact, she might even have preferred a bed of nails, but none appeared to be handy. She could always beat her head against the wall until she was bloody and unconscious, but she'd developed a certain fondness for the silk clothing that rat bastard had brought her, and she didn't want to ruin them. She was going to take them back to L.A. with her, have them professionally cleaned, and wear them without a second thought.

He'd known. The whole goddamn time he'd known that she had a crush on him. How could Summer have told him? For that matter, how could Summer have known? It had been embarrassing enough to admit it to herself—she was hardly going to confess her adolescent fantasy to her wise older sister. All she'd done was drop in the occasional question now and then—that shouldn't have been enough to tip Summer off. And she had taken the photos off the disk in Summer's digital camera last time she came to visit. Most of them were of Japan and California and her beautiful husband. But there were a few, just a few, of Reno. And what was the harm in up-loading them into her computer, as well?

Why would they tell him? It wasn't like she was going to be anywhere around him. And it was going to be over and done with as soon as she found a decent-enough lover to carry through with the job. All right, maybe she'd come running to Japan with the subconscious hope of seeing Reno once more, after that initial look two years ago. But really, it was just a remnant of her odd, old/young life.

So she'd walked right into it, with Reno know-ing all the time that she had a sophomoric passion for him. He must have been laughing at her wasted attempts at pretending he annoyed her.

No, that wasn't true. He really did annoy her. He was a smart-aleck pain in the butt, with the emotional availability of a soap dish. And if she had supernatural powers, she'd vaporize him as he lay stretched out on the cot, his long legs dangling over the edge.

So her ridiculous crush on him was gone,

wasn't it? Had vanished the first time he knocked her out. Or it was definitely gone when he pushed her out of the car on the snowy mountain. Maybe not till he tricked her into the capsule hotel and put his hands on her with insulting ease.

Or maybe she'd held out until she'd actually had sex with him. That was enough to get her over him, wasn't it? His ice-cold rejection the next morning?

And yet she'd made love with him on that very cot, only a matter of hours ago, all the while knowing he was a son of a bitch.

Okay, but now she really hated him. No hesitation, no caveats, no doubts. There was no coming back from his final, insulting rejection.

She closed her eyes, envisioning a solid chunk of the ceiling suddenly coming loose and landing square on the cot, squashing him like a bug. It was a lovely thought. Or maybe running him down with a car, so that he stood there, watching her coming and knowing that there was no way he could escape her murderous wrath.

No, she just needed to let go. She'd been used, shamed, insulted, abandoned. And, all right, so she'd had a crush on him. That was over and done with, and wasn't coming back. She knew him too well, knew the way his mind worked. His casual cruelty was a dead giveaway. He had no reason to be so vicious—he could have gotten rid of her just as efficiently without hurting her. And suddenly she knew why.

She pushed herself to her feet, using the wall to brace herself. Reno would have heard her move, but he remained stretched out on the cot with deceptive laziness. He turned his head as she approached, his cool expression wary.

"Are you planning to beat me to death with a purse?" he asked, looking up at her.

It was tempting, but she'd abandoned her makeshift weapon. "Why are you afraid of me?" she said, her voice perfectly calm.

"I'm not afraid of anything or anyone."

"Of course you are. Every time you get close to me you turn around and say something vicious. What do you think I'm going to do, cling so tightly that you can't get free? Do you hate all the women you sleep with?"

He watched her, his eyes wary. "You're not a woman I sleep with," he said. "You're not someone out for a good time with no strings attached, and that's the only thing I'm interested in. The problem is," he said, rising on his elbows to look at her out of his wicked eyes, "you're just too tempting. If I'd just kept my hands off you in the first place, then we wouldn't be having this conversation. But if you'll remember, you asked me. Hell, you demanded. And I've never been the kind of man to resist an offer like that."

"And last night?"

"I was bored."

A knife, she pictured dreamily, stabbing straight into his heart. "It's a great deal too bad that I shot the man who was about to kill you. I should have let him do it and saved myself a great deal of trauma."

"You'd be dead, Ji-chan."

"Then neither of us would have to worry, would we?"

"What do you want from me?" he asked. "Because I can tell you right now, whatever it is, I can't give it."

She was silent, looking down at him. His long body was stretched out on the cot, and his white shirt was unbuttoned. She could see the scrapes and bruises marring his smooth, golden skin, and she hoped each one of them was painful.

"I was going to say I want an apology, but come to think of it, even that's not good enough. I want you to keep away from me. We're related by marriage, but if we make an effort, we won't have to be in the same room with each other once we get out of here."

The slow smile that crossed his face was both ironic and fatalistic. "I don't know if we're getting out of here, Ji-chan. But I promise you, if we survive, you'll never have to see me again. Does that satisfy you?"

"Yes," she said, her voice cool. "Now, get the hell off the cot and let me sleep. I was here first— I claim rights to it."

His soft laugh was as irritatingly seductive as always. Why didn't he have a light, breathy voice? Why was his voice, whether he spoke English or Japanese, so distressingly deep and warm? Asshole.

He rose, and she backed away to make sure he wouldn't brush against her. The instinctive retreat seemed to amuse him even more, and she wondered what would happen if she kicked him.

She knew what would happen. He'd already warned her—if she hit him again, he'd hit her back. If she kicked him, he'd put his hands on her, and then all hell would break loose. Because he wouldn't hurt her, no matter how much he threatened. He'd put his hands on her, and then she'd be lost again.

"Thank you," she said in a clipped voice, moving around him to stretch out on the cot. It was sheer will that kept her there, trying to look relaxed.

It was warm. Warm from his body. It was like a virtual embrace, his heat to the cot to her body. Goddamn it. And if she closed her eyes, it was even worse.

And then he was standing over the cot, and she froze, waiting for him to touch her. Why the hell had she demanded the cot? Was she asking for trouble? Was she wanting him to start this all over again?

"Here," he said, yanking something from under her feet. It was the thin blanket they'd left, and he covered her with it, careful not to let his hand touch her. It smelled like sex, it smelled of almond soap and Reno, and she wanted to throw it back at him.

But that would be letting him know she was still vulnerable. And she wasn't. She was going to lie here and go to sleep and wait for her brother-in-law to rescue her.

He heard the noise before she did. She'd been drifting off into an uncomfortable sleep when Reno moved, immediately on full alert.

"What's happening?" she said sleepily, as she heard the noise outside the door.

"I think they decided not to wait," Reno said in a grim voice. He grabbed her hand and hauled her out of the bed, and she didn't protest. "Stay behind me," he said.

The door slammed open and four young *yakuza* pushed in the room, and Jilly had a sinking feeling in the pit of her stomach. These were like *yakuza*-boy, not the exquisitely polite Hitomi-san. These were trouble.

It took her a minute to even begin to understand the conversation. It was in Japanese, and the intruders spoke with a strange accent, rolling their *R*'s, using phrases Jilly hadn't learned in her intensive study. Reno was answering them the same way, even with the rolling of the *R*'s. And then the words began to make sense.

The leader, a slightly older gangster with a high shellacked pompadour and sour expression, was the spokesman. "We're taking her," he said. "Hitomi-san has decided she has no use. Your grandfather has barricaded himself in his rooms, and she will be of no help in getting to him. We have orders to kill her, show her body to the *oyabun* to prove we will stop at nothing, and then dispose of her body."

"That would be a mistake," Reno said, his voice calm and almost bored—as if he were discussing different ways to cook fish. "The Americans get very upset if their people meet with trouble in Japan, and this one is a young, pretty girl from a good family. Her face and name will be in newspapers all over the world, and the authorities will not let her disappearance go unnoticed. They will search until they find her."

"We know how to dispose of a body, Shinoda-san," one of the younger men said with a sneer.

"They will look until they find her," Reno said. "And if they don't, they will keep looking. The police, who turn a blind eye to most things, will be on notice. You will make life much more complicated for Hitomi-san and the family."

"Hitomi-san's orders are clear. If your grandfather is presented with the dead body of the *gaijin* he will realize he is defeated." Two of the men started approaching, and Reno grabbed Jilly's arm and pulled her tight behind him.

"You can't take her," he said. "If you need a dead body you can take me instead."

"We could do that," the spokesman said, raising his gun.

"Matsumoto-san!" Hitomi's voice was sharp as he appeared in the doorway. "What is taking you so long?"

"He's being difficult, trying to save the life of the girl by offering his own." The tone of his voice expressed his opinion of such idiotic behavior.

Hitomi looked at Reno, shaking his head. "You've spent too much time among *gaijins*,

Hiromasa-san. You're forgetting that for each one lost, there are a dozen to take their place."

"If you want to kill her, you have to go through me first."

"So romantic," Hitomi said with a sigh. "It must be the tainted blood of your American mother. We can work out a compromise. Your grandfather has a small group guarding him, and we can't break in. I've already lost seven men trying. I had planned to drop the body of the girl in front of the door with the assurance that you and his great-nephew would be the next, but I am flexible. You can take the girl and get him to open the door."

"And then what?"

"And then we discuss the future with your esteemed grandfather. His ways are old-fashioned and impractical. It's a new world, and he's keeping his men from earning the kind of money they deserve. It's time for him to step down and a new order to take his place."

"And you will run that new order," Reno said. "I don't think my grandfather will agree."

"I don't think your grandfather will have any choice, once he fully understands the situation. We can do this the easy way or the hard way, Hiromasa-san. It's up to you. This way you might have a choice of saving your *gaijin* girlfriend. Otherwise you'll both be dead."

"I thought you were waiting to get your hands on Taka," Reno said.

Hitomi's smile was chilling. "We have him, Hiromasa-san. My men found him outside the compound. He hasn't been talking, but he's not going to be able to come to your rescue. You're on your own."

Reno's body didn't move, but she could feel the momentary shiver that hit him. Was it defeat, despair? Disbelief?

"Then it would appear we have no choice. I'll get grandfather to open the door for you, if you let the girl go."

"Not until we are able to talk to your grandfather."

"And what makes you think I believe that you'll let her go?"

"We are all honorable men, are we not?" Hitomi said with an expansive gesture. "We do not kill for pleasure, but rather for the greater good. If we do not need the *gaijin's* death, then she will go free."

And if Reno believed that, he was more gullible than he appeared to be.

"Yes," he said. "But let me explain the situation to her in private. You know she can be impulsive. I want to make sure she behaves herself. I wouldn't want her shot accidentally."

"Nor would I," Hitomi said with a small bow.

Reno bowed back, and Jilly wanted to scream. They were talking about murder and betrayal and they were fucking bowing to each other?

"I'll give you five minutes," Hitomi-san said. "If it takes any longer, we'll shoot her, anyway."

The men left, leaving the door unlocked, and Reno turned to her, grabbing her arms and speaking in low, hurried English. "We're in trouble. They've got Taka, and they want me to get my grandfather to open the door so they can talk to him. They claim you're worthless to them, but even so, when I give the signal I need you to fall to the ground, roll into the nearest corner you can and pray."

"You want me to what?"

"You heard me. I tried to get them to take you as bait," he said, trying for his lazy smirk. "I thought they could rough you up and drop you outside his door and then Ojiisan would have to negotiate, but they insisted on taking me instead."

She looked at him for a long, endless moment. "Reno-chan," she said gently in Japanese, "I understood almost every word you were saying."

He'd been cool, almost off-hand, but now he looked shattered. "Your Japanese isn't that good."

"It's good enough to know you offered to die for me. Why?"

"Don't complicate my life further, Ji-chan. It's family honor. They say they've got Taka, and my grandfather's life is at stake...."

"You don't think they have Taka?"

"Not necessarily. But we can't count on him showing up. Right now it's up to me, and I don't need difficult questions or you to distract me."

And then it hit her, with blinding simplicity. He cared about her. It was the last thing he wanted, the reason why he kept pushing her away. But the bottom line was, he cared about her, whether he would admit it or not.

"What are you smiling for?" he demanded, indignant. "We'll probably be dead in another hour."

"Yes," she said, leaning forward and kissing him lightly on his beautiful mouth. He was too astonished to duck. "But you love me."

"Don't be insane...."

"We're going to die, Reno. You shouldn't die with a lie on your lips. You care about me, and you don't want to. It's that simple and so obvious I should have realized it before. You love me."

"And you've lost your mind," he said, exasperated. "I don't blame you—you aren't used to this kind of life. If we somehow manage to survive, you'll realize how ridiculous that is."

"And if we don't survive?" she asked, surprisingly calm and happy.

"Then you can die believing I love you," he snapped. "In the meantime, keep your head down." He turned and started for the door, keeping a hold of her hand, and then, at the very last minute he stopped, turning back.

"I don't love you," he said. And he pulled her into his arms and kissed her, a kiss of passion and desperation, a kiss of deep currents and longing. "I don't love you," he said again.

"Of course you don't," she murmured happily. And she followed him out the door, into the lion's den.

# 18

Hitomi-san and his small army were waiting in the hallway with surprising patience. Jilly had long ago lost track of what day or what time it was; the interior corridors of the old warehouse didn't give her a clue, and she suspected that the *yakuza* didn't keep regular hours. It felt like the black side of midnight, or the approach of a dark, rainy dawn. It was a time when people were murdered, and babies were born. And as far as she knew, no one was pregnant.

They trudged through the dark corridors, and Reno still kept her hand tight in his. As long as he held on, they weren't going to die, she told herself. If he let go, anything could happen.

The *oyabun*'s rooms were on the top floor of the warehouse. For some reason Jilly had thought they'd be taken back to the room where she'd first met him, but the black-lacquered doors were different from the red ones of the throne room.

Two armed men were stationed outside the door. They were older, and when Hitomi approached them they blocked the way, even as they bowed politely. "The *oyabun* is not receiving."

"The *oyabun* will receive me. I have his grandson and his *gaijin* girlfriend, and I'll cut both their throats if he doesn't agree to talk with me."

The guard didn't blink. Now that Jilly had a chance to look at him she realized he was very old, maybe as old as Ojiisan himself, and his companion wasn't much younger, whereas Hitomi's men were all in their twenties and thirties. Even Hitomi had to be in his forties at the most. The elderly *yakuza* pulled a cell phone from his pocket, and to Jilly's astonishment it was decorated with tiny charms hanging off it, just like a Japanese schoolgirl's. The man punched in a text message, then folded his arms and waited.

Hitomi-san stood there, seemingly peaceful, while a skinny young man beside him began cleaning his fingernails with a very large knife. The knife that was supposed to slash their throats? She only hoped it was sharp and fast.

Reno must have sensed her tension, because he squeezed her hand, a small gesture of reassurance that was so unlike her bad-boy Reno that she was even more convinced they were going to die. She only hoped they killed her first. She really didn't want to see Reno die, his red blood mixing with his flame-red hair on the cement floor.

The older *yakuza* picked up his phone and squinted at the screen. He moved it closer to his eyes, then farther away, and Hitomi's patience seemed to be slipping, as evidenced from the tapping of his foot on the floor. Finally, the elderly guard reached into his pocket and pulled out a pair of horn-rimmed glasses and set them on his nose. Then he took them off again, pulling a handkerchief from his pocket and wiping the lenses. She felt a faint tremor run through Reno, and if it weren't an impossibility, she would have thought he was laughing.

Finally the old man seemed able to read the screen. "The *oyabun* is ready to receive you," he said, opening the door behind him. "Follow me."

A gesture from the knife-wielding *yakuza* made it clear they were to proceed. Maybe as a human shield—they couldn't shoot Hitomi if Reno and a *gaijin* stood between them. Could they?

She almost couldn't believe the suite of rooms belonged in the warehouse. The carpeting was thick beneath her feet, and she realized that everyone—assassin, guard and gangster alike—was taking off their shoes. She kicked off her sneakers, and her toes sank into the thick plush. It was white—the blood would make a terrible mess.

The furniture was white leather with black accents, the paintings on the wall were modern and abstract. There were at least a dozen men lined up against the far wall, all of them elderly, dressed in dark suits, their hands clasped in front of them. She wondered how many fingers they had among them.

In the middle sat the *oyabun*. Reno's grandfather looked even more tiny than he had three days ago...or was it four? He seemed to have shrunk, and the lines in his face were set into even deeper grooves as he surveyed the newcomers. Kobayashi's massive form was directly behind him, a watchful presence.

Hitomi-san moved forward, past Reno and Jilly, and gave Ojiisan a deep bow, one that might have denoted humility if he weren't trying to overthrow the old man.

"Oyabun," he said, "we have a great many things to talk about."

"I fail to see it, Hitomi-san. You're a cheap gangster with no honor or values. I have nothing to say to you."

Hitomi straightened, and his face showed no emotion whatsoever. "You have no choice in the matter, Oyabun. We have matters to discuss, and if you refuse, we must use force. I don't think you want to see your grandson die before your eyes."

"I will if I must. He's been raised to live and die with honor. A concept that must be strange to you." Even in Japanese, the old man's tones were withering.

"You live in the past, old man," Hitomi said, dropping his attempt at courtesy. "Your men are sick of it. You've denied them opportunities that would enrich them and their families. You've betrayed your *kobun* by your old-fashioned ways."

"Because I refuse to get in the drug trade, Hitomi-san? Because I find intimidation and the murder of innocent people to be a betrayal of all our organization has stood for? We are one of the oldest families, and we have always looked out for the welfare of the common people."

"Oh, cut the Robin Hood crap," Hitomi said, and even Reno was startled. "The *yakuza* haven't been the protector of the average family since before the war. The power is being taken by gangs like the Yamaguchi-gumi and other *gurentai*. There is no room for old-fashioned *bakuto*—the world has changed, and the *yakuza* has changed with it."

"I have not changed," the *oyabun* said with great dignity. "And I will not. Nor will my men."

"You mean, the old men who still listen to you? Their time is past. The young men have allied themselves with me, and we will take over the running of the organization. You will be treated with the honor and respect owed to our elders, but you will no longer be able to tell them what they can do."

The old man didn't look impressed. "And my grandson and his friend? And my nephew, Takashi?"

"Your grandson and nephew will have a choice. They can follow me, pledge their loyalty to the new order, or they can die."

"Fuck you," Reno said in English. The phrase was universal, and Hitomi shot him a cool look.

"Behave yourself, Grandson," the old man said calmly. "I believe Hitomi-san has the controlling hand today."

"And you think he means a word of what he says? Even if I wanted to be a part of his gangster army, it would do no good—he'll see to our deaths the first chance he gets."

"So little trust," Hitomi-san said sadly. "The girl, however, is a problem."

"You could let her go," the old man suggested in that calm, controlled voice. "She is no harm to you. She doesn't understand a word you're saying, and even if she could get someone to listen to her, they'd never believe her. Just drop her off at the American consulate and she will no longer be a problem to you."

"Your grandson tried to convince me of the same thing. I'm afraid I am too thorough a man to let small details slip my attention. I can promise we can make her death fast. Miyavi-san is very experienced."

The man with the knife looked up and grinned, an evil expression that was far too cheerful. Jilly moved a little farther behind Reno, and she couldn't help it; she pressed up against him, needing to feel him, his warmth and strength. They weren't getting out of this, she knew it. And damn, her mother was going to be pissed.

"Kobayashi-san," Hitomi said, and the huge man moved to the center of the room. "Now is the time to show your loyalty to the new order. Hiromasa-san is correct—we would never be able to trust him. I want you to hold him while Miyavi-san finishes the *gaijin*. If he struggles, kill him."

Jilly waited for Reno's grandfather to protest, but the old man said nothing, bowing his head and putting his hands together. Reno's hand tightened for a moment, and then released her; instead, he pulled her arms around his waist so that she was plastered up against his back, and his grip was unbreakable.

"Touch her and you die," Reno snarled.

"And how are you going to manage that, young hothead? You have no weapons, you're outnumbered. Miyavi, Kobayashi, do as I ordered. Unless the *oyabun* has something to say."

Hidden behind Reno's back she could barely see a thing, but the old man gave a slight, imperceptible nod that might have been a reprieve. Except that the nasty-looking Miyavi kept coming, and Kobayashi was approaching, as well, and she and Reno were both going to die.

With a swift push, she went flying backward, into Kobayashi's waiting arms, and Reno kicked out in a blur of motion, knocking the knife out of Miyavi's hand, another kick landing to the side of his head. He collapsed in a boneless heap, and Reno scooped up the knife, grabbed Hitomi and pressed it against his throat before the rest of his men could make a move.

She didn't understand his barked-out words, but the message was clear. Come any closer and Hitomi would die.

Kobayashi released her, setting her carefully

aside, and moved back to the *oyabun,* his head lowered in an attitude of obedience.

"You should never underestimate the house of Shinoda, Hitomi-san," the old man said in a quiet, commanding voice. "We don't take well to threats, whether our honor or our women are threatened."

She understood that statement well enough, and so did Reno, and she half expected him to push Hitomi away and announce to the world and to her that she wasn't his woman. But Reno didn't move, his face a blank mask of rage, and there was a thin trickle of blood beginning to slide down Hitomi's neck and onto his expensive shirt.

"It won't do any good to kill me, Oyabun," Hitomi said in a cool voice. "There will be others who follow me. Your time is done—the world has changed and there's no place for you in it. Hiromasa will only have time to kill me before my men open fire, and then you will all be dead, and…"

She saw the movement of the *oyabun*'s hand. Even Ojiisan was missing parts of his fingers, and she watched with stunned detachment as he brought his hand down. And then everything was a blur of noise and fire and blood—moving so swiftly her brain couldn't comprehend it, moving so slowly every moment was etched on her eyeballs.

Reno drew the knife across Hitomi's throat, slicing deep, letting the body drop as he jumped out of the way as the *oyabun*'s old men opened fire.

Someone pushed her down on the floor—she wasn't sure who, and she lay facedown on the thick white carpeting, her arms over her head, trying to shut out the noise, the smell of death that filled the air with such a miasma of dark evil that she wanted to choke. She thought she was screaming, but noise thundered around her and she may have only whimpered.

The gunfire suddenly stopped, and all was eerily silent. Someone was on top of her, and when he released her, she didn't move, didn't want to see. From a distance she heard Reno's voice, talking to his grandfather in frantic Japanese.

If she just stayed like this, she wouldn't have to see, she told herself. The guns had stopped— no one was likely to shoot her at this point. If she didn't move…

"Get up," Taka said, and the sound of his voice was enough of a surprise that she lifted her head. "We need to get the hell out of here."

The room looked like a scene out of *Hamlet*. Bodies were everywhere, staining the deep white carpet with dark pools of blood. She let Taka pull her to her feet, looking for Reno amid the carnage.

He was kneeling by his grandfather, who lay across the leather couch, held in loving arms by the loyal Kobayashi, who had tears streaming down his broad face. The old man's suit was dark with blood, but there was a peaceful expression on his face, and Reno leaned forward to catch his soft words, nodding and answering just as quietly.

"We need to get out of here, Jilly," Taka said, impatient. "The rest of Hitomi's men are on their way—I blocked the elevator but it won't take them that long to make it up the stairs."

"But Reno…" she protested.

Reno must have heard her voice. He looked away from his grandfather, into her eyes, and it was the face of a stranger. A dealer of death.

"Take her," he said.

Taka clamped his hand on her arm, but instead of dragging her away, he took her over to face the dying *oyabun*. He bowed low, and out of instinct Jilly did, too, her eyes filling with tears.

The old man smiled faintly, and he murmured something, but it was too soft for Jilly to hear or understand, and then Taka was pulling her away, and there were tears running down his face, her cool, emotionless brother-in-law.

And then she didn't have time to think, or to cry, or even to breathe, as Taka dragged her through the back of the room, out into a darkened corridor.

She didn't waste her time arguing. She could smell the chemical odor of gasoline and something else, and she knew, even without asking, what was going to happen. There was no pulling away from Taka's iron grip, and when they reached the bottom of the endless flights of stairs and crashed out into the bright winter dawn light, she collapsed in the dirty, packed snow.

"Reno...?" She was gasping for breath. "You left him behind!"

"Summer would kill me if anything happened to you," Taka said, not even winded. "And Reno can take care of himself. We've got to keep moving. The place is going to blow. Uncle had charges set all over the place."

"Why?"

"So there'd be no chance Hitomi's men would take over the family. Ojiisan's men were honored to die with him."

"Not Reno!" She scrambled to her feet, ready to race back to the building, but Taka caught her easily.

"Reno can take care of himself," he said again.

"In the meantime, you need to get the hell out of here. There are going to be a lot of questions, and I don't want you around to answer them."

"Please, Taka," she begged as he dragged her away from the building. "Let's just go back and make certain."

"You'll forget all this," Taka said. "This was just a short nightmare that's no part of real life." There was a small gray car outside on the street, and he pushed her into it. She had no idea whether he'd brought it or stolen it, spur-of-the-moment. All she could see was the compound, the smoke curling out of the upper-floor windows.

They were three blocks away when the explosion hit, so powerful that the car skidded beneath the shock. The streets were almost deserted—Taka didn't slow down, and his face was grim.

"You can't just drive away!" she cried.

"Yes, I can." He didn't even blink when the fire engines raced past them, heading for the warehouse. His face was set in stone, and if she couldn't see the marks of tears on his face, she'd have thought he was without feeling.

"What if he dies?" she whispered.

"Reno has nine lives. At most he's used up six of them."

"And Ojiisan?"

"He's gone," Taka said, his voice flat and emotionless. "You were honored to have even been in his presence."

"But what did he say to me? What were he and Reno talking about?"

"I couldn't hear," Taka said, but she didn't believe him. "And it no longer matters—it's over. Next time maybe you'll listen to your sister when she tells you not to visit. We'll come to you."

She slumped back in the seat, closing her eyes. At that moment she wanted to strangle her intractable brother-in-law, but there was nothing she could do. She was going home, bloody and bruised but in one piece, and sooner or later she'd get over it. Get over Reno. And move on with life.

In the meantime, all she could do was something she seldom considered. She prayed.

Reno closed the old man's eyes, then took a step back. Kobayashi still held him, and he was sobbing, his great chest shaking with it. "We need to leave, Kobayashi-san," he said patiently. "He wouldn't have wanted you to die with the rest of them."

"My place is here," he said with great dignity. "I served him in life. I will not abandon him in death."

Reno nodded. He was running out of time, and his grandfather's words still echoed in his brain, his heart. "This is a good death for him, Kobayashi-san. An honorable death. He would want you to go on. You have more to do in this life."

Kobayashi didn't answer, and Reno gave up. Once he'd left the world of sumo, Kobayashi's life had been tied up with Reno's grandfather—without him there would be nothing. If he chose to die with Ojiisan, then that was his choice.

Once Reno started moving, he acted quickly. He was sticky with Hitomi's blood—Jilly had seen him kill the man. That should have finished things once and for all, and he could breathe a sigh of relief. If Taka did what he knew he should do, Reno would never see her again. It was a time of endings. A time of new beginnings.

He set the charge the moment before he slid out the first-floor window. The place would go quickly—there'd be no escape for Hitomi's soldiers. They would all die, and the ancient organization would disappear, but its name and reputation would stay intact. An honorable anachronism in the world of brutality.

He was just past the outer wall when the place exploded, and he didn't look back. Jilly and Taka would be long gone, and he had the pieces of a life to pull back together.

A light snow began to fall again, covering the dirty slush that filled the gutters. He walked on, his cowboy boots making a crisp noise on the empty sidewalks, as he disappeared into the early-morning light.

# 19

"You need to get over this, darling." Lianne Lovitz came to stand over her recalcitrant daughter, clearly annoyed. "You can't spend weeks moping. It depresses me, and you know how I hate to get depressed. Besides, the semester started last week, and you only got as far as the driveway before turning around and heading straight back to bed. You need to snap out of it."

Jilly looked up. She had managed to drag her sorry ass out into the fresh air, and she lay on a chaise by the heart-shaped pool, covered from head to toe in baggy jeans and an oversize T-shirt, sunglasses firmly on her nose. Not that the air was that fresh, of course. First there was the smog, second there were the brush fires currently scouring the canyons. The scent of smoke lingered on the air like a nervous memory.

Lianne, of course, was dressed in the skimpiest excuse for a bikini, which looked magnificent on her perfectly toned and sculpted body. Jilly tilted her head, surveying her mother. She had no idea how old Lianne actually was; she'd told so many lies she probably didn't know herself. The finest surgeons in the world continued to ensure that Lianne was perfect, particularly if one didn't look too closely or expect an actual expression to mar her beautiful face.

"Snap out of what?" Jilly said in an emotionless voice. "I'm absolutely fine. I was thinking I may take the semester off. I'm just not in the mood for Mesopotamian archaeology."

Lianne shuddered dramatically. "I can't imagine why you ever could have been. If you want to stay home, that's fine with me, but you need to at least pretend to be happy."

"Why?"

"Because I need happy people around me. I'm much too sensitive to other people's feelings, and it upsets me to be surrounded by unhappiness." Lianne took a sip of her Perrier. "Really, darling, I don't know how you can be so thoughtless. You know how I am."

"Yes, Lianne. I know how you are," Jilly said listlessly.

"You need drugs," Lianne said, sitting down

beside her on the adjoining chaise. Lianne was five foot three inches of perfection, and from the time Jilly turned twelve and begun to tower over her mother, she'd always felt like an awkward, hulking giant. "Some kind of antidepression thing. It will fix you right up—I'll have Dr. Medellin prescribe some Prozac and some tranquilizers." She wrinkled her perfect nose, possibly the only feature on her beautiful face that hadn't been tampered with. "Perhaps some of the new diet pills. I've heard they do wonders."

"I'm not fat, Lianne," Jilly said, unable to summon her usual outrage.

"There's no such thing as being too rich or too thin," Lianne replied. "Wouldn't you be happier in a size four?"

"I'm almost six feet tall, Lianne. I'd look like a scarecrow." Though, come to think of it, that wasn't a bad idea. Apart from her nightly quart of Ben and Jerry's, she hadn't had much appetite. Maybe she ought to just stop eating entirely, so that she could waste away—and then he'd be very very sorry.

Not that she was thinking of him. She didn't even know who "him" was. She was just tired, and her mother was being even more annoying than usual.

"But clothes hang so much better when you're a little bit underweight," Lianne said.

"How would you know—you never wear any clothes," Jilly grumbled.

Lianne's hurt silence was evocative enough. Jilly should have known she wouldn't let it go at that. "You've been spending much too much time with your half sister. Summer was always unsympathetic, and now that you've come back from Japan you've been almost as bad. God knows why you wanted to go there, anyway—it's filled with foreigners. Your sister may have been crazy enough to move there, but you're my brilliant daughter. You should know better."

"Summer's got a Ph.D. in art history, Lianne."

"Yes, but it took her the normal amount of time to earn it. And she didn't even get into Harvard— she had to make do with Stanford."

Jilly opened her mouth to protest, then shut it again. She just didn't have the energy.

"I'll make an appointment with Dr. Medellin," Lianne said. "And with my nutritionist, and my astrologer and my aesthetician."

Jilly stayed silent. Lianne was like a wave washing over her—all she had to do was keep her footing and she'd ebb away soon enough.

But Lianne hadn't moved. She was looking at

Jilly more closely than she usually did. "Your sister tells me you fell in love."

"Summer's crazy. It's pregnancy hormones."

Lianne shuddered. "Don't remind me. I refuse to be a grandmother. I'm much too young."

At another time Jilly would have easily distracted her—Lianne was always much more interested in discussing her own issues than anyone else's, but even in the interest of self-preservation she couldn't rouse herself. All she could do was run.

"I'm going out," she said, pushing off the chaise.

Lianne brightened. "Well, that's a good thing. Maybe you'll stop moping. Are you going shopping?"

"Yes."

"Where? I could come with you."

"Little Tokyo."

Lianne made a face. "I swear to God the Japanese have been nothing but trouble in my life. First there was Summer's nanny, who turned her against me, then there was that crazy cult leader, then your sister marries someone who has all the warmth of Dracula, and now you come back from Tokyo looking like someone ate your dog. They eat dogs over there, you know."

"No, they don't, Lianne."

"I think we should go to Paris. We could get you some new clothes."

"No, Lianne."

"Then why are you going to Little Tokyo? Why drive into the heart of downtown L.A. when you're depressed? It's not going to cheer you up. What's there that you can't find just as easily in Beverly Hills?"

There must be some way to shut her mother up. "A Hello Kitty vibrator?" she suggested.

Lianne shrieked—Jilly wouldn't be surprised if she put her hands over her ears and began singing loudly to drown out the sound of her voice. Typical Lianne—for all her lack of modesty with her own knockout body, she was ridiculously prudish then it came to her daughter's sexuality. Then again, it might have been something as simple as not wanting to be old enough to have daughters who were sexually active. Or inactive, as Jilly intended to be for the rest of her life.

"I'm kidding, Lianne. I'm just going to the grocery store."

"For heaven's sake, why? We have a cook."

"I want octopus."

It was enough to silence her. Jilly could feel her mother's eyes on her as she headed for the ten-car garage, but she didn't look back. Despite the bright Southern California sun she felt like ice, and she wasn't going to let anything break through her cool, unearthly calm.

Driving in L.A. traffic was enough to keep her mind off other problems, but the moment she parked she realized she'd made a huge mistake. No one had flame-red hair and red teardrop tattoos. There were no tall, leather-clad bad boys lurking around every corner. There was nothing for her here.

There was, however, food. She found her sister's favorite restaurant, not much more than a diner, and ordered miso soup and *oyakudon*. Her mother was right about one thing, she had to get it together. The longer she stayed inside and moped the worse things got. And even Ben & Jerry's wasn't doing it for her.

She wandered through the neighborhood, past the Otani Hotel, through the Zen garden. It didn't feel like Tokyo—there wasn't the buzz, the energy. There wasn't Reno.

And God knows what she was looking for. She needed to look forward, not into the past. She needed to get over it, get back to school, start a new life.

She glanced up at the replica of the old Japanese fire tower. She'd spent a fair amount of time in Little Tokyo with Summer when she was growing up, but everything looked and felt different now. Later, after a lot of time had passed, she was going to have to go back to Japan, get outside the city, see things. She'd come back with the impression of noise and light and blood. And sex.

There had to be a lot more to it. There had to be some kind of Zen serenity if she looked for it.

It was getting dark, and the evening rush-hour traffic had picked up. It was going to take her forever to get home, assuming that was where she wanted to go. She stood patiently at the intersection with a crowd of people, waiting for the light to change, when someone bumped into her. Hard. Hard enough to make her lose her balance, and she went sprawling forward, directly in front of the rush of traffic.

She heard someone scream, and she tried to scramble to her feet as the headlights bore down on her, and then there was the slam of brakes, horns honking, as someone dragged her out of the road, onto the sidewalk, and she half expected to look up and see Reno.

"You should be more careful, miss," the tired-looking man said. "You could have been killed."

"Thank you," she said shakily, rising to her feet. The light had changed, and people were moving forward, though there were a few curious glances in her direction. She followed them, heading for the parking lot, her hands and knees scraped from her fall.

It wasn't until she got back in her car that reaction set in. She was shaking, badly, and she leaned back, closed her eyes and took deep, calming breaths.

It had almost felt as if someone had shoved her. But that was impossible—it had to be post-traumatic stress or something ridiculous like that. Or maybe, just maybe, she'd done it on her own, unconsciously.

No, that was ridiculous. She was over him, completely, and she wasn't going to go wandering out in traffic like some pathetic loser. She was getting on with her life.

She pulled out into the evening traffic, heading up toward the Hollywood Hills. Maybe her mother was right, maybe she needed Paris. Someplace where she wouldn't keep looking for Reno around every corner, where she wouldn't imagine his eyes on her wherever she went.

She wiped the tears off her face as she sped up. She'd never been one to cry—it wasn't her style. She'd grown up tough and calm and capable. When your own mother was a spoiled child, someone had to be the grown-up—and when Summer wasn't around, the task had fallen to her.

If Lianne was joking about Paris, which she might very well be, then she could go to England, visit Peter and Genevieve Madsen. The countryside in Wiltshire was a good place to heal. She'd watched her sister make peace with her life there—she could probably do the same.

But her sister had had a happy ending. Taka had come for her in the end. That wasn't going to happen with Reno. No one was coming for her. There was no happy ending.

The truck came out of nowhere. It slammed into her lightweight Honda, pushing her toward the side of the road, to the edge of the overpass. She stomped on the brakes, trying desperately to steer, but the car was still moving, and she knew she was going to die. Her car was going to tumble over the bridge and land on the freeway below in a heap of twisted metal, and probably burst into flames, as well…and then the air bag exploded, the car slammed to a halt and everything went black.

For Reno the decision had been simple enough. Cleaning up the mess left by the destruction of the compound and the organization was a major undertaking, and there was no way both of them could head to L.A. Taka's wife was pregnant, and the safety of his sister-in-law was a matter of family honor. Reno was the only one who could possibly go.

That didn't mean he was happy about it. He needed time and distance for Jilly Lovitz to fade into an uncomfortable memory, and it was taking more of both than he would have liked.

He couldn't even screw her out of his system. He'd gone out prowling a couple of times, looking for fast, satisfying sex with one of his old girlfriends, and ended up coming home alone. He couldn't even jerk off—he kept seeing Jilly, feeling Jilly. It was no wonder he was a hypersensitive bundle of nerves, snapping at everyone.

And really, flying to L.A. was probably just a case of overreacting. There was no one left alive who could possibly want to hurt her, and both he and Taka would be more obvious targets. Taka's intel had to be faulty, even if he got it directly from Peter Madsen.

According to Peter's sources, someone had been watching the Lovitz mansion, following Jilly the few times she left the house. Which brought up any number of questions. Were they after Jilly's father, whose financial dealings were definitely shady? Ralph Lovitz was a financier, a fancy term for an upper-class robber baron. Were they after Jilly's bat-brained mother, who'd almost gotten both her daughters killed a couple of years ago when she joined a doomsday cult? The Lovitzes could have acquired any number of enemies, even with their hedonistic L.A. lifestyle. Or were they after Jilly—and who on earth could want to hurt her? She'd only been a peripheral complication with Hitomi and his grandfather, and everyone involved in that was dead, the family disbanded. Maybe it was an old boyfriend, except that she hadn't had boyfriends. All he'd had to do was kiss her to know that she'd had a ridiculously small amount of experience.

Another question loomed. Why wasn't she leaving her parents' mansion in the Hollywood Hills? Shouldn't she be back at school by now, getting on with her life? She wasn't the kind of woman to mope around; he'd made it clear that he had nothing for her, and she'd left without argument. She was a practical young woman—she'd be completely over him. Hell, she was probably doing a better job of it than he was.

Not that he was having a problem. Hell, no. He'd known from the very beginning that she was trouble, and he'd done his best to keep her at arm's length. So his resolve had faltered a couple of times, and he'd managed to enjoy himself a little too much. So what? It was over, ancient history.

But if someone was actually watching her, trailing her, then he needed to make certain she wasn't in any danger. Reason stood that there was no one left alive who should want to hurt her.

But he was going to have to make sure.

He couldn't sleep on the flight across the Pacific, as nervous as a cat. The other members of first class weren't particularly happy to be sharing that rarified air with a flame-headed, tattooed punk, but they were too polite to object, and he stretched out in the little pod that they called a first-class bed, trying to tell himself this was a wasted trip. He hadn't had a decent night's sleep in two weeks, not since the compound had blown and Ojiisan had died, and an airplane wasn't going to remedy that. All he had to do was make certain she was safe and head straight back. She would never even know he was there.

Ojiisan owned a great deal of real estate in Southern California—his grandfather always believed in diversifying—and Reno could have chosen his lodging among hotels, condos and even several empty houses in the more expensive sections of the city. Instead, he went for an airport hotel and a rented sedan. In Los Angeles he didn't have the unspoken protection of the police, and he needed the ability the blend in.

The black suit he traveled in was unimpressive—one would have to look closely to see it was a thousand-dollar silk one. He headed into the bathroom of the suite, staring at his reflection for a long moment.

"Only for you, Ji-chan," he muttered. Picking up the pair of scissors, he cut through the waist-length braid, dropping it onto the marble bathroom floor.

By the time he was ready to leave, Reno had disappeared. Hiromasa Shinoda was in his place, the ubiquitous dark glasses shielding the tattoos. He'd considered getting makeup to cover them, but at the last minute gave up. As long as he kept the shades in place no one would see them, and wearing sunglasses day and night wasn't that odd for Southern California.

He tied what was left of his newly dyed black hair in a small tail at the back of his neck. She'd look at him and never recognize him, he thought grimly. He could find out what the fuck was going on and she'd never know.

He was just about to leave his suite when his cell phone vibrated, and he picked it up, staring at the screen. Then he began to swear.

# 20

Everything hurt. Jilly didn't want to open her eyes—the light overhead was too bright and whatever she was lying on was too narrow. She knew where she was without looking—the sounds and smells of a hospital were unmistakable. She wondered idly if she was going to die. The thought wasn't particularly distressing, as long as it didn't hurt too much. She'd dodged a bullet, literally, so many times in the past month that maybe her time had run out. She ought to be able to summon up some kind of emotion, but right at that moment all she wanted to do was breathe. And not hurt.

"Oh, my sweet baby!"

*Shit.* Lianne was there. Jilly opened one eye, very carefully, to look at her mother.

Lianne was exquisite, of course, dressed in a designer evening gown and her diamonds. "Hi,

Ma," she said, her voice a croak. "You didn't have to dress up just for me."

Lianne did her version of bursting into tears. It never involved actual eye-leakage, which would smear her makeup, but Jilly could tell by her expression that she was relatively disturbed.

"I'm fine," Jilly said, not quite convinced of it.

"You never call me 'Ma' anymore!" Lianne sobbed.

"Don't worry about it. I think they've got me on drugs."

"Of course they do. You were in a car accident!"

"I remember that much," she said dryly. "Who hit me?"

"It was a hit-and-run. It was just lucky there were people around to call the police and the ambulance. Your car almost flipped over onto the freeway."

Jilly tried to sit up, but her head started whirling, and she sank back again. "Hit-and-run?" she echoed. Not happy, definitely not happy. An accidental fall in front of oncoming traffic could be explained, a hit-and-run accident within a half an hour of the fall was just a little too coincidental.

Except who would want to hurt her in L.A.? All the bad people were dead, weren't they?

"I want to go home," she said after a moment.

"And I'll take you home, sweetie. Tomorrow. They want to watch you overnight, make sure you're all right. And I have a charity thing that I can't miss, so it works out better this way anyway."

*Of course you do,* Jilly thought, feeling put upon. "What exactly is wrong with me?"

But Lianne had already risen, ready to be off. "You'll have to ask the doctor about that. Apart from a sprained ankle, I think you're just badly shook up, but they want to be sure before discharging you."

"Great," she grumbled. "I survive a car crash and my injuries aren't even interesting. Are you sure? I can't even open one eye."

"It will be fine once the swelling goes down. They're going to move you to a private room in a little while. You just get a good night's rest and I'll have the chauffeur pick you up in the morning."

Jilly closed her eyes again. Whatever they were giving her was knocking the hell out of her. She was just as happy to sleep. "Goodbye, Lianne," she said, dismissing her.

Even with her eyes closed she could feel her mother's hesitation. "Baby, if you want me to…"

Jilly opened her eyes again, ignoring how much her head hurt. "Yes?"

Lianne bit her artificially enhanced lip. "If

you want me to, I can come back with Jenkins in the morning. If you want my company. I can change my plans."

"No need, Lianne," Jilly said, closing her eyes. And a moment later her mother was gone.

She really must be pumped full of drugs, Jilly thought, as tears seeped out from behind her closed eyes. She had no more illusions about Lianne, and hadn't had any since she was twelve years old, maybe even younger. She'd just been feeling so vulnerable recently, and the drugs were breaking down any of her lingering defenses. She hadn't needed a mother in a long time. She needed to remember that.

It was a good thing Summer wasn't around. Jilly had had a hard-enough time convincing her sister that nothing had happened with Reno. Summer had come racing back to California as soon as she heard what had happened. And she knew Jilly far too well. Right now there was nothing she wanted to do more than bawl her head off, and Summer, already skeptical, would jump to conclusions. And really, she wasn't crying about Reno. She was just crying.

She tried to shift on the narrow bed, then realized she had things attached to her. IVs and blood-pressure monitors and even something attached to her finger. Whatever they were giving her was doing a decent job of killing the pain— maybe just a little bit more would knock her out completely. If only she could find a button to push.

A little oblivion, just for the night. Tomorrow she'd deal with her aches and pains, accept the fact that her mother had the emotional attention span of a gnat, and she'd make plans. She wasn't sure what those plans were going to be, but they'd include being far away from here. Far away from anything at all familiar.

Tomorrow she was going to figure out where to run. One thing was certain—she wouldn't come back until she damned well wanted to.

It would serve Reno right if she just disappeared. Not that she knew where he was. Her misery had nothing to do with him, and no one would be likely to tell him she was gone. She'd managed to convince her sister nothing had happened, and Taka would politely ignore anything he'd happened to observe.

No, she would run as far and as fast as she could, and she wouldn't come home until she'd made peace with everything.

It should only take a decade or two.

In the meantime she was going to sleep. If someone would just come in and give her more…

* * *

Reno had been perfectly willing to mug a doctor in order to steal his coat and name tag, but in the end it had been much simpler. The locker room was easily marked, no one was inside, and no one bothered with locks. It was a shame—he was in the mood to hit someone—but he accepted the fact that life was going to give him a break. The coat he found was a little small but it still fit, and it belonged to Dr. Yamada. Perfect. He grabbed a stethoscope and went out to prowl the midnight floors of the hospital.

No one gave him a second glance. He'd grabbed a pair of weak reading glasses—the bottoms of the frames were just enough to distract from his tattoos. They gave him a headache, but that was the least of his problems. Studious Dr. Yamada could move through the floors without anyone giving him a second glance.

It took him almost an hour to find her. She was in a private room at the end of one of the darkened corridors, and he managed to bluff his way past anyone who questioned his presence. The night staff was just as happy to leave him alone, and no one noticed when he slipped inside her room, closing the door silently behind him.

He was half afraid he'd be too late. Whoever

had tried to kill her could have gotten there ahead of him, finished the job. But he looked at her and breathed a sigh of relief.

She looked like hell. She had stitches on her cheekbone, bruises on her pale skin and one eye was swollen shut. She was lying in the hospital bed and she looked very small for such a force of nature.

He grabbed the chair and propped it under the door handle; no one would be coming in without giving him plenty of warning. He took his gun from his belt and set it on the table, looking down at her.

Her one good eye fluttered open, staring up at him. She was drugged up the ass, looking at him with muzzy wonder. "Who are you?"

He'd forgotten his changed appearance. "Your doctor," he said, wishing he'd grabbed an operating mask at the same time.

And then she smiled, a dazed, dreamy smile. "You're Reno," she murmured happily. "I knew you'd come."

She didn't know anything; he could tell from her movements and slurred speech that she was too drugged to realize what was going on. Tomorrow morning she'd think it was just a morphine dream, or whatever it was they were giving her. In the meantime, he was going to give in to temptation, do something he'd never be able to do in real life.

"You're imagining me," he said softly, kicking off his shoes. "I'm just a dream. You won't even remember me in the morning."

For once she didn't argue. Maybe that had been the trick—he should have just kept her drugged and docile while they'd been on the run in Japan. And then he saw the tears begin to slide down her bruised face.

"How badly are you hurt?" He should have checked her chart on the way in, but he'd wanted to get out of sight as quickly as possible.

"Nothing interesting," she said, sounding faintly disgruntled. "Just a sprained ankle and some bruises. It's my heart."

"Your heart?" he echoed, panicked. "Do you have internal injuries…?"

"It's broken," she said, soft, plaintive, the tears still sliding down her face.

He muttered a curse. It was just the drugs talking, but he could feel his own heart twist inside. She lay in the middle of the wide hospital bed, but she was looking very small, and he simply climbed up beside her, pulling her into his arms with exquisite care, not wanting to hurt her any more.

She let out a small sound, and for a moment he thought it was a cry of pain, but then she moved closer, putting her face against his shoulder, and he could feel her crying. "I missed you," she said, her voice muffled.

"I know." He held her gently—she suddenly felt fragile, and he'd almost been too late. He didn't want to think about what would have happened if she'd gone over that bridge. He didn't want to think what would have happened to him. He'd lost Ojiisan, the most important person in his selfish, miserable life. If he'd lost her…

He wasn't going to think about the fact that she wasn't even his to begin with. All he wanted to do was hold her while she cried, hold her while she slept, watch over her for as long as he could.

And then, once she was home and safe, he was going to kill the man who'd done this to her.

He remembered what he'd told her. If he ever felt in danger of falling in love, he'd lie down till the feeling passed. He hadn't been fast enough. She'd gotten to him, the way no other woman had been able to, ruining his life, ruining his sex drive, ruining everything. All he wanted was her, and right now all he wanted was to hold her, take care of her.

He was totally fucked up. But the good thing was, he could get over it. So he was temporarily insane. He had enough strength of will to fight it, to walk away from someone who didn't fit into his plans for his life.

And he would. Once he was sure she was safe.

For now he'd hold her. Stroke her hair, put his lips against her forehead. And not think about anything at all.

"I want some of those drugs you gave me last night," Jilly said brightly. She was dressed in the clothes Jenkins had brought her, ensconced in a wheelchair on her way out of the hospital, and the studious young resident was fiddling with her discharge papers.

"Drugs?" the woman said. "Are you in pain?"

"Not particularly. But I had the best dream of my life." The effect was lingering even now—she could still feel Reno's arms around her, smell the almond soap that he liked, feel the beat of his heart. She felt happy for the first time in weeks, and if it was caused by drugs, she wanted more of them.

"Sorry, we're not responsible for dreams. If you need a prescription for pain, I can give it to you."

"Never mind," Jilly said, defeated. "The next one would probably be a nightmare. So I can leave now, Dr...." For some reason she wanted to call the young woman Dr. Yamada, but considering that she was a Nordic blonde, that name seemed unlikely. Jilly checked her name tag. "Dr. Swensen," she said.

"Just as long as you promise to take it easy for the next few days. You've had a nasty shake-up, and you're lucky you didn't have a head injury."

Jilly wasn't as convinced of that; the hallucination last night had been so real, felt so real. But she wasn't about to say anything—she wanted to get the hell out of there, back to the safety of her family's gated Hollywood mansion. If fate was kind enough to send her the same dream, or maybe even a more sexually active one, then she'd be happy. Otherwise she'd just sleep.

She glanced up once as Jenkins helped her into the backseat of the limo. Her body still hurt—for having no real injuries she was feeling like shit, and she could only see out of one eye. She'd taken a fleeting look at herself in a mirror after the nurse helped her dress, and shuddered. It was a good thing it had only been a dream—she looked like a witch who'd met the wrong end of a broomstick.

The day was dark, ominously so. "Is it going to rain, Jenkins?" They hadn't had rain in weeks, maybe months, according to the KTLA weather report.

"It's the fires, miss. They're looking bad this

year. That's smoke overhead. A good rain might help, but there's none expected."

Jilly tried to summon up a shred of anxiety. "We're not anywhere near the fires, are we?"

"We'll get word if we need to evacuate, miss."

That wasn't the most comforting response he could have come up with, but she wasn't going to worry about it. The chance of the wildfires making it all the way to the Hollywood Hills was unlikely. There was a hot breeze blowing, bringing smoke on the air. It was late for the Santa Ana winds, but the dragon breath had an angry feel to it.

By the time she managed to limp into the house she was ready to collapse, and the sight of her mother waiting for her in the hallway didn't help matters. Until she took a closer look. Lianne was wearing her traveling Armani, and her matched luggage was waiting in the hall.

"You're leaving?" Jilly said, trying to keep the hopeful note out of her voice. The last thing she wanted was Lianne in her nurturing-mother role. Lianne would have thrown herself into it with a vengeance, and it could be really annoying when she did. Right now Jilly just needed peace and quiet, not Lianne hovering.

"Darling, I forgot that I promised I'd meet your

father in Prague. I can always cancel my flight if you want—I hate to leave you here all alone."

Jilly wondered exactly what her mother might do if she asked her to stay. It was almost worth it, just to watch Lianne try to wriggle out of it. "I'll be fine. And I won't be alone—Consuela and Jenkins will be here."

"Well, actually, I hadn't expected you were going to be here. After all, the semester started last week, and I've never known you to skip school in your entire life. I told them they could have the week off. Consuela's already left, and Jenkins and his wife have a vacation planned. The gardening staff will be here, but God only knows if any of them speak English."

Jilly was so used to her mother's casual racism that she didn't rise to the bait. "I'm perfectly capable of being on my own here." She limped into the living room, sinking down on the couch carefully. The room was dark from the smoke-filled sky outside, and she turned on one of the lights. "As long as I have Diet Coke and a television I'll be fine."

"Of course you will. And we have the best security system in the city. Not that there'll be any problem—there never is. Even so, I put in a call to the temp agency and they're sending a couple of people out after the weekend."

"I'll be fine. I don't want strangers wandering around here."

"You need to do this for me, sweetie. I won't have a moment's peace in Prague if I'm worrying about you being home alone."

Jilly resisted the impulse to growl. "Whatever makes you happy, Lianne," she said.

Her mother smiled brightly. "I had Consuela make up some meals for you, and you can have any kind of food in the world delivered. By Monday you'll have company."

"All I intend to do is watch TV and sleep."

Her mother beamed at her. "Oh, and there's one more thing. Just a tiny little favor."

Jilly had infinite patience with her self-absorbed mother, but it was wearing very thin indeed. "Of course," she said, stifling a sigh.

"I was supposed to do an interview with a young man from the *Times*. He wants to hear about the Lovitz Foundation. I thought he might be a nice distraction for you—he's supposed to come by tomorrow afternoon."

"I don't think so…"

"He's young and Asian, sweetie. I thought you might enjoy it. I can always do the interview by phone but you can imagine what a pain that would be with the time difference. You know as much about the foundation as I do, and it might help get you over whoever it was in Tokyo that's made you so mopey."

"He can wait until you get back. I don't need any young Asian men in my life, thank you very much. And nothing happened in Tokyo—I'm just tired."

Lianne managed an ineffectively long-suffering sigh. "It would really set my mind at ease if you…"

"I'm not meeting with your reporter, Lianne," Jilly said in a dangerous voice. "Go to Prague and leave me alone."

Her mother actually pouted, something she did quite effectively with her collagen-enhanced lips. Her mother was the epitome of a trophy wife, married to a man who was twenty-five years older than she was, surgically enhanced to look half her age, with all her energy and attention centered on Ralph Lovitz. She genuinely loved her fourth husband enough to stay with him for the last twenty years, which still amazed Jilly. She had no illusions that either of her parents was particularly faithful, but at least they were discreet, and their affection for each other was undoubtedly real.

"I don't know why you have to be so difficult," Lianne said with just the trace of a whine. "I'm just asking for a little peace of mind."

Jilly had spent most of her adult life protecting Lianne. "You'll have to find it on your own, Lianne," she said wearily, closing her eyes.

She knew her mother stood there for a while, trying to outlast Jilly, but she was no match for her daughter's stubbornness. Jilly waited until she heard the main door shut, until she heard the distant sound of the limousine starting down the long driveway. And then she opened her eyes, grabbed the remote control and turned on *Animal Planet.*

Mindless sex and violence, just what she needed, she thought, stretching out on the over-stuffed sofa to watch the lizards dance. To hell with her mother, to hell with Reno, to hell with everything.

As long as it was her and the lizards, things would be just fine.

# 21

The fires were getting closer. KTLA was covering them with breathless anticipation, and even their usual tongue-in-cheek joviality seemed on the wane. It was late when Jilly dragged herself out of bed, and if anything, she was even more achy. The house was deserted, for maybe the first time in her life. Her mother always kept a skeleton staff on, particularly if her young daughter was at home. But Jilly was a grown-up, and the locked gate was security enough. Who would want to hurt her?

Whoever had shoved her in front of traffic. Whoever had slammed into her with a truck, trying to push her off an overpass, and taken off before anyone could catch him.

She shook herself. Whether she was being paranoid or not, she was safe here. And there was a panic button in the security panel that went directly to the police.

And there was no reason for her to be in any danger. Everything that happened in Japan was resolved—no one would be coming after her. Ojiisan was dead, along with both his men and his enemies. And she'd never been more than a pawn in their entire game—it wasn't as if she had possessed any kind of intrinsic value. She'd been in the way, and as soon as the dust settled, or even before, she'd been sent back home. Apart from a rush visit from her sister and a few phone calls, everyone in Japan had forgotten she existed.

Probably.

She'd been half tempted to call Summer, just to set her mind at ease, but in the end she resisted. Summer would just ask more questions about Reno, then follow it up with a loving lecture on how Reno wasn't even remotely viable as…what? A boyfriend? A lover? Something even more?

She didn't need her sister to tell her that. She didn't need to be reminded. Bad boys, while delicious, weren't for brainiacs like her.

She used her mother's marble shower with the built-in seat, letting the hot water stream down over her. Her body was a mess—her torso was a mass of bruises, and the mark the seat belt had made across her chest was far from attractive. For an accident with "no interesting injuries," it had certainly made her look like shit. Fortunately no one but a doctor was going to see her naked for the rest of her natural life, so she didn't need to worry.

At least the swelling in her eye had gone down, and she could see out of both now. She dressed carefully in loose khakis and a T-shirt, not bothering with a bra; no one was around, just the gardener she'd spotted, lurking among the roses, and it was too much trouble to fasten it.

Then she remembered Reno's reaction to her lack of a bra, and was half tempted to take the trouble.

She had to stop thinking about him. She was seeing him everywhere—she even thought the new Hispanic gardener looked like him, that is if Reno stooped, had short black hair and worked as a gardener. She should have fought harder for drugs—a prescription—at the hospital. Dreams or no, a little oblivion would be a treat.

The windows in her mother's suite didn't open, but she craned her neck, looking at the darkened, smoke-filled sky. It should be safe enough, up here in the Hills. And as Jenkins said, there'd be plenty of warning if the fires came closer; California was very good at getting people evacuated. But even through the air-purified, hermetically sealed house she could smell the smoke in the air, and it made her nervous.

Hell, everything was making her nervous. She made her way down the backstairs to the kitchen, barefoot and hungry, heading straight to the freezer. A little of Ben & Jerry's Chunky Monkey should do the trick. Bananas for fruit and nuts for protein—very healthy. Add chocolate chunks for serenity and she had the perfect meal. She opened the giant freezer, grabbed a pint and headed for the long copper counter that was Consuela's pride and joy, grabbing a spoon and a stool and digging in.

It was early afternoon—she'd almost slept the clock around—yet it was unnaturally dark. She could see the new gardener out there, doing something with the Hawaiian orchids.

She watched him as she ate the ice cream, savoring each bite. If she half closed her eyes she could almost imagine it was Reno. Except that he didn't move with Reno's pantherlike grace, and Reno wouldn't have been caught dead in baggy khakis and a green work shirt. Besides, there was no mistaking Reno's glorious hair.

She pushed away from the counter, heading in to the screening room with her pint of ice cream, now half gone. There were televisions in almost every room of the house, and usually she preferred a room with windows, but the overcast sky was making her edgy, and the gardener was making her think too much about Reno. She needed a nice weepy movie to take her mind off things.

She put the ice cream down on one of the plush reclining seats and began scrolling through the DVDs loaded onto her father's state-of-the-art player. *Titanic* or *Steel Magnolias* would be nice and cathartic—she could sit there and sob and get at least a little bit of relief from the pressure building inside her. *Mommie Dearest* would be another distraction—Lianne's typical abandonment was more of an irritant than ever. Or she could really ask for trouble and watch *Akira Kurosawa*. And imagine Reno's throat impaled with arrows.

No, *Ghostbusters*. That and *Galaxy Quest* were surefire cures for what ailed her. She pushed the buttons, grabbed the rest of her Chunky Monkey and settled in to watch.

She must have fallen asleep again. When she woke the screen was blank, the little bit of ice cream she hadn't devoured was melted in the bottom of the cardboard container, and the doorbell was ringing.

That didn't make sense—no one could get through the security gates to the main door without being buzzed in, and she hadn't been so knocked out that she could have sleepwalked.

She almost dumped the melted ice cream in her lap when she sat up. She set it on the floor, then headed into the main part of the house, turning on lights as she went, trying to brighten the awful smoky gloom that hovered outside.

She wasn't stupid enough to open the front door without checking—she pushed the intercom button, and for a moment panicked. The neatly dressed young man in the video cam looked like Reno.

"Yes?" She couldn't help it—her voice wobbled.

"Miss Lovitz? I'm Lee Hop Sing from the *Los Angeles Times*. Your mother said you'd be willing to talk to me about your recent trip to Japan and your father's foundation."

*Shit.* Of course he wasn't Reno. He looked younger, his face was broader, and of course his hair was all wrong. *Double shit.* Her mother hadn't canceled the interview—typical Lianne.

"How did you get in? The front gates are kept locked." She sounded rude and suspicious, but she didn't care. She wasn't in the mood to deal with the press, particularly if they reminded her of someone she didn't want to be thinking about.

"The gardener was leaving as I arrived. He let me through. Is this a bad time, Miss Lovitz?"

Someone was going to have to speak to the

new gardener—she certainly didn't want strangers just wandering up to the house.

But the reporter looked perfectly normal. He was neatly dressed, with his black hair slicked back from his broad face, a far cry from a leatherclad bad boy. And knowing the press, he'd keep coming back.

"All right," she said, pushing the code to unlock the door. "But just fifteen minutes." She opened the door.

He was shorter than she was, but then, a lot of men were. He was carrying a laptop case, and he looked as harmless as Jenkins.

"We can talk in the living room," she said, leading the way. "Though I don't know that I have anything interesting to say. The foundation is my father's work—he's always had a lifelong interest in the environment. I don't have much to do with it." In fact, Ralph Lovitz didn't give a rat's ass about the environment, but he had enough sense to find a worthy tax dodge that would offset some of his less environmentally friendly investments.

"And your recent trip to Tokyo?"

She stopped and looked at him. "Just a visit to my sister," she said. "Nothing to do with anything. Would you like something to drink? Some coffee?"

"Tea would be lovely," the man said. His

voice was lighter than Reno's, faintly accented. She kept thinking there was something familiar, something she was missing. But she had no doubt she'd never seen this particular young man before in her life. It must just be part of the emotional hangover that she couldn't seem to get rid of.

"Make yourself at home," she said. "I'll get us some tea."

It took her for freaking ever. She didn't know where Consuela kept the tea, or the teapots, and she wasn't going to touch the Japanese pottery her sister used when she was here. She was moving slowly; she felt as if she'd been tossed in a blender. She finally made do with some Lipton tea bags and a couple of mugs, even as she could hear Summer mentally chastise her. The water took forever to boil, and by the time she rounded up milk, sugar and a tray, she'd probably left the poor man alone for half an hour. He was sitting on the sofa, small feet neatly together, a small digital recorder on the table. He'd put his briefcase down somewhere, but it probably didn't matter. She just had to remind him to take it with him when she managed to get rid of him.

"Sorry it took me so long," she said briskly.

"Not a problem. I hope you don't mind if I tape you? That way I can be sure I quote you correctly."

"There really is nothing to quote, Mr. Lee," she said, setting the tray down by the recorder. "I think you're wasting your time."

The recorder was already blinking, a slow, steady red light, which seemed odd. She sat in the armchair across from him, reaching for her mug, and he did the same.

And then she saw his hand. Parts of two fingers were missing, one from the first knuckle, the other from the second. And she set her tea back down, suddenly sick.

"Is something wrong, Miss Lovitz?"

*Fuck. Hop Sing. That was the stereotypical character on* Bonanza. *She'd spent hours watching Western reruns on* TVland *in her youth. No wonder something seemed familiar.* "Not at all," she said in an even voice. *Where the fuck had he put his briefcase?* "I just forgot the plate of cookies I set out."

"I don't need any cookies."

"I do." She scrambled to her feet, and he rose, as well, and suddenly he didn't seem so short and sweet at all, and he was reaching in his coat for something.

She grabbed her scalding tea and threw it in his

face, his screech of pain following her as she took off at a dead run. He was close behind her, and she tossed over chairs and tables as she ran, anything to slow him down.

She made it as far as the kitchen when he caught up with her. They went down on the slate floor, and Jilly kicked at him, desperate, furious, breaking free for a moment and scrambling away, only to have him grab her again as she tried to leap across the counter.

He grabbed her ankle, trying to haul her back, but he'd underestimated her. The knife block was there, and she picked up the whole damned thing, slamming it down on his head.

He slid to the floor, a silent, boneless puddle, and she leapt over him, still frantic. She didn't know whether he was unconscious or dead—blood was already pooling beneath him, and she wanted to throw up.

She needed to get the hell out of there, before he came to, before someone else showed up. She was still barefoot and she didn't care, racing to the huge garage and grabbing the biggest car she could find, her father's bright yellow Hummer.

The keys were on the rack by the door, along with the automatic opener, and it started up with a powerful roar. She didn't wait for the door to open completely—she drove so fast she clipped the roof of the car, and she could just imagine Ralph Lovitz's reaction.

She tore down the driveway at full speed, pushing buttons on the automatic gate opener. It didn't move. She forced herself to stop for a moment, reentering the numbers that had to be right.

It was jammed. Keeping her trapped inside, with either a *yakuza* killer or a dead body, and God knew who else. The gardener must have been part of the plan, as well—no wonder he seemed to be lurking near the house every time she looked.

She put the car in Reverse, backing up about twenty feet as she fastened the seat belt with shaking fingers. And then, putting it in Drive, she floored it, slamming toward the gates like a bright yellow battering ram.

It was like hitting a brick wall. The front of the Hummer made little more than a dent, and then the air bag went off, scaring the hell out of her. Second air bag in three days, she thought, coughing. She flailed around, yanking the keys out of the ignition and stabbing at the inflated bag, and it collapsed. She turned the car on again, put it in Reverse and floored it again. It didn't move, the tires spinning beneath her. The grille had gotten caught in the mangled gate, and she was trapped, well and good.

She scrambled out of the Hummer, looking back toward the house. There was no sign of life in the shadowed afternoon, and the smell of smoke was stronger still. The fires couldn't be coming that quickly, could they? She headed toward the high stone walls surrounding the property—she'd tried to climb over them when she was younger and had failed totally—the top was strung with electric wire. But right now she was between a rock and hard place, and she wasn't going to stay there and let someone—

The hands reached out from behind, hard, hauling her back, and she kicked out, instinctively, panicked. A moment later she was slammed up against the stone wall, staring into the face of an angry stranger, dressed in loose khakis and a work shirt. A tall, angry stranger, with black shoulder-length hair and red tears tattooed on his cheekbones.

"What the fuck are you doing?" Reno demanded.

# 22

She didn't even question his presence. "I'm trying to get the hell out of here. I don't know whether I killed the man in the kitchen or not, but I'm not staying here a moment longer." And then it hit her. "What did you do to your hair?" she demanded, horrified.

"You should be asking me what I'm doing here."

"Okay, what the hell are you doing here?"

"What do you think I'm doing? Trying to save your life. Again."

"So how did a *yakuza* hit man get past you?" she said, cross. "You're doing a lousy job of saving me. And I certainly don't need any favors from you."

"I'm not. This is for your sister."

There wasn't room enough to hit him, and she wasn't going to cry. "So who's trying to kill me this time? And why? I thought I was safe once I got out of your country."

"Damned if I know. Taka got word that you were being watched, and he sent me to check it out. I was looking for a back way out when your friend got in. Who have you managed to annoy now?"

"Were you at the hospital two nights ago?"

"What hospital?"

She should have known that part was still a dream. "Why are the *yakuza* still after me?"

"What makes you think it's the *yakuza?*"

"The man in the house is missing part of his fingers. It's either an industrial accident or he's part of your organized-crime family."

"All members of my grandfather's organization are dead. He has to be from some other family."

"Then what's he doing here?"

She'd forgotten how cold and dangerous Reno could look. The shorter black hair was all wrong, everything about him was wrong, and what the hell was he doing there, making her hurt all over again?

"I want you to find someplace to hide while I check this out. The garage is secure—I checked it out yesterday. Go in there, lock it, and don't open it until either I or the police tell you to."

"Go to hell."

"You're not going to give me attitude, are you?" he demanded, wearily.

"That's all I've got for you." She brought her

knee up, hard, fighting dirty, but he jerked out of the way in time. Leaving her room to run.

She took off across the wide, manicured lawn, running toward the house. She needed to grab her cell phone, call 9-1-1, and the hell with Reno and everyone else who was placed on this earth simply to make her completely insane.

He caught her by the swimming pool with a flying tackle that sent her sprawling on the grass, and a moment later he was on top of her, rolling her over beneath him so that she could look up at him in the smoke-filled dusk. He was staring down at her, and the expression on his face was unreadable. Was it anger? Disdain? Hatred? Or something else?

"You're going to get up and do exactly what I tell you to do," he said in a deceptively soft voice. "Or I swear to God, I'll let them kill you."

"I'm sure you're tempted," she shot back, squirming. "But then you'd have to come up with a good excuse for Taka, and I don't think you have it in you. Get off me!"

He didn't move, straddling her, ignoring her struggles. It only took her a moment to freeze. He was turned on.

"You sick bastard," she said, fighting it. Not him. Fighting the heat that had pooled between her legs.

He climbed off of her, hauling her up beside him, his grip like iron. "Healthy," he said. "Are you going to do what I tell you?"

"Fuck, no."

Before she could stop him he picked her up, tossing her over his shoulder like a sack of potatoes. She beat at his back, but he was impervious, skirting the pool, heading for the garage.

The moment they were in the shadows he veered to the right, to the pool house, kicking the door open and shutting it behind him. The pool house had been closed up for years—Lianne preferred to spend her time in the sun, and no one had ever really liked the place but Jilly. There was an old mattress on the floor, and she used to curl up there and read, safe and secure and hidden just on the rare chance that Lianne or Ralph would remember she existed and start to look for her.

It hadn't changed—if anything it was dustier, but the mattress was still there, and he dropped her down on it, making no effort to cushion her fall.

"Goddamn it!" she said, furious. "I was just in a car accident. You might at least be a little gentle."

"I'm not feeling gentle right now," he growled. "If I stay around you a minute longer I'd probably strangle you. I'm going to check the house, see if your supposed *yakuza* is really dead. And then

I'm going to have to find a way to get you out of here. You screwed up the front gate, big-time, and the service entrance has been locked from the house. We can't get out that way, either, unless I disarm it."

"I know how to turn it off," she said, starting to get up, but he put his hands on her shoulders and shoved her back, hard.

"You'll stay here or I'll tie you up."

"Promises, promises," she muttered. "And you can just stop throwing me around and hurting me. I'm fragile."

"Ha! You're as fragile as a sumo wrestler. And trust me, I'm pulling my punches. I could hurt you a lot more."

"If that's what turns you on," she snapped, grabbing at the loose jacket he was wearing.

He swore, foul and dirty, pulling out of the jacket and moving away. "Coward," she said, mocking.

He froze. The dusty, deserted pool house was silent, the windows so dirty she could barely see the huge house beyond it. He turned to look back at her for a long, thoughtful moment, then headed for the door.

She was tempted to throw the jacket at his head, tempted to find something, anything, to hurl at him, but she simply sat there on the mattress, defeated.

He didn't open the door. He locked it. And then he turned back to look at her in the dusty stillness.

"What do you want from me, Ji-chan?" He sounded older, tired, not the smart-ass, smirking punk she was used to. He sounded as wounded as she felt.

*Your head on a platter? Never to see your face again? For you to be eaten by hungry tarantulas? Nothing was bad enough.*

She looked up at him, opened her mouth to rip him a new one. But only one word came out. "You," she said.

She wasn't sure what she expected. Was he going to walk away from her? Bring the force he'd threatened? He moved across the deserted pool house to the mattress, squatting down beside it, close enough to touch her. "Someone is trying to kill you, Ji-chan," he said softly. "I haven't had sex in three weeks, not since you left, and I'm not the kind of man who goes without sex easily. You need to let me go and try to save your life, because otherwise I won't be able to keep my hands off you."

"Why haven't you had sex in three weeks?"

"Because you weren't there. And unfortunately I don't want anyone but you. Now, let me go and find a way to keep you safe."

She reached up her hand and touched his face.

His skin was smooth, warm, and the new, shorter hair was in his eyes. She pushed it away. "Safety is overrated," she said. And she leaned up and kissed him.

For a moment he didn't move, and his mouth was hard, stubborn beneath hers. Then something seemed to break inside him, and he pulled her into his arms, his mouth open, devouring hers with a hunger that was both startling and just right. It didn't matter that her body ached from the accident—she melted against his hard strength and warmth and wanted to sink into his bones, his skin, disappear inside him.

She pulled him down onto the mattress, the mattress where she'd daydreamed about her perfect lover. She pulled her demon prince down with her, pushing at his clothes, reaching for his zipper with fevered hands, and he was yanking her pants off, throwing them across the room. He pushed her trembling hands away and released himself, fully erect, and she wanted to touch him, to put her mouth on him.

"If we're stupid enough to do this, we're going to do it fast," he muttered, pulling her legs apart.

"But I want—" He pushed inside her, one hard, deep thrust that filled her, so powerful that she was shaken, hot, and the first orgasm hit her.

He withdrew, just enough, his hands cradling her head, his luscious mouth skimming over hers. "You want what? This?" He thrust all the way in again, hard enough that she almost bounced off the mattress, hard enough that another small climax washed over her body.

"I want—" Another thrust cut her words off once more, as prickly waves of sheer, gorgeous lust took over. "I want I want I want…"

He was moving fast, his narrow, hard hips driving like a piston, and she wrapped her legs around him, pulling him in deeper still, twining her arms around him, kissing him, her mouth open, her legs open, her heart open. She wanted all of him inside her, every way he could take her. She wanted to lock him tight in her body and never let him go. She wanted to suck his cock and take him up the ass and anything she could possibly think of, and then do it all over again.

He was hot, sweaty, and so was she, their bodies slapping together in the stillness, and she could feel the final explosion building, and she knew she was going to scream, that nothing could stop her, she was going to shatter and cry out….

He'd braced himself with his hands on the mattress as he drove into her, and she grabbed one hand, slapping it over her mouth, over her lips, as the last barrier shattered, and she was gone, dissolved in a white-hot flash of pure response, and she could feel him jerk inside her, spilling into her, and she wanted more.

And then there was nothing left. She collapsed on the mattress, unable to catch her breath, letting the last remnants of orgasm tease her body, and she closed her eyes. Every bone in her body had melted, and when he pulled away from her, she couldn't even summon the energy to pull him back. She just lay there, sprawled on the mattress, her shirt still on, in a state of such perfect bliss that it ought to be illegal.

The perfect bliss was shattered when she was hit in the face with her discarded pants. "Get dressed, Ji-chan," Reno said. "We could have gotten ourselves killed."

She opened her eyes. She didn't want to, she didn't want to move. She wanted him to come back. But the cold Reno was back, and she sat up, reluctantly doing what he'd told her to do.

His back was to her, and he was flexing his hand, wrapping something around it. She managed to get to her feet, though there was no question her legs were shaky, and moved over to him. "What's wrong with your hand?"

He cocked an eyebrow, and a trace of Reno's

old smirk crossed his face. "Never put your hand in the way of a bitch in heat."

"No, you throw cold water on her," she said, feeling as if she'd been slapped. She took a step back from him, the color flooding her face, when he caught her and pulled her back, up against his body, ignoring her indignant struggles, wrapping his arms tight around her. "I like you in heat," he said softly. "And you can bite me anywhere you want."

She wasn't appeased. "I think I'd be happier punching you."

"You can try," he said, his voice light. "You aren't going to stay here and let me see what's going on, are you?" He sounded resigned.

"No."

"Then at least stay back. I didn't bring you this far to lose you now."

The moment his grip loosened she pulled herself out of his arms. "I'm not yours to lose," she snapped.

"Aren't you? We'll see about that." And he unlocked the door, pushing it open into the smoke-filled air.

"The fires must be spreading," she said, coughing. "The air wasn't this bad before."

"Maybe someone's helping."

If anyone was left inside the main house, he was probably dead—there were no new lights to spear through the gathering darkness. She headed for the kitchen door, knowing Reno was behind her, knowing he was ready to throw her to the ground and out of the way of danger at a moment's notice, but she refused to think about it. The kitchen door had locked automatically when she ran out, but she knew the code by heart and punched it in. The lock clicked open, and she stepped back. "On second thought, I'll let you deal with it," she said.

"On second thought, I'm not letting go of you." He caught her arm, and his hands hurt. He pulled her into the house, turning on the kitchen lights. The *yakuza* hit man was where she'd left him, rivers of blood pooling beneath him. His throat cut.

"I thought you said you hit him," Reno said, not loosening his grip.

She froze, staring down into the man's sightless eyes. "I didn't use a knife," she said in a low voice.

"Someone did." He leaned down to take a closer look, and since he wasn't letting go of her she was forced closer, as well. The smell of blood and death was overpowering, the smell that had haunted her for what seemed like forever.

"Please," she said, trying to pull away.

He ignored her, turning the man over, ignoring the blood. "Shit," he said.

"Shit what? Do you know him?"

He took the gun from the holster under the dead man's arm and handed it to her. "Don't use that on me," he warned her.

He looked at the man for a moment longer, then finally moved away, and she allowed herself to breathe again. "He's Hideto Nakamura. He's never been part of the Japanese branch of my grandfather's family—he's always lived here—but he has a connection. One that's impossible."

"You want to explain it to me?"

"He's dead," Reno said, his voice flat. "This doesn't make sense. You need to do exactly what I tell you—"

"How many times have I heard that?" she said.

He frowned at her. "I'm going to get you out of here before I get rid of the body. We don't want anyone asking questions that you aren't going to want to answer." He dragged her through the kitchen, ignoring her struggles.

She tried holding back, but it was useless. He was too strong. "I don't mind talking to the police. Why don't we call them?"

"The phone lines are cut, and the cell-phone

signal's been jammed. Nakamura was always good with electronics. The question is, who hired him?"

"And who killed him? And where is he?"

"I am here, Lovitz-san."

Reno swore, spinning around. Kobayashi had loomed out of the shadows, calm and gentle as always. Even splattered with blood.

"I thought you died with my grandfather, Kobayashi-san," Reno said in a calm voice. He'd finally released her, and she knew what he wanted her to do. He wanted her to run. She didn't move.

"I wanted to, Hiromasa-san. It would have been my great honor. But I knew I had to avenge him before he died."

"Why would you need to avenge him? Hitomi and his men died in the explosion."

"The girl," Kobayashi said, his voice mournful. "If she had not come, this never would have happened. I hoped my nephew would take care of her, make certain the blood price had been paid, that my master would be avenged, but he failed me. Not once, not twice, but three times."

"What do you mean?" Jilly said, still in shock as she looked up at the gentle giant with blood on his hands.

"He was to push you in front of traffic. When that failed, he tried to drive you off the road, but instead you were rescued. And he let you escape today. He has dishonored me. Such carelessness had to be punished. But it is my fault, as well—the task should have been mine to complete."

Reno stood very still. "Are you going to kill me, as well, Kobayashi-san? You know my grandfather loved me—he would never have wanted you to hurt me. And you heard what he said to Ji-chan before he died. Are you forgetting that?"

Kobayashi's broad forehead wrinkled for a moment, and Jilly realized at that moment that Ojiisan's bodyguard was bat-shit insane. "She is supposed to die. Someone must pay for the master's death."

"But why her? She had nothing to do with it."

Kobayashi blinked. "Everything was good until she came. The *oyabun* knew what Hitomi-san was trying to do, and he had it well under control. Until she came into things and destroyed everything. She must die."

"You know you have to kill me first," Reno said, his voice soft, implacable.

"I will do what I have to do."

Reno moved away from her, toward Kobayashi, and his eyes glittered in the shadowy hallway. "You can try."

Kobayashi stood still, his massive body blocking the exit. "It won't do you any good, young master," he said. He was holding something in one meaty hand, something small and delicate. It was the digital tape recorder her supposed interviewer was going to use. He clicked it, and Jilly closed her eyes, expecting a thundering explosion. Nothing happened. Until she heard the crackling.

"My nephew already set the charges. He thought we were going to leave before the house burned, but that was never my intent. We will all die here, and join my master…."

"Ji-chan, run!" Reno shouted as he leapt toward Kobayashi.

He was like a spider on a giant warthog. Reno was tall, but bone-ass skinny compared to Kobayashi's massive bulk, and the big man tried to shake him off like the annoyance he was.

But Reno was clinging, slamming his elbow into the man's neck, and the two of them were crashing against the furniture, Reno's wiry strength little match for Kobayashi's massive determination.

Suddenly she realized what she was holding. Nakamura's gun. It was too much like the gun she'd used in Reno's apartment, and her stomach lurched again. "Stop it!" she cried, but her voice was drowned out by the grunts and thuds of their uneven battle.

And then Reno was down, smashed against the floor, unmoving, and Kobayashi turned to her.

She could hear the crackle of the fire, feel the heat begin to build. Smoke was billowing around the outside of the house, and the drapes in the living room caught, bursting into flame. She pointed the gun at Kobayashi, but her hands were shaking so much she could barely keep it still.

"A bullet won't stop me," Kobayashi said gravely. "This is what must be. You and the young master will die, and be reborn...."

She cocked the gun. She wasn't even sure how she knew how to do it, but she pulled back the slide, hearing the chamber click into place. "I'm not ready to be reborn," she said, her voice as shaky as her hands. "Get away from Reno. We're getting out of here."

He started toward her, keeping between her and Reno's unmoving body, and there was no way she was going to run out and leave him. It was all or nothing.

"I've killed before," she warned him, but the gun was shaking even more, and all she could see was the man she'd killed in Reno's apartment, his head blown half off.

Kobayashi said nothing, he just kept coming. If his hands had been around Reno's neck, she could have pulled the trigger. Anything short of that and she was helpless.

She saw Reno move, just a tiny bit, and knew she had to get Kobayashi away from him. She threw the gun at him, then took off across the marble floor, heading for the long, sweeping staircase that was her mother's pride and joy.

The fire was spreading, rapidly, moving through the first floor of the mansion. The nephew must have used some kind of accelerant to make it go so fast, and the heat was coming at her in waves, thick and deadly, following her as she ran up the stairs.

She could hear the fire engine sirens, but they were far, far away. She moved fast, scrambling up the steps two at a time, ignoring the pain in her ankle. As she raced by the first landing she looked out the window—the fire engines were trying to get through the gate that was blocked by the crashed Hummer. She'd sealed her own fate.

Kobayashi was coming up the stairs after her, faster than she would have imagined the big man could go. Flames were already licking their way up the wallpaper at the top of the staircase, dancing across the landing to the bedrooms. The bedrooms would go quickly, and then there'd be no escape. And Reno was down there in that inferno.

Why the hell had she thrown the gun at him? Why hadn't she just capped Kobayashi between the eyes and dragged Reno's unconscious body out of harm's way? She'd picked a hell of a time to get squeamish.

And then she saw Reno, taking the stairs three at a time, racing to catch up with them, just as Kobayashi caught hold of her loose T-shirt, hauling her backward.

She lost her footing, her sprained ankle buckling beneath her, and she struck out at him, but he was too big, too strong. She felt him pick her up, carry her to the edge of the marble railing, and she knew she was going to end up smashed in a bloody puddle on the marble floor almost two flights down, and there was nothing she could do about it.

She kicked uselessly, she scratched at his face, but he was impervious, carrying her to the edge as if she were a sacrificial cow.

And then Reno reached them, and his headlong charge left all three of them sprawled on the hard stone stairs. Reno kicked at Kobayashi's head, but the solid blow didn't slow him down, any more than the follow-up hits to his neck and kidneys. Kobayashi was simply beyond feeling pain, and he was dragging Reno toward the railing along with Jilly, impervious.

He was hauling her across the marble steps, painfully, and she looked up at the huge man, clenched her hand into a fist and slammed it into his testicles.

Kobayashi let out a high-pitched squeal, momentarily taken off balance, releasing Jilly, and Reno took advantage, slamming his leg up high against Kobayashi's head, again and again, until the big man fell across the wide stone railing, momentarily dazed, trapping Reno's body beneath his, pinning him there.

Reno shoved, as hard as he could, but Kobayashi didn't move, and the flames had spread down below, filling the stairwell, starting to eat their way up Lianne's organic-grass stair runner.

"Get out of here!" Reno shouted, his voice muffled as he struggled with the huge man's weight.

Jilly didn't hesitate. She took a flying leap at them, and a moment later Kobayashi went over the side, landing on the marble floor two flights below with a sickeningly wet-sounding splat.

Blood was pouring down Reno's head, and he was cradling his arm, but he managed to get to his feet. "Come on," he said. "We have to get out of here."

The flames had reached the bedrooms, billowing out of the open doorways above them, and the smoke was getting so thick she could barely see him. They hadn't gotten this far only to burn to death. "You're supposed to be the rescuer," she said, choking on the thick smoke. "I don't suppose you have any suggestions?"

"It's your goddamned house," he said in a raw voice. "You tell me."

"Come on." He was too busy cradling his arm with his other hand, and he couldn't drag her and haul her anywhere. The blood was getting in his eyes, and she took a moment and tried to wipe some of it away. His blood, on her hand. Proof of life, she thought. They weren't ready to die.

She went up the last few steps of the massive staircase, into the fiery heat, knowing he was following her. "Keep low," he shouted at her, and she ducked as the smoke swirled overhead.

The only windows that opened in the house were those in her bedroom—Ralph and Lianne Lovitz preferred their air processed. The fire was just beginning to eat through the wallpaper on her bedroom wall, the awful girly stuff her mother had chosen, and she watched it go with mixed feelings. She headed for the casement windows, ready to shove them open when he stopped her.

"Wait," he said, panting. "It could cause a backdraft and burn us to a cinder."

"We don't have any other choice," she said. "The swimming pool is down below. If we can just jump out far enough, we'll be okay. Otherwise we'll both be dead, so we might as well go for it. Just answer me one question."

"I'm not answering anything…"

"What did your grandfather say to me before he died."

"You speak Japanese!" he snapped.

"I couldn't hear him."

"It doesn't fucking matter."

"What did he say?"

Exasperated, Reno ran his hand through his thick hair. "He said 'Welcome to the family, Granddaughter,'" he snarled.

"In that case, maybe it's worth living after all," she said.

He moved away from her and shoved her door closed with his shoulder, cursing as it burned through the rough shirt. "That should slow it down." He caught her hand in his, and shoved the casement windows, leaning over to look down at the pool below. He turned back, and there was an odd light in his eyes. "Did I ever tell you that I can't live without you?" he said.

"No," she said. "You can tell me about it when we survive." She could barely breathe, death was eating its way toward her, and she wanted to laugh out loud with the joy of it.

He shook his head, and then grinned at her, Reno, even with the shorter black hair, the bad boy who liked to live dangerously. "Come on, Ji-chan. We don't have all day." He grabbed her hand, and they ran, throwing themselves through the open window with all the force they could muster.

She lost her hold on his arm as she went sailing through the cool, smoky air, and then the water went over her head, and she was choking, her feet touching the bottom of the swimming pool and then pushing up, up, until her head broke the surface.

"Reno!" she screamed.

He bobbed up beside her, and he looked as if he'd just taken his favorite ride at Disneyland.

"Right here, Ji-chan."

"Bitch in heat?" she said. And she punched him in the jaw as hard as she could. Watching with satisfaction as he sank back down beneath the chlorinated water.

# 23

"We've been seeing a little too much of you lately, young lady," the emergency-room doctor said. "Twice in three days is not a good thing."

Jilly tried to summon a smile, not quite sure if it was working. Her sprained ankle felt as if it was broken, though they assured her it wasn't; she had burns on the left side of her body, bruises just about everywhere else; and it was sheer luck she hadn't drowned.

"Have you been depressed? Feelings of worthlessness? I can arrange for someone to talk to you."

She stared at him for a moment. "I'm not suicidal. Someone was trying to kill me."

He patted her hand. "Let me call the social worker."

"I don't need to talk to someone. I need to go home."

"The police are wanting to talk with you, as

well. You've been through a shock—it's no wonder you're disoriented."

"I'm not disoriented!" she said. "Where's Reno?"

"North of Las Vegas, last I heard," he said.

Kicking him would send her off to the psych ward immediately, so she restrained herself. "The man who was brought in with me. Where is he?"

"Mr. Shinoda? He was treated and released."

Of course he was. Gone without a word. Probably halfway to Tokyo by now, and unless some other maniac surfaced to try to kill her, she wouldn't see him again.

Of course, she could always egg someone on. He'd assured her that anyone who spent time around her would wind up homicidal. That hadn't happened until she ran afoul of him, but if it was that easy, she could doubtless get someone to try to strangle her if it would bring Reno back.

She was out of her mind. He was gone, and good riddance. "I want to go home," she said again.

"I'm sorry, Miss Lovitz, but right now there's no home to go to. Your house is gone, and the entire neighborhood has been evacuated. You must have some friends in the area, someone you could stay with for the time being? The police have been in touch with your parents and they're flying home, but in the meantime you need—"

"In the meantime I need to get the hell out of here," she said. She smelled of smoke and chlorine, every inch of her body ached, and her heart, already smashed into little pieces, had somehow managed to re-break. Falling in love had to be the stupidest thing imaginable. Reno was right—if you feel it coming on, you just lie down until it passes.

"Would you like us to call someone for you?"

"I need a taxi to take me to the Beverly Hilton," she said. "Nothing else."

"Wait right here and the social worker will be with you."

He disappeared before she could make another protest, and she bit back a snarl. One that she swallowed, as she suddenly realized the name tag on the elderly doctor's coat. *Dr. Yamada.*

Dr. Yamada had climbed into bed with her and held her, kissed her, and it certainly wasn't that annoying old man. There was an observation window overlooking her cubicle, and she could see the good doctor in earnest conversation with a policeman and a woman who looked like a jailhouse matron. Probably the social worker, but she wasn't sticking around to find out.

She slipped off the table, wincing as she put

her weight on her sprained ankle, and began moving toward the back of the cubicle, when the enveloping curtains were pulled back. He was there after all, a bandage across his forehead, his arm in a sling, his bad-boy smile in place, despite the fact that she'd managed to split his lip when she'd punched him.

She managed not to throw herself into his arms. She froze, looking at him. "You never told me. What happened to your beautiful hair?"

"I needed to blend in. You can't guard someone if you stand out like a parrot."

"You cut it for me?"

She was waiting for a denial, but none came. "Someone was following you. I needed to make certain you were safe. I got here a little late, though. You were already in the hospital."

"And you were there, too."

He didn't deny that, either. "You want to get the hell out of here? They were talking about putting you under psychiatric observation when I went by."

He was going to kill her. He was going to break her heart all over again, in tiny little pieces. She should just lie down and wait for it to pass. But she only wanted to lie down with him.

"I thought you'd be halfway to Tokyo by now," she said, stalling.

"Not without you."

Oh, man, she was so screwed. He was bad enough when he was giving her shit. Right now he was looking at her as if she was the most precious thing on earth, and she knew what she looked and smelled like. The world had turned upside down.

"I don't suppose you love me," she said. "Even a little bit?"

"Don't be an idiot, Ji-chan. Why else would I be here? Now, do you want to stay here or do you want to prove you're really crazy and come with me?"

"Will you grow your hair again?"

"If you want me to."

"Then tell me."

"You're not going to make this easy, are you? Su-chan warned me about you."

"She warned me, too. Tell me."

He let out a long-suffering sigh. *"Aishiteru,"* he muttered.

"In English."

"I love you."

She beamed at him. "I love you, too. Now, let's get the hell out of here."

"Holy motherfucker, yes!" he said, relieved. And a moment later they were gone.

*International bestselling author*

# PAM JENOFF

Two years after the Nazis were defeated, Marta
picked up the pieces of her life and left Poland.
She has started over in London with her husband,
a British diplomat, with whom she shares a
companionable, if passionless, marriage.

But Marta's new life is anything but simple. A
new war has been brought home to her doorstep:
Communist loyalists have infiltrated British
intelligence, and the one person who holds
the key to exposing the leak is connected
to Marta's past. There is a traitor
amongst them who needs to prevent
Marta's involvement, and no one
can be trusted.

# THE DIPLOMAT'S
*Wife*

"[A] moving first novel...
Jenoff succeeds in humanizing
the unfathomable as well as
the heroic."
—*Booklist* on
*The Kommandant's Girl*

*Available wherever
trade paperback
books are sold!*

MIRA®

MPJ2512

# ANNE STUART

| | | |
|---|---|---|
| 32500 ICE STORM | ___ $6.99 U.S. | ___ $8.50 CAN. |
| 32478 ICE BLUE | ___ $6.99 U.S. | ___ $8.50 CAN. |
| 32356 COLD AS ICE | ___ $6.99 U.S. | ___ $8.50 CAN. |
| 32273 THE DEVIL'S WALTZ | ___ $6.99 U.S. | ___ $8.50 CAN. |
| 32171 BLACK ICE | ___ $6.99 U.S. | ___ $8.50 CAN. |

*(limited quantities available)*

| | |
|---|---|
| TOTAL AMOUNT | $ _____ |
| POSTAGE & HANDLING | $ _____ |
| ($1.00 FOR 1 BOOK, 50¢ for each additional) | |
| APPLICABLE TAXES* | $ _____ |
| TOTAL PAYABLE | $ _____ |

*(check or money order—please do not send cash)*

To order, complete this form and send it, along with a check or money order for the total above, payable to MIRA Books, to: **In the U.S.:** 3010 Walden Avenue, P.O. Box 9077, Buffalo, NY 14269-9077; **In Canada:** P.O. Box 636, Fort Erie, Ontario, L2A 5X3.

Name: _____
Address: _____ City: _____
State/Prov.: _____ Zip/Postal Code: _____
Account Number (if applicable): _____

075 CSAS

*New York residents remit applicable sales taxes.
*Canadian residents remit applicable GST and provincial taxes.

**MIRA®**

MAS0508BL